"Surprise!"

From her place in the crowd, Blythe watched Duncan's face. Except for the widening of his eyes, his surprise would have been difficult to detect. His chagrin, however, was flagged by a crimson stain that washed up his neck to suffuse his features.

He stood tall and handsome, attired in a dark, conservatively cut suit, handmade Italian leather shoes and a pointed party hat.

Laughter bubbled up in Blythe's throat, but she managed to choke it down. The picture of the arrogant CEO as birthday boy was hilarious.

"Go ahead and laugh," Duncan told her morosely.

"It's not that bad," she sympathized. "Martha and Amelia just wanted to do something special for you."

"I would have settled for an ice-cream cake."

Blythe looked up at him. Suddenly she felt there was no place on earth she'd rather be at this moment than here.

ABOUT THE AUTHOR

We at Superromance are pleased to welcome Terri Lynn to our family of authors. Terri is a talented writer who worked as a stockbroker before leaving that position five years ago to write full-time. Terri was born in California and has spent most of her life in the South. Eventually, she settled in Florida, where she still lives with her husband, Gregory. *Uncommon Stock* is Terri's second published book. Her next Superromance novel, *Rightful Place,* will be available in July.

UNCOMMON STOCK

TERRI LYNN

Harlequin Books

TORONTO • NEW YORK • LONDON
AMSTERDAM • PARIS • SYDNEY • HAMBURG
STOCKHOLM • ATHENS • TOKYO • MILAN
MADRID • WARSAW • BUDAPEST • AUCKLAND

Published February 1993

ISBN 0-373-70534-4

UNCOMMON STOCK

Printed in U.S.A.

To my husband, Gregory,
who has given me the precious gift of time
Thank you, my love

CHAPTER ONE

"*CHURNING,* not earning. It looks as if there's been churning in your account." Blythe Summers ran her fingertips over the smooth length of her cartridge pen as she waited for a response from the two silver-haired ladies sitting across the desk from her.

Long-time widow, Martha Bevane, and her spinster sister, Amelia McKeon, had told Blythe they'd lived in Atlanta, Georgia, for over eighty years before they'd decided to move here to Winter Park, Florida, three years ago. They had come to see her yesterday on the recommendation of one of their friends. By the end of the meeting they'd become Blythe's newest clients.

With their prim buns, pearl earrings and expensive, flowered silk dresses, the two members of old Atlanta aristocracy could have passed as twins, but Blythe knew Martha was Amelia's senior by a year.

Now they regarded Blythe with faded cornflower blue eyes from across the wide expanse of polished rosewood.

Forced to meet those gazes, Blythe felt her anger resurge with the memory of yesterday's discovery. The copies of their ledger sheets had revealed the loathsome crime in the neat black-and-white columns of numbers.

"Is that good, dear?" asked Martha. "I don't think Raymond ever explained churning to us." She looked to her sister for confirmation, and when Amelia shook her head in agreement, continued. "Perhaps he was saving it as a surprise."

No doubt, thought Blythe grimly. Raymond Fosker, their previous stockbroker, had probably planned to spring his surprise as he drove his Rolls-Royce off into the Georgia sunset, on his way to early retirement and the good life.

"No, ma'am, churning is *not* good. If your ledger entries are correct, it means Mr. Fosker traded excessively in your account, for the sole purpose of his own gain."

The sisters looked at her with such helplessness and shock Blythe wished she could wave a magic wand and make their account whole.

The churning wasn't the only bad news. Faced with telling them about all the inappropriate investments sitting in their account—such as that oil exploration limited partnership—she felt like the owl telling Thumper his little brothers and sisters would likely end up as sleeves on some hooker's coat. She wasn't sure how strong their hearts were, but she knew hers was getting fainter as two sets of innocent blue eyes regarded her.

Blythe cleared her throat. "In addition to the churning, there are investments in your Durnam Sims account I consider highly inappropriate for the goals we discussed. What goals did you set with Mr. Fosker?"

The elderly sisters looked at each other, then at Blythe.

"I don't believe we discussed goals, dear," said Martha. "We just told him we wanted to learn about investing, but didn't know how to choose things. Raymond said he would be happy to advise us."

Blythe swallowed a groan. After that conversation dear Raymond had probably danced with glee.

Enough said about investments for now. They'd still be in the account when it transferred to her here at Stewart Duke.

"Did you send your letter to Durnam Sims?" Blythe asked.

Martha smiled. "What letter, dear?"

Blythe laid down the pen before she snapped it in two. She took a deep breath and smiled. "The letter requesting your securities be released to your new account here."

Amelia's and Martha's eyes widened simultaneously. "Oh, my," Amelia murmured. "We forgot."

"Under the circumstances, I think it would be wise to get a letter in the mail immediately, don't you?"

Blythe instructed her sales assistant to type a transfer letter to be signed by Mrs. Bevane and Miss McKeon. Minutes later, Ginny brought the paper in, and the clients signed their names.

As Blythe saw the two women to the front door in the lobby, Martha reached over and patted her hand. "Your mother must be very proud of you, dear. We know you'll take good care of us."

Blythe had informed Tom Jarzabek, her own manager, of the situation. As soon as she double-checked the facts, Blythe planned to advise Martha and Amelia of options open to them if they wanted to try to rectify their loss.

Back in her office, she frowned at the ledger copies on the desk in front of her. Lowlifes like Fosker violated the trust of clients and splashed mud on all the decent brokers in the securities industry.

The branch manager of Durnam Sims had neglected his responsibility to oversee the activities of the registered representatives in his office. Had he read his copies of the statements, the churning would have been detected long ago.

Ginny Rodriguez, Blythe's sales assistant, walked into the glass-walled office and placed a stack of letters to be signed in front of Blythe. "Those ladies need someone to help them," Ginny commented.

"I went over the case with Tom earlier this morning. It's a little unorthodox, but he's going to call the manager at Durnam Sims. That way, if the situation is what I think it is, the account can be immediately frozen so Fosker won't have access while we're waiting for the securities to transfer."

Ginny nodded. "Good. I'll bet those ladies have been sheltered most of their lives. Don't they have a financial manager?" When Blythe shook her head, Ginny said indignantly, "And what about their family? Their family should be protecting their interests."

Blythe agreed. "They're very trusting and it looks like some—" her face darkened "—some *scum* took advantage of it. We'll help them. When there's something we can't or shouldn't handle we'll supply them with names of competent professionals."

"Like an attorney?"

"If it comes to that." Blythe hoped it wouldn't.

"I still say their family should be helping them. It's just not right." Picking up the last signed letter, Ginny returned to her desk outside Blythe's office.

It didn't seem right to Blythe, either.

NEVER AGAIN, vowed Duncan McKeon as he tipped the taxi driver and hefted the suit bag onto his shoulder. Never again would he fly coach. It was *worth* the price of a first-class ticket to insure against sitting so indecently close to a nervous, chattering woman who had not quite perfected the art of applying makeup with a trowel.

All he'd wanted on the flight from Atlanta to Orlando was a little sleep. Instead, out of a sense of— what? Southern chivalry? More like stupidity—he had listened to the first-time flyer's life story and all her hopes for the future told nonstop at high speed.

She'd gotten sick, and his monogrammed linen handkerchief had fallen victim to cheap, red lipstick and worse.

With a pang of regret, Duncan let himself into his aunts' house through the imposing front doors. The handkerchief had been a gift. He could recall the redhead's face but not her name. Beautiful, he remembered. She'd been smart enough to see early on he wasn't looking for a wife, that he already had a possessive mistress—Macrocosm, Inc.

It was Macrocosm that brought him to Martha and Amelia's house now. Central Florida Software had made a surprise offer to buy his company. Instead of sending the appropriate vice president, he'd taken the opportunity to go to Florida himself, which would allow him an overdue visit with his aunts. His attorneys would fly in for the meetings.

The house was silent. He strode across the foyer, down the hall and into the kitchen. Opening the back door, Duncan peered into the dimly lit cavern that served as a four-car garage. The 1972 baby blue Cadillac Martha refused to part with wasn't there. Rarely did either of his aunts go anywhere without the other, which meant no one was home.

Duncan retraced his steps to the high-ceilinged foyer and climbed the sweeping stairway. In the bedroom they kept ready for him, he heaved his suit bag onto the large bed, set his briefcase down and began to unpack.

When everything was in its place, he stripped and stepped into the shower, allowing the hot spray to wash away his tension and travel-grime.

Ten minutes later, clad in jeans, scrubbing his wet hair with a towel, he heard the inside garage door open, and the low murmur of his aunts' voices. He tugged on a T-shirt, stuffed his feet into a pair of canvas deck shoes and went to greet them.

"Duncan!" Amelia hugged him and brushed a kiss on his cheek. "Welcome home."

Duncan smiled. "Thank you." Both ladies refused to acknowledge he had a home of his own in Atlanta.

It was Martha's turn to embrace her nephew. As if reading his mind, she said, "Your home is where your family is, dear."

Amelia opened the refrigerator and took out a pitcher of mint-sprigged tea. She poured a glass and offered it to him. He accepted it gratefully. No one made tea like Aunt Amelia, and she always brewed it fresh for him.

After downing half the glass, Duncan allowed himself to be directed out to the screened area around the pool. He slouched slightly in the peach-colored patio chair, stretching his legs out in front of him, crossing them at the ankles. Seated amid the palms and hanging orchids, he finally relaxed.

"How was your trip, dear?" Martha asked.

He smiled sourly. "About what I could expect on a Tuesday."

"Oh, my."

"What have you ladies been up to this morning?" Duncan asked. "Playing bridge?"

"We went to see our stockbroker," replied Amelia, reclining demurely on her favorite chaise longue.

"Stockbroker? I didn't know you had a stockbroker. So you finally decided to invest the money?"

"Yes, dear." Martha absently smoothed the side of her stylish coiffure. "We gave it a great deal of thought and decided you were right. Investing your gift would give us experience in overseeing our finances."

It pleased Duncan to know his aunts had taken his advice. His gift of "play money" had been given with no strings attached, but with the suggestion they use it to learn about investment. Duncan had even presented them with an elegant leather ledger. At the time, Martha and Amelia had shown a marked disinterest in the subject. They knew Duncan would handle whatever needed to be taken care of.

"That's great!" He clapped his palms together and rubbed them. "Are you having a good time with it? Have you parlayed the money into your first million, yet?"

A peculiar look passed between the elderly sisters. It puzzled Duncan, making him vaguely wary.

"If you lost some money, that's to be expected," he reassured them. "The market is unpredictable. Before you buy a stock you have to study the company, the industry... What? What is it?"

Amelia had risen and walked into the living room. She came back to hand him a leather-bound ledger. As Duncan took it from her, the confused concern he saw in her face had him immediately looking toward Martha. Her expression mirrored Amelia's.

He came over to sit on the edge of Martha's chaise longue. "Now look," he told them firmly. "When I gave you this money it was with the stipulation you not worry about it. It's play money. There's more where that came from. If the investments you picked didn't pan out, that's the way it goes sometimes."

Martha looked down at her perfect manicure for a moment then raised her eyes to meet his. "We didn't actually *pick* the investments. That's why we never told you what we had decided to do with the money. Oh, we wanted to make you happy and be daring enough to make those decisions, but it just seemed so intimidating. We let our broker choose." She laid her hand on his arm in appeal. "Amelia has never handled stocks and whatnot, and my dear Horace used to take care of such things for me. You do understand, don't you, Duncan?"

He looked at Martha, then Amelia. "You didn't pick your stocks? Did you always accept your broker's recommendations?"

Martha sighed heavily. "Always."

"Did you give the broker power of attorney?"

"No. We aren't completely foolish."

Duncan opened the ledger. He scanned the transactions, which had been meticulously recorded, just as he'd shown them to do. The more he read, the tighter the muscles in his jaws bunched.

The neat pages screamed of a stockbroker's rapacious greed.

Rage bubbled up in Duncan like the poisonous brew in a demon's caldron. Who could slither so low as to steal—for, in fact, that's what it was—from two trusting little old ladies? Two sweet, charming women who had, over the years, sacrificed so much for their only nephew?

Furious, he slammed the ledger closed. Long ago, Duncan had learned the best way to extract vengeance was through an offender's wallet. That was the way he would handle this matter.

"Please get me your statements." He stared at the ledger, conjuring a mental vision of a stockbroker clad in a dark, hand-tailored suit, weeping and writhing on a medieval rack.

"We don't have them, dear," Martha said.

Duncan reluctantly released his daydreams and turned to look at his older aunt. "You didn't throw them out, did you?" He remembered all the bank statements they had pitched, along with their canceled checks, until he had realized what they were doing.

"Yes. But we recorded everything in the ledger first, just as you showed us. Odd. The broker wanted the statements, too." Martha smiled uncertainly.

I'll bet, Duncan thought darkly.

"What's your broker's name?" he asked. "I'd like to pay a call."

"Oh." Martha disappeared into the kitchen. When she returned she handed Duncan a business card. It read: B. K. Summers, Certified Financial Planner. The name of a prestigious brokerage house was given, along with its Winter Park address.

Duncan held up the card. "This is your broker?" he asked, wanting to be sure.

"Yes, and we're so fortunate." Amelia beamed.

He stood. "I think I'll just pay a little visit to B. K. Summers. Sort of introduce myself."

"That's nice, dear. Breeding tells."

Maybe he could manage to get at least *one* blood-curdling shriek out of Summers while he was there, Duncan thought hopefully.

"I DON'T CARE if he's *Adonis,* he doesn't have an appointment and I don't have time to see him!" Blythe's look dared her sales assistant to say anything more on the subject.

Blythe's stern aqua glare didn't have the power to quell Ginny as it had so many others. Instead, the petite, dark-haired woman calmly continued. "I was only passing along what Lucy said. More to the point, however, he's Amelia McKeon's nephew. That makes him Martha Bevane's nephew. Your newest clients, remember?"

"Thank you for spelling it out for me, Ginny. I never would have been able to make the connection."

The sales assistant ignored the sarcasm. "Shall I tell Lucy to send him in?"

"Did anyone think to ask *why* he's here?" Blythe glanced at her watch impatiently. The market was moving! She should be calling clients right now.

"It's not Lucy's job to ask why someone comes to see a stockbroker. But I have some idea. It must have something to do with Martha and Amelia's decision to have their account set up as Joint Tenants with Right of Survivorship with their nephew, Duncan Keir McKeon. He's probably dropped by to bring back the forms you sent and to meet his aunts' broker."

"Okay. Buzz Lucy and tell her I'm on my way." This wouldn't take long. Blythe left her office and walked down the carpeted corridor toward the reception area.

The brokerage office was alive with frenzied activity. Telephones, typewriters and voices combined to form a constant blizzard of sound. The market was going up.

The lobby of Stewart, Duke, Renken and Koenig, Inc., venerated member of the New York Stock Exchange, was richly contemporary in midnight blue, white marble and Lucite. The receptionist, Lucy, caught Blythe's eye and nodded slightly in the direction of a dark-haired man.

Tall and long-limbed, he stood looking out the glass double doors, his back to the room. His charcoal gray suit of imported cloth was tailored to a perfect fit across his broad shoulders.

As if he sensed her approach, the man turned, revealing high, sculptured cheekbones and long, oblique eyes of a startling silver gray.

Duncan McKeon was handsome, Blythe thought, impressed. Unusually so. Exotic.

"Mr. McKeon," she said. "I'm Blythe Summers."

Astonishment registered on his face. "B. K. Summers?"

His aunts had evidently not mentioned the gender of their broker.

She offered her hand and sought to put him at ease with a warm smile.

Burning fury flashed in those argent eyes like noon sun on a diamond. He made no move to take her outstretched hand.

Blythe lowered her hand to her side. She had no idea why this man was angry, but after his rudeness, she wasn't sure she cared.

Blythe's smile lost its warmth. She had too many clients and too little time to have patience with such behavior. Her irritation, caused initially by his interruption of her frenetic day, flared into dislike.

"Did you bring the forms?" she asked coldly.

Black eyebrows drew down like an advancing storm. "The only thing I've brought you, Miss Summers, is bad news."

Showing this boor the exit would give her satisfaction. Only the thought of Martha and Amelia restrained her from exercising that pleasure. If this was the best their family could provide for them, they needed her badly.

She considered his behavior might stem from the fact his aunts' stockbroker was a woman. It would not be the first time she'd encountered that reaction. Her dislike grew.

She met his stare with a reflection of arctic fjords. "What bad news is that, Mr. McKeon?"

"Do you have an office where we can talk?" It was more a demand than a question.

"This way." Turning on her heel, she walked back down the hall to her office, not bothering to see if he followed. She moved around to her side of the desk. With a flick of her hand, she waved him to one of the two client chairs. Blythe settled into her high-backed executive chair.

McKeon placed his briefcase on the seat next to him and opened it. He withdrew a book.

"Miss Summers—"

"Ms. Summers," Blythe corrected. "Or Mrs. Summers, if you prefer." A frosty, totally insincere smile curved her lips. He didn't reply immediately. *Thrown off his timing,* she thought smugly.

"Mrs. Summers," he began again, holding up the leather-bound book, "does this look familiar?" His words were softly spoken, and perfectly controlled. It was the tone of his voice that caused her to regard him with masked wariness.

"Should it?" His aunts, she recalled, had carried a ledger with them on their first visit. She'd made copies of its pages.

"This is my aunts' ledger. It's a record of every transaction since they opened their brokerage account." He lowered the book to rest on the case. "Your ignorance of its existence doesn't surprise me."

He was watching her closely.

An ugly suspicion began to form in Blythe's mind.

"This firm keeps accurate records of all transactions, Mr. McKeon, and I keep a separate record of my own for my clients." With effort, she maintained her polite facade.

"Yes." Sarcasm edged his voice. "I suppose you would keep a separate accounting of your clients' transactions."

Blythe was careful to display no emotion as, under the desk, she tensed and relaxed her thigh muscles in an effort to relieve some of her anger. Before she flung her hand-blown paperweight between those silvery eyes she wanted confirmation of the purpose of his visit.

"Please get to your point." Her voice was as cool and hard as steel.

His eyes darkened. "Is your game so commonplace you can't remember my aunts' account? How long is the average life of your accounts? Or should I ask how *short* they are? I'll bet they're all highly profitable."

Blythe's suspicion ignited into cold fury. "Say what's on your mind, Mr. McKeon."

"I've seen what you've been doing in my aunts' account—buying securities then quickly selling them to buy something else. No gain for your client, but a nice commission for you! What kind—"

"Churning."

"Do you mind clarifying that?"

"What you describe is called 'churning.'"

Duncan McKeon's face flushed with anger. "So we're down to the niceties, are we? This type of swindle has a *specific* name. What you've done is unethical, illegal and low. You've betrayed a trust. No matter *what* you call it, it's stealing."

McKeon, Blythe decided, was not aware of the recent change in brokers.

She eyed the man sitting across from her. The skin across the high planes of his cheekbones was taut, his mouth drawn in a hard line.

"Mr. McKeon, I have not churned your aunts' account."

"Do you expect me to believe it just 'happened'? Or are you implying my aunts came up with all those lousy investments and forced you to buy them?"

This man is going to feel like the idiot he's acting when he learns the truth, Blythe thought, savoring the sharp blade of her malice.

She could hardly wait to tell him.

"I expect nothing of you." *Certainly nothing remotely akin to intelligent thought.* "I told you I didn't churn your aunts' account because it's the truth. Martha and Amelia came to see me only yesterday to set up a new account."

McKeon raised a dark eyebrow. "Oh, come on. You can do better than that. It's certainly not good enough to keep me from going to the Securities and Exchange Commission."

It was almost too tempting to let him humiliate himself in front of some SEC minor official.

Suppressing her smile at the thought, she decided to end this confrontation. Even an erroneous accusation of dishonesty could taint a career.

Blythe locked gazes with him. "I've told you I'm not responsible for what went on in your aunts' account. I don't even have the securities yet. You need to discuss this with them, Mr. McKeon."

"I did discuss it with my aunts, Mrs. Summers."

She could feel the blood drain from her face. "*Martha and Amelia* told you I had churned their accounts?" Blythe clenched the paperweight. "Tell me what they said," she demanded. "Exactly."

He seemed a little surprised by her reaction. "They told me they had invested money. That they had been too intimidated to choose stocks or other investments by themselves, and had relied entirely on the suggestions of their broker. They were distressed, Mrs. Summers. Their losses are substantial. They trusted you."

"Then what was said?" Blythe persisted.

He glared at her. "This is a farce, and you know it. Stop wasting my time."

"*Then what was said*. Exactly, Mr. McKeon." Blythe struggled to retain her composure.

"Then I read the ledger, asked who their broker was and Martha gave me your card."

"Your exact words, please."

"This is getting us nowhere." He stood and reached for his briefcase. "I'll take the matter up with your manager."

Rising to her feet, Blythe fought to keep the urgency from her voice. "It's important, Mr. McKeon. Please tell me exactly what you said before your aunt gave you my card."

He hesitated, studying her face. "All right. I said, 'What's your broker's name? I'd like to pay a call.'"

Inside her chest the muscles loosened from their knots, and Blythe breathed a relieved sigh. "I *am* your aunts' broker. In order to pay a call on the man who *was* your aunt's broker, the one who took advantage of Martha and Amelia's inexperience, you'd have to go to Atlanta."

His eyes narrowed.

She withdrew a copy of the signed transfer letter from the file of her newest clients and handed it to McKeon. "Check the date on this against the date of the latest transaction in your ledger."

As he compared the ledger against the copy of the letter, he went still. Gradually deep color crept up his neck to suffuse his face.

Blythe sat back in her chair and waited for his apology. It had better be *very* good.

He cleared his throat. "I don't suppose we could back up and start over?" he asked. His lopsided grin was audaciously charming.

Blythe slowly shook her head, unsmiling.

McKeon looked away, his flush growing darker. He cleared his throat again and directed his gaze back to her. "Mrs. Summers, I was wrong. I'm deeply sorry. My aunts..." He spread his hands. "I'm sorry."

Still too furious to formally accept his apology— uninspired as it was—Blythe responded with a curt nod.

He was as far as the door before Blythe stopped him. "Mr. McKeon."

He paused, his hand on the knob.

"Would you please explain to your aunts they have Raymond Fosker to thank for the present condition of their account. I do not churn, sir, and I've never thought oil exploration or windmills suitable investments for the elderly."

McKeon turned to face her. "I promise to make your innocence quite clear to my aunts." He opened the door and strode down the hall toward the heavy glass doors.

Blythe stared, unseeing, at the files on her desk. She hotly resented being accused of an act as despicable as churning. Not only was it a slur against her integrity, such an accusation could easily become a destructive rumor.

A broker's reputation was the foundation of her business. Blythe had learned that lesson the hard way, but she had learned it well.

She'd worked hard for her sterling reputation. It hadn't been easy, thanks to her late husband, Promise-Them-Anything Andrew. In order to get people to invest their money with him, he had told them what they had wanted to hear rather than what they should have heard.

By the time she'd discovered how he worked, she was already married to him.

Once she was on to Andrew, Blythe always went back to the client to explain the true nature of their investment before the trade was made. She believed it preferable to have no client than one who had unrealistic expectations. Occasionally someone became so disgruntled the business would be withdrawn. When that happened, Andrew became furious with her.

His philosophy had nearly cost Blythe her career as a registered representative. She had been the wife and partner of a lying thief—guilt by association. Only the fact that no one had been "taken" once Blythe had become Andrew's partner had saved her.

Maybe she should call Martha and Amelia to make sure their nephew explained things correctly.

If she did call, might she not be doing to McKeon what so many had done to her—unfairly assuming the worst?

She decided to give him tonight to straighten out the confusion with his aunts. Tomorrow, she'd call Martha and Amelia and satisfy herself they understood the truth.

Duncan McKeon had descended on Blythe like an avenging archangel, but he'd walked out like a man highly embarrassed. The more she thought about it, the more Blythe believed his intentions had been good—much better than his communication with his relatives.

His angry face with those quicksilver eyes and that arrogantly sensual mouth slipped into her thoughts. Blythe's immediate impulse was to thrust the unwanted image from her mind, but she stopped.

The high-voltage energy Duncan McKeon radiated posed no threat to her, she told herself, nor did his exotic good looks.

No doubt about it, though. Martha and Amelia had one fine-looking nephew.

Thank God he was such a jerk.

CHAPTER TWO

THEY'D DONE IT to him again!

Once, just once, he wanted to get a straight story from his aunts.

Duncan's frustration chewed at him as he turned the key in the ignition and felt the engine respond. He flexed his hands on the steering wheel, willing his temper under control.

He should have seen it coming, Duncan steamed as he guided the Cadillac into the flow of traffic. It wasn't as though his aunts hadn't muddled the facts before. He knew they didn't do it intentionally, bless their hearts, but somehow, with their cooperation, circumstances always conspired to leave him looking like an idiot.

It was a pattern that seemed doomed to repetition. In its first phase, his aunts found themselves in difficulty, either of their own making or someone else's. It didn't matter. Phase two brought their appeal—mute or verbal—to him, and the arousal of his admittedly excessive protectiveness. This was the part where those sweet, generous, sometimes infuriating ladies managed to put a warp in reality. Phase three, the denouement, always ended with a humiliating bang. In his attempt to rescue, he discovered the situation slightly skewed. And always, he ended mired in the ludicrous.

His life had been less stressful since his aunts had decided to move from Atlanta to Winter Park. They had moved into the mansion Martha's late husband, Horace—dead forty years now—had built in 1935.

Duncan had helped them settle into the enormous pink stucco monstrosity in which previously only tenants and caretakers had dwelled. Before he allowed his aunts to move into the house, however, he'd arranged for modernization. He remembered it well. In one of the many mix-ups all too common with his elderly aunts, he had nearly been electrocuted by an angry electrician.

Yes, with Martha and Amelia in Winter Park, Duncan enjoyed living in Atlanta more than ever. Of course, he thought with a stab of guilt, Macrocosm was headquartered in Atlanta. He was owner, chief executive officer. What could he do?

It wasn't as if he'd abandoned his aunts. At least once every month or so he spent a weekend with them. His conscience twinged. All right, so it had been three months since he'd last been to Winter Park. The discussions with Central Florida Software might be over after the first meeting, or they might go on for weeks, possibly months. Naturally he couldn't afford to stay here months, but he was prepared to spend three weeks with interim trips to Atlanta. No doubt he would spend most of his time outside of the CFS negotiations untangling Amelia and Martha's checking account and finances, but he'd also find time to take the ladies out to dine, and bask in their doting affection.

Turning into the tree-shaded neighborhood where Martha and Amelia resided, Duncan reluctantly recalled his first reaction to the stockbroker. He'd assumed B. K. Summers was male. He'd envisioned

Summers as an oily-haired weasel who would probably make excuses for his unethical actions. The
problem would then either be resolved by the broker
and his manager, or Duncan would go to the Securities and Exchange Commission.

The real B. K. Summers had been something of a
shock.

Instead of a shifty, beady-eyed man, Duncan had
been faced with a tall, slender woman, whose cobalt
blue suit did not quite conceal her voluptuous curves.
She wore her silver blond hair pulled back in a royal
chignon from which wisps escaped to float in moonlight tendrils at her nape, and along each elegant
cheek. Pale brows arched over large, widely spaced
aqua eyes. Her nose was short and straight, and the
Cupid's bow top lip of that luscious mouth was
slightly fuller than the rounded bottom one.

Duncan would have preferred confronting the weasel.

His arrival at his aunts' place interrupted further
thoughts of Mrs. Summers as he pulled the car off the
brick street, into the driveway marked by pink stuc-
coed posts on either side.

His aunts greeted him with such loving smiles Duncan felt like a traitor for his earlier thoughts. He gave
each an affectionate peck on the cheek.

"How was your visit, dear?" asked Amelia.

Duncan winced at the memory. "Very enlighten-
ing. Ladies, we have to talk."

"Oh, how nice. It's been months since we've sat
down for a good chat." Martha went to the cupboard
and took down a plate. "We have cake." She paused,
frowning. "It's three hours until dinner time. Surely
the cake won't spoil your appetite." Turning to her

sister, she asked, "Do you think cake will spoil Duncan's appetite?"

Amelia gave the question some thought. "No," she decided. "Three hours should be long enough."

"Oh, good." Martha looked back at Duncan. "It's devil's food chocolate with mint frosting. Your favorite."

Duncan listened tolerantly to the exchange, having long since given up trying to explain that a full-grown man usually had some idea of when he should and shouldn't eat. He was almost thirty-four, but they fussed over him as if he were still twelve.

The prospect of ingesting Aunt Martha's cooking was sufficient to demolish even the heartiest of appetites. Duncan would never consider telling his elderly aunts it had been Eula's cake he'd enjoyed so much. Eula, the cook who had been with Martha and Amelia for years, had moved with them to Winter Park. After her first traumatic encounter with a palmetto bug—a giant, flying cockroach—followed by an unwanted visit from one of the many tiny lizards that inhabited the garden and the plants of the pool area, Eula had packed her bags and returned to her home city.

The mansion's size dictated the need for staff, but when Duncan had tried to hire them Amelia and Martha had balked. *They* would learn to cook. They also refused any help other than the weekly lawn service and cleaning team. When he had asked them why they refused adequate help—he knew money couldn't be the reason—they had informed him they were getting back to their roots.

That had been three years ago. No extra help had been hired, but the would-be cooks ate out a lot. He suspected they were weakening.

Out in the pool area Martha and Amelia set three glasses of lemonade, a fork and one plate bearing a large slice of cake on the wrought-iron table.

Yum, he thought morosely.

"Do you need to see this, dear?" Amelia asked as Duncan took off his suit jacket and hung it on the back of a chair. She handed him an envelope.

Curious about the look that passed between the women, he examined the opened envelope in his hand. It was addressed to his aunts and it bore the return address of Stewart, Duke, Renken and Koenig, Inc., postmarked yesterday.

It consisted of three forms with signature lines highlighted in transparent yellow ink, a return addressed envelope, postage guaranteed and a letter. He unfolded the last item and read.

Dear Martha and Amelia:
Thank you so much for opening an account with me and with Stewart, Duke, Renken and Koenig. I will do everything in my power to maintain your confidence in me and in this firm.

Enclosed are the papers necessary to include Mr. McKeon on the account as Joint Tenant, as you requested. His signature is required on those lines indicated in yellow. Please return these forms in the enclosed envelope.

Should you have any questions on your account, or on investments, please do not hesitate to call. I will contact you when your securities arrive from Durnam Sims Securities in Atlanta.

The letter was from B. K. Summers.

Reliving his earlier embarrassment, Duncan slowly lifted his face toward the screen dome and closed his eyes. Mortification trickled in until he burned with it.

He had built a prosperous corporation through cool consideration. By taking time to learn as much about the matter at hand as possible he usually made the best decisions. Success had attended his philosophy. It was only when he spent much time in close proximity with Martha and Amelia that he ended up looking like an impetuous nitwit. And now he'd unjustly accused a woman he had never met before of cheating little old ladies!

Duncan lowered his head to stare at the letter in his hands. He had slandered his aunts' broker, an innocent woman whose livelihood might have been ruined by such misconceptions. He winced inwardly as he remembered he'd refused to shake B. K. Summers's hand.

Recalling Martha and Amelia, Duncan glanced around. They were no longer there. He was alone with his disgrace.

As if on cue, Martha's voice sang out to him. "We'll be right back, dear."

Duncan sighed.

The women walked out of the house to join their nephew. Amelia smiled as she picked up her glass of lemonade and settled onto a chaise longue. "Martha and I were just trying to decide where you were going to take us to dinner. Someplace nice." Her blue eyes twinkled.

He tried for a smile. It came out a grimace. "Of course." Duncan regarded the sisters sitting in their deck chairs, looking so sedate. "Mrs. Summers did not churn your account. Your securities haven't even been transferred from Atlanta, yet.''

Martha and Amelia stared at him, their expressions startled.

"Well, of course she didn't," said Martha. "We signed the forms only yesterday."

Amelia shook her head sadly. "It seems Raymond was no gentleman."

"We called Stewart Duke," said Martha, "but you'd already left."

"What did you call for?"

"We weren't sure how long you'd be, and we wanted to make certain seven o'clock reservations for dinner suited you."

Duncan cleared his throat. "What did Mrs. Summers say?"

Amelia smiled knowingly. "Only that you had been in, and had been under the impression she was the one responsible for the churning."

"It was Ginny who told us how offensive you were," Martha offered. "We talked to her after we spoke to Blythe. Apparently Blythe was quite annoyed with you."

"Who's Ginny?" Duncan asked.

"Ginny is Blythe's sales assistant. They've worked together for years."

Amelia leaned forward, catching his attention. "Why do you keep calling Blythe 'Mrs.'?"

"Because that's what she said she was. Mrs. Summers."

"Oh. Well . . . I guess if that's what she wants . . ."

"Amelia," Martha said, "maybe we're surprised such a young widow insists on that title, but it's her right. Perhaps it's to keep all those brash young men at bay." Her merry gaze danced to her nephew, then back to her sister.

"A widow?" Duncan croaked, with a sinking feeling. This was getting steadily worse. Next he expected to hear his lovely victim was suffering from an incurable disease and had only one month to live.

Amelia took a sip of her lemonade and leaned back in her deck chair, smiling. "Now, about dinner. Is seven o'clock all right?"

Duncan nodded.

"Oh, good."

They dined at Beau Jardin in Altamonte Springs. The restaurant was a quiet, old mansion surrounded by gardens. The excellent food, serene vista and pleasant company should have insured an enjoyable evening, but Duncan's thoughts kept drifting back to the scene at Stewart Duke. The beautiful Blythe Summers had made time for him in her obviously busy schedule. He, in turn, had refused to shake her hand, had insulted her and accused her of being a thief.

He wasn't usually like that! he protested silently. This sort of thing only happened when he got around his aunts. But would the stockbroker with the green-blue eyes believe it?

As coffee was served at the end of the meal, Martha and Amelia assured their nephew they forgave him his blunder.

One voice, however, was absent: the husky alto of Blythe Summers.

She must think him a fool. What other conclusion could she draw? The thought that she might hold him in contempt—or worse, see him as a clown—gnawed at him. Still, he reasoned, the damage was done.

As he escorted his aunts across the parking lot to their Cadillac, Duncan decided he wouldn't let Blythe Summers write him off as a fool.

A BANGING on the front double-glass doors interrupted Blythe and Ginny as they went over a proposal Ginny had typed.

It was eight-thirty at night, too late for clients. Another Stewart Duke broker would have his own key. The two women exchanged glances.

"Maybe it's that nephew of Martha and Amelia's," Ginny suggested.

"I doubt I'll ever see *him* again. After his behavior this morning he probably won't want to show his face in this office ever again." Blythe fished the ring of keys from her purse. Together she and Ginny walked down the hall to the doors.

A tall, young woman with long, red hair stood under the outside light, with lowered head, pounding on the heavy glass.

Blythe paused in the darkened lobby. From the corner of her eye she could see Ginny look up at her questioningly.

That height. That fiery hair...

"Fiona!" Blythe dashed to unlock the door. "It's my sister," she explained to a startled Ginny. Finding the right key among all the others took frustrating seconds, but finally it was in the lock. Blythe jerked open the door and pulled Fiona inside.

Then she hesitated, uncertain, as they faced each other. Just before Fiona had left for Alaska, three years ago, the younger woman had been aloof, almost withdrawn.

But no longer. Laughing, Fiona surged forward and grabbed her sister in a fierce hug. "Say something!"

Blythe returned the hug instantly. "I'm glad you're back," she said unevenly into the flame-colored hair. They rocked back and forth, neither making an effort to break the embrace. "How long will you be here?"

"Looks like I'm back for good."

"Great!" Blythe nodded, enormously pleased.

"A-hem." Ginny looked at them expectantly.

"Oh, sorry." Blythe released her sister and turned her to face the sales assistant. "Ginny, I'd like you to meet my kid sister, Fiona Burnett. Fiona, this is my friend, my self-appointed nanny and sales assistant, Ginny Rodriguez."

The tall redhead and the petite brunette exchanged amenities, then Ginny said, "Victor's going to wonder if I ran away from home. You two try to stay out of trouble. Fiona, it was nice meeting you. I'm sure I'll see you again."

"Wait a minute, Ginny. I'll give you a ride to your car."

The trio walked outside, where Blythe's Volvo was parked in the brokers' area. Blythe helped her sister heft two large suitcases into the car's trunk.

"Only two suitcases? Fiona, you *left* with more than that."

Fiona shrugged. "I was ready to go. I just tossed some things into suitcases, and left the rest in Alaska."

They let Ginny off at her car and headed home. When they reached Blythe's house, they set the luggage in the guest room and Fiona treated herself to a tour of the rooms she had not seen in three years.

"Gee, you've really changed things," Fiona called as she wandered from room to room, ending in the kitchen where Blythe had put the kettle on the stove and arranged lemony butter cookies on a china plate.

Fiona selected one and took a healthy bite. "It's good to see you haven't lost track of the really important things in life." The rest of the cookie disappeared. "Tea and cookies."

Blythe flashed her sister a smile. "Yes. Well, Mom raised us right. Time passes and fortunes change, but lemony butter cookies and tea are always the same. A woman can depend on them." Trays of cookies and pots of tea had importance in lives with few constants, Blythe reflected sadly.

"Mmm," agreed Fiona through a mouthful of another cookie.

The kettle sang its steamy song and Blythe set about preparing their tea. She dropped a cozy over the porcelain teapot, and carried the ladened tray out to the screened porch, which provided a lovely view of the lake. Fiona followed behind with the platter of cookies.

Only the tinkling of wind chimes in the breeze broke the stillness of the spring evening as they sat down at the small round table.

"The weather here is great, isn't it?" Blythe asked, her question heavy with meaning. She darted a glance at her sister and proceeded to pour their tea.

Accepting the steaming cup, Fiona laughed. "You mean as opposed to the weather in Alaska?"

"I was simply hoping you'd admit this isn't such a bad place to live."

Surprise widened Fiona's eyes. "I never thought it was a bad place to live!"

"Then why did you leave?"

"As I told Mom at the time, I'd spent my entire life in the Sun Belt. I wanted to try something else. She was in New York, and you were married. Alaska had always intrigued me." She shrugged. "I just hadn't intended to stay so long."

"What made you change your mind?" Blythe picked up a cookie and took a bite.

Fiona pushed a strand of hair behind her ear and shifted in her chair. "I'd expected to stay a year, year and a half. I wanted to be more than just a tourist."

"You were gone three years." Blythe tried to keep the statement from sounding like an accusation.

The younger woman turned her face up to the skylight, a rectangle of star-dotted black in the ceiling. Russet hair rippled down her back and her pale skin reminded Blythe of pearls. The lovely green eyes were closed. Finally Fiona spoke. "I liked Alaska, but last year I was ready to come home. Two years was long enough."

Blythe remained silent and waited.

Fiona stared down into her teacup. Long seconds of silence made it clear that what she was about to say would be difficult for her. "Then I met a man," she began slowly. "There was an immediate attraction. We both liked the same foods, we laughed at the same jokes, we enjoyed the same books. It's hard to put into words." Fiona glanced up at her sister. "He's wonderful, Blythe. You'd like him. Being with him made me feel whole, and very much alive. One thing led to another and we moved in together. He asked me to marry him, but I was *afraid!* I kept thinking about...well, about the way we grew up." Absently she ran her finger around the rim of the teacup.

"Someday I'd like to have children and I don't want that for them."

Blythe was careful to keep her voice neutral. "And you think you can give your children a more secure life by not getting married?"

A smile attempted to assert itself on Fiona's lips and failed. "It doesn't make much sense, does it? All I know is that I didn't want to get married until I could work out my confusion."

"No one can fault you for that. What happened?"

"All I wanted was to be with him. I just wanted to continue the way we were." A small sob caught in her throat. Fiona blinked rapidly and took a deep breath. "He kept on, about getting married. You know, a little whisper here, a note with a flower there. Bringing it up at dinner now and then, and sometimes, when we made... at night." Fiona squeezed her eyes shut and shook her head in angry frustration. "I just couldn't take any more of it. I *wanted* to marry him, to make him happy. *Us* happy. God, I just couldn't do it!" Her fragile features twisted in grief.

Swiftly rounding the table, Blythe perched on the arm of the chair and gently pulled her sister close to her side. Fiona clung to her.

"Maybe you just need some time away from him, to think," Blythe murmured, stroking her sister's hair soothingly.

Fiona drew a shuddering breath. "I sneaked away, Blythe. I waited until he was at work, then I threw my clothes into my suitcases and I left. He's hurt, I know it, and probably worried about me. I'm such a coward. You never would have done something like that. Would you?" The tears came and Blythe held her sister, feeling the slim body quake. Finally the weeping subsided, softening to small hiccuped gasps.

Blythe leaned back to examine Fiona's sorrow-stained face, knowing a sorrow of her own. "Why didn't you call me?" *Why have you shut me out of your life?*

Tear-bright eyes met Blythe's. "I'm sorry."

"You were never very good at writing letters, either."

"What Ethan and I had seemed almost too perfect. I was sure it couldn't last, that it would only be a matter of time until it blew up in my face. I was afraid if I wrote how I felt about him it might doom our... love."

Fiona's hesitation over the last word caught at Blythe's heart. How well she knew the difficulty of verbalizing that emotion. That one small word encompassed such a deep well of self. To speak it was to risk rejection. It opened you to hurt.

Fiona blew her nose. In a muffled voice she continued. "I told him everything, you know. What our life was like, growing up. How I was feeling. Blythe, he was so good, so understanding. Then when I moved in with him..." Fresh tears threatened to spill over.

"Yes?" Blythe encouraged gently.

"I was embarrassed to tell you we were living together."

"Oh, come on." She found that hard to believe.

"I was!" Fiona insisted. "And I'm not looking forward to telling Mom, either," she muttered.

"Now *that's* a different story," Blythe agreed. Their mother was a great believer in marriage. Five trips to the altar had demonstrated that.

Fiona hugged her sister. "I'm glad I've got you."

"I'm glad you're finally home, kiddo. I only wish it was under better circumstances."

Fiona blew her nose again and hiccuped. "You wouldn't have run, would you? You've always been strong."

Blythe thought about it. "I don't know, Fiona. I've never had a man love me the way it sounds Ethan loves you." There had been a time when she'd wished for such a thing. But that was before her marriage to Andrew. She was wiser now.

"Blythe, do you think we're going to end up like Mom?"

Each of Madeline Rousseau's marriages had ended in divorce. After the last, she had moved to New York City and thrown herself into a new career. The past was something the three women did not discuss. To hear Fiona broach the subject now gave Blythe the true measure of her sister's turmoil.

In the balmy warmth of the evening, Blythe shivered. The question summed up that secret, shadowy fear that had haunted her since the decline of her relationship with Andrew. Though she kept telling herself such a concern was ridiculous, she knew enough about the hidden poisons of the mind to wonder. And that, in itself, might be part of a self-fulfilling prophecy. With one marriage chalked up to her discredit, had she already started down the road her mother had forged?

"Do you think she's unhappy?" Blythe countered.

Fiona gave this question a moment's consideration. "No," she answered slowly, as if uncertain her answer made sense. "She's beautiful, and interesting, and fun. Men are just naturally attracted to her. And I think she likes them as much as they like her." She shook her head. "No, I don't think she's unhappy. I hope not. And I've never doubted for a minute that she loves us, that we're important to her."

"I've wondered about whether or not I'll become another Madeline Rousseau," admitted Blythe. The fear was like a toxic cloud: drifting, insubstantial, virulent. "But I have to believe we're both capable of loving a man for a lifetime. And if we're careful, we'll each choose one who can return that love."

Blythe clung to that hope. Loving had never been the problem. She had given her love to each new father Madeline had brought her—until she had learned the vows of forever were good for only a few years. Even Andrew had not kept his promise. The divorce papers had been in process at the time of his fatal automobile accident.

No, it was trust she didn't have. And now she knew Fiona didn't have it, either. Blythe couldn't bring herself to tell her grieving sister trust was something learned, and they'd had little opportunity to learn it.

She read the signs of fatigue in Fiona's streaked face. "It's late. After you've spent so much time traveling I'm amazed you haven't already crashed." She hugged her sister. "I missed you."

Later, settled in the warm nest of her bed, Blythe found the conversation with her sister running through her mind like an endless loop. Both of Madeline Rousseau's daughters were unsure. Each harbored the same irrational, insidious fear. Blythe had tried to circumvent it through logic. Fiona had allowed it to rule her.

Both had failed.

CHAPTER THREE

BLYTHE SPENT the next morning calling up stock quotes and other investor information on the Quotron with her right hand, while flipping the pages of her account books with her left hand. She cradled the telephone handset between shoulder and jaw. The market was moving up and a number of her people were in position to take profits.

By eleven o'clock she had a kink in her neck, but she also had several orders to her credit and many pleased clients.

She picked up yellow legal sheets covered with scrawled notes and numbers and walked out to her sales assistant's desk. "Ginny, I need this proposal typed. I have an appointment with the Breslers Thursday morning."

Ginny nodded as she accepted the papers. "What about Mrs. Bevane and Miss McKeon's proposal? They're scheduled for Monday at one."

"Here 'tis. Pretty incredible. I wouldn't have put them into these things—" she waved the page listing the elderly women's current investments "—even if they had begged me for the most speculative stocks and limited partnerships I could find. I think the ladies should sic their nephew on their *ex*-broker."

Ginny whistled softly. "Oh, you're mean."

Blythe feigned an expression of wounded innocence. "Just trying to save the taxpayers a little money. Think of the time and trouble the Securities and Exchange Commission would be saved if Super Nephew swooped down and wrung a confession out of Fosker."

"His heart's in the right place. Everything else he has is, too." Ginny sighed. "He's the best-looking man I've seen in . . . well, ever. Nice buns."

"How could you tell?" Blythe asked. "He had a suit on."

With a sniff of disdain, Ginny rolled a finished proposal out of her typewriter. "Some of us aren't blind, Ms. Summers."

"Be nice, or I'll tell Victor you've been ogling the male clients again." Blythe could anticipate the handsome Victor's response. He'd pat his wife on the fanny and grin, then inform Blythe he had no fear—Ginny might look at other men, but she came to him for action.

"Good heavens, look at that!" Ginny's brown eyes widened as she stared past Blythe. Quickly Blythe turned around.

Coming down the aisle was the largest, most elaborate floral arrangement Blythe had ever seen. Lilies, orchids and roses were accompanied by blooms unfamiliar to her. Their colors and delicacy were breathtaking. Only the legs and feet of the delivery man were visible. "B. K. Summers?" his muffled voice asked.

"I am." Blythe raised her hand, then realizing he couldn't see her gesture, quickly lowered it.

"Where can I set this?"

She guided him into her office and hastily cleared a space on the credenza.

Seconds after the delivery man left there was a crowd in the office.

Blythe stared at the extravaganza in wonder.

"Who sent it? Someone special?" asked Leonard Brock, a broker who specialized in bonds.

"I don't know." Immediately Blythe looked for the card, thinking the delivery man might have made a mistake. She plucked the envelope from the holder but refused to open it while Leonard stood so close.

"I'll bet this is from You-Know-Who," Ginny said. Her dark eyes twinkled.

"You-Know-Who?" Leonard prompted.

His reputation as a notorious gossip was well-deserved and Blythe had no intention of providing any grist for his mill. "Just a client who was rude," she told him.

"His regrets are very expensive." Leonard eyed the arrangement. "These aren't exactly dandelions."

"They are beautiful, aren't they?" Blythe smiled, hoping Leonard would leave.

"Must've been quite an insult," the bond specialist persisted with a smirk.

Blythe gazed at the arrangement. "He must have thought so," she murmured.

Leonard gave up and left. Ginny watched him walk back toward his office as the rest of the group drifted away. "Leonard is such a busybody," she muttered.

Blythe glanced at the card, then reached out and softly touched the petal of a rose with her fingertip. "Ginny, how did you know these were from Mr. McKeon?"

The sales assistant sighed and rolled her eyes heavenward, as if praying for patience. "You always underestimate your attraction for the opposite sex."

Ginny stood on her toes, trying to peer over Blythe's shoulder. "What does the note say?"

Blythe studied the scrawled message, then handed the small gilt-edged card to her friend. "Hardly professing his undying admiration," she commented dryly.

"'My apologies for yesterday,'" Ginny read aloud. "'Please believe that first impressions are seldom reliable.'" She looked up at Blythe. "Notice he said '*first* impressions.' How can you have a first without at least a second? He'll call," she announced smugly.

Scowling, Blythe snatched the card from Ginny's hand. Unable to squeeze between the desk and the flowers, Blythe settled into a client chair.

Five minutes later her telephone buzzed. Suspiciously she glared out her glass wall to see Ginny smiling back at her with angelic sweetness. Pulling the phone around to face her, Blythe lifted the handset to her ear.

"Duncan McKeon is on the line," Ginny sang.

Blythe's eyes narrowed. "Did you call him?"

"No," Ginny replied, sounding wounded. "I certainly did not." Her voice perked up. "I told you he'd call. Just call me Madame Dora."

"More like Witch Hazel," Blythe muttered, half under her breath.

"I heard that! He's all yours."

"No! Ginny, wait—!"

"Hello?" asked a new voice. "I'm holding for Mrs. Summers."

"This is she." *Sound professional. That's it: professional. He's probably used to women melting all over him. Well,* I'm *not going to.*

"Mrs. Summers, I want to apologize for my rudeness yesterday." His voice was a rich baritone—a fact easier to discern when it was not raised in anger.

"You did that yesterday, Mr. McKeon. And I've just received your lovely flower arrangement. It really is most . . . impressive. Thank you."

"Then I'm forgiven and you'll have lunch with me?"

That smooth devil. "Yes, you are forgiven, and no, I will not have lunch with you." *Of course, not, Summers, you'd rather eat a turkey sandwich at your desk. Again.*

The masculine voice on the other end of the line sounded genuinely disappointed. "Then I'm not forgiven. Not really."

"I make it a practice, Mr. McKeon, to have lunch only with those little old ladies whose accounts I've targeted to churn." *That's for yesterday!*

There was a pause. "I very much want to take you to lunch, but I draw the line at donning a blue-rinsed wig and sensible shoes."

Blythe pictured the imperious Duncan McKeon in a lavender wig and orthopedic wedgies. She choked back laughter, managing to convert it to a cough.

"Look," coaxed that spine-melting, butter-cream voice, "I know I behaved badly. You'd be perfectly justified if you pitched the flowers out the window and hung up on me. I'll make you a deal. If you let me take you to lunch, we'll go to a place that serves crow. I'll order a nice big helping and eat it while you watch."

Blythe knew she was justified in refusing to accept his apology. But she also knew it was probably difficult for him to apologize. She decided she could afford to be gracious.

"That won't be necessary, Mr. McKeon." She paused as she considered his invitation. "Lunch at The Gardens would be pleasant. Say today at twelve?" That gave him less than thirty minutes to hightail it over to the restaurant, which was a few blocks from Stewart Duke.

"Fine. I'll meet you at your office."

"I'd rather meet you at the restaurant," Blythe said primly.

"Am I forgiven or not?"

Blythe hesitated. "Yes, you are."

"Then I'll meet you at your office."

After she hung up, Blythe refused to satisfy the curiosity she knew must be consuming Ginny. Instead, she grabbed her purse and fled to the ladies' room where she freshened her makeup, smoothed her hair and told herself accepting the luncheon invitation had probably been a mistake.

ATTIRED in a hastily donned burgundy polo shirt, dark gray cotton slacks and loafers, Duncan walked into the plush lobby of Stewart, Duke, Renken and Koenig, Inc. He supposed it would be too much to hope his last visit had not attained him notoriety. Inwardly he sighed. The sooner he faced this down, the better.

He summoned a winning smile for the receptionist and told her he was there to see Mrs. Summers. The pretty blonde stammered the news of his arrival into her telephone headpiece.

Duncan wished he had that effect on his aunts' stockbroker. Convincing her to have lunch with him had been downright awkward. For a minute there, he'd thought she would refuse his invitation. But then, she had good reason to want nothing more to do with him.

"Mr. McKeon?" The familiar alto voice was unintentionally sensuous. He looked up to see Blythe standing before him.

"Mrs. Summers?" The prospect of spending time with this woman suddenly looked more appealing. He smiled his pleasure and was delighted as her captivating lips curved up in answer.

Duncan opened the door for Blythe. "After you, *madame.*"

"*Merci.*"

"I love a woman who speaks French!" he exclaimed, suddenly feeling as relaxed as if they had been friends for years.

They walked briskly to the restaurant, where they were ushered to a table in a corner that afforded them a certain amount of privacy. Skylights provided the lovely garden room with natural illumination, enhancing the pristine pink of the linens.

A waitress brought them menus. Silently they studied the list of offerings. Seconds passed, then minutes. Blythe decided on the club sandwich and laid her menu neatly in front of her. When Duncan glanced up at her, then returned his attention to making his selection, she wished they'd get the conversation started. She found the silence awkward.

After the waitress had taken their order, Blythe asked, "So, what brings you to Winter Park, Mr.

McKeon? Are you mixing business with the pleasure of seeing your aunts?''

"Yes. I've got some business that may keep me here a while.''

She waited, but when he made no effort to elaborate on the nature of his concern she knew he didn't wish to discuss it. Politely she moved to another subject. "Well, I'm certain your aunts are happy you're here.''

"Can I persuade you to call me Duncan, instead of Mr. McKeon?'' he asked.

"Yes, you can, by calling me Blythe.''

Color crept up his high cheekbones. "I guess I need to explain why I called on you yesterday.''

"I thought you made that very clear before you left.''

He studied his water glass for a few seconds, then looked up, locking eyes with her. "You aren't going to make this easy, are you?''

Blythe felt a shock at the jolting impact of his gaze. She suppressed the urge to look away, forcing herself to maintain that disconcertingly intimate contact. "I . . . Reputation is very important to a broker, Mr. —''

"Duncan.''

"—Duncan. People are concerned about the individual who handles their nest eggs, and the funds that will one day pay for their children's educations. Would you allow someone you distrusted to invest your money for you?''

He opened his mouth to say something, seemed to think better of it and shook his head.

"I thought not. You'd be foolish if you did.'' She leaned slightly forward, her forearms resting on the edge of the table. "I've worked hard to establish a reputation for excellence. When someone trusts me enough to make me their broker, I take it very seriously. Over the years I've built a respectable business in an industry that doesn't always get the best press. It doesn't always deserve it. But brokers, on the whole, are hardworking, honest people."

"I never said they weren't. I was concerned about one broker—the one who ripped off my aunts."

"And you thought I was the guilty party," she supplied dryly.

"Let me explain."

Blythe leaned back in her chair, ready to listen.

"Martha and Amelia have led sheltered lives. They were raised to believe discussing money was vulgar. Their father, my grandfather, took care of the finances. For the year Martha was married her husband, Horace, handled all that. Neither lady knows anything about managing money. Now I take care of their regular accounts and they think I'm brilliant."

"And you don't want anyone to blow the whistle on you, is that it?"

He laughed. It was a rich, rumbling baritone. Like a net, it spun out and captured her. "You could say that. Martha and Amelia have played an important part in my life and I'd like to maintain my status of being reliable and omniscient."

"Sounds like you and your aunts are close."

His smile gentled. "When I was a kid they came to all my ball games. They were always room mothers. Martha even ran for PTA president, but she wasn't elected." Duncan chuckled. "I think she was relieved."

No wonder he's so protective of Martha and Amelia, Blythe thought as she studied the man across the table. She found herself beginning to like Duncan.

"It bothered me they had missed the experience of controlling their own finances. I didn't want them to worry about it, though, so a couple of years ago I gave them a gift of money. I suggested they invest it and use it to learn how to make capital grow. It was their play money. I gave them the ledger I showed you, and taught how to enter each transaction." He lifted one shoulder in a slight shrug. "They showed absolutely no interest in investing, so I didn't press." His smile faded. "Eventually they entrusted it with a broker, and he took a very personal interest in it. But I didn't learn about it until yesterday. I thought the money was still sitting in their bank. When I found out the account had been . . ." He groped for the word.

"Churned," she supplied.

"I was furious. You know the rest." His color had deepened again.

A wistful longing to know such care from a man drifted through Blythe. In surprised alarm she quickly crushed it.

"Why did your aunts open the account in Atlanta if they live here?" she asked.

"When I asked them that, they told me they felt the money was safer in Atlanta, because that's where I was. They were planning to tell me as soon as they worked up the courage to get more involved in selecting the securities. But then, based on a recommendation from friends, they decided to switch to you. That's how the . . . misunderstanding . . . happened."

"Oh, lucky me." Blythe could well imagine his fury at discovering Amelia and Martha had been swindled. All things considered, perhaps his behavior had been quite civilized.

His expression was serious. "I hate to think what kind of a crackpot you thought I was. I *can* use the past tense, can't I?"

Before she could answer, their food arrived. When they were alone again, Blythe smiled at Duncan.

"You know, I was surprised when the flowers arrived this morning. I don't think I've ever seen such a gorgeous arrangement. And your call to invite me to lunch. Duncan, that took courage. Most people would never have worked up the nerve to face me again. Your apology is accepted."

He inclined his head in acknowledgment. He flashed a grin, revealing even, white teeth. "For a minute there, you had me sweating."

She reached nervously for her water glass. "Oh? How?"

"I make it a practice, Mr. McKeon," he mimicked the prim tone she had used with him over the telephone, "to have lunch only with those little old ladies whose accounts I churn."

Blythe groaned. "I really was that ungracious, wasn't I?"

"You were," he agreed, with a wicked smile.

"Well, you deserved it."

"I'm a swine."

"I won't argue with that," she agreed lightly.

"What! After everything you put me through? I deserve a medal for patience."

"Everything I put *you* through? You stormed into my office and accused me of *theft!*" She was leaning forward, over the table.

He leaned forward until they were nose to nose, only a pause apart. "You *could* have *told* me immediately my aunts had just opened the account with you! Instead, you allowed me to go on and on!"

Suddenly Blythe realized how near he was. His eyes. So silvery gray. And such thick, black lashes.

He was looking at her mouth. Was he thinking of kissing her?

She reminded herself she was a respectable businesswoman sitting in a Park Avenue restaurant.

Blythe eased back in her chair. Duncan withdrew to his own side of the table.

They spoke of the weather, comparing Atlanta and Winter Park, then moved on to other neutral topics. Gradually Blythe regained most of her inner composure, but there remained an awareness of Duncan, an electric current that hummed just under the surface of her skin.

"Amelia told my sales assistant you own a computer software company," she said. "You built it up from scratch. Macrocosm, right?"

"Yes." Duncan settled back, looking at ease. "Macrocosm, Inc. is the name of the company. We started out as a software house specializing in the hospitality industry." His expression was that of a proud parent trying hard not to boast about his achievement-oriented child. "We've expanded into other fields now. Education, government, industry, medicine. But I still have a special affection for the hospitality division."

Their waitress stopped at their table briefly to collect their dishes and to pour steaming coffee. Blythe waited for hers to cool a little. "Why did you decide to base Macrocosm in Atlanta? Aren't most of the hotels concentrated in Florida, Hawaii and California?''

Duncan paused as he lifted the cup to his lips. ''I live in Atlanta.''

''What's it like, being CEO of a software house in the hub of the South?'' Blythe smiled.

''It's probably about the same as being CEO of a software house anywhere else in the United States.''

''Which is . . . ?''

''Hard work.''

''Do you travel much?''

''More than I like. Lately it seems as if I spend my life on planes.'' He grimaced good-naturedly.

''Oh? Anyplace exotic?''

''Definitely.'' Duncan laughed. ''Mysterious Orlando, center of the Worlds.'' Though a city in its own right, Winter Park was considered part of the Greater Orlando Area.

''Gee.''

He leaned toward Blythe, conspirator-fashion. From under lowered lids he glanced first to his right, then to his left, and leaned a little closer. ''I was warned about coming here,'' he told her sotto voce. ''Too many people have been known to visit this area and refuse to return to the ice and snow. We suspect the water.'' Again he looked in either direction and his voice gave melodramatic import to his words. ''Sink holes.''

Delighted to find this playful side of Duncan, she moved slightly closer. Blythe could feel his warm breath on her cheek. It sent a tingle down her back. ''You're not—?''

''Yes. The Federal Sink Hole Inspector.'' Duncan nodded solemnly.

She pressed the knuckles of one hand to her lips. Pale eyebrows drew up in feigned shock.

"I'm incognito," he whispered. "As a tourist."

"Does that mean you wear tasteless flowered shirts and baggy walking shorts?"

"And sandals over knee socks."

"My lips are sealed."

His quicksilver eyes lowered to gaze at her mouth. Once again his strong masculine aura vibrated against her senses, like a wand to a tuning fork. Again she pulled away.

"Have you always lived in Atlanta?" she asked.

"Always."

She couldn't recall ever having met anyone who'd lived in one town all his life.

"What about you? Are you a native Floridian?"

Blythe smiled. "I think there are only about twenty *native* Floridians left in Florida. The rest have moved up to North Carolina. By today's standard, though, I'm almost a native. I've lived here twenty years. Originally my family is from Virginia."

Duncan studied the woman across from him. He'd been tempted to kiss her when he'd found her so close earlier. Her eyes had widened, and her mouth—that ripe, soft mouth—had parted slightly, as if in surprise. He'd wanted to bury his hand in her hair and take her lips in a heated kiss.

It surprised him, this sharp attraction to her, but he didn't know why it should. She was intelligent and beautiful. But her life was here, and his was in Atlanta. He didn't need complications.

Blythe glanced at her watch.

"I lost track of time," Duncan said. "Can I assume two hours is not the standard stockbroker lunch?"

She smiled, and Duncan absorbed its warmth. "Yes," she said. "But there are exceptions."

"Like today?"

"Like today."

Were these other exceptions shared with men who also found themselves attracted to her? Men who lived in Winter Park? The thought brought Duncan an instant of dissatisfaction.

He walked her back to the lobby of Stewart Duke where they said goodbye. Blythe thanked him for lunch. Smiling, she turned and walked down the hall that led to her office.

It irritated Duncan to see her so apparently unaffected by him. Pushing open the heavy glass door and stepping into the bright spring sunshine, he decided Blythe's indifference alleviated any temptation to initiate a long-distance affair. With his aunts' dependence on him, and the demands of Macrocosm, he had enough to handle.

Not three seconds after Blythe entered her office and started sorting through pink telephone messages, Ginny appeared in the doorway. "Well? How did it go?"

"Ginny, it was lunch, not a betrothal."

"One step at a time." The sales assistant slipped into a client chair. "Did he grovel for your forgiveness?"

"Certainly not."

"Good. Any of your other feebs would've. I had a feeling about this one, though."

"Good for you. Now, if—"

But Ginny was not to be put off. "Did you have an enjoyable time?"

Yes. She had. It had been…well…*fun.* Blythe tried to recall the last time she'd had that much fun. Frowning, she realized she couldn't remember. It had been too long. That thought gave her pause, demanded that she take a good look at her life. *Later.*

"I had a very pleasant lunch," she answered noncommittally.

"Did he ask you out?"

"Of course he did." Blythe played dumb, knowing full well what Ginny meant. "That's why we went to lunch." It was difficult to look innocent under such scrutiny.

"Did he, or did he not ask you out *again?* You know I'll get it out of you eventually, so you might as well tell me now."

"No, he did not ask me out. Okay? Satisfied? Can we get back to work now? I've already goofed off longer than I should've."

"I was wrong about him," said Ginny, disgust plain on her face. "He's just another turkey." She stood up and walked out of the office. "Call your sister," she threw back over her shoulder.

For a moment Blythe sat and stared into space. She was getting nothing accomplished today. The hour she had allotted for lunch had turned into two. Two marvelous hours, filled with the company of an extremely attractive man. It seemed impossible something as simple as lunch could have been so enjoyable. Maybe Ginny was right to nag her so relentlessly to "get out."

Actually she did get out. She attended an occasional play, went to dinner, went to a party now and then, always on the arm of a handsome escort. She liked the men she dated. And they liked her. It was quite safe.

Blythe didn't think Duncan McKeon would be at all safe. Her attraction to him was difficult to analyze. That disturbed her.

She'd been in the company of good-looking, intelligent men before. With McKeon there was something more, something she couldn't quite define. It was out of her previous experience.

She palmed her paperweight. Martha and Amelia's nephew had apologized effectively. Very effectively. There wasn't much chance of his magnetism becoming a problem, though. He'd made no move to continue their acquaintance.

Resolutely, Blythe pushed Duncan McKeon out of her mind, and dialed her home number.

"Hi," Fiona's voice greeted her. There was a pause. "I called Mom."

"I don't suppose you kept in touch with her any more than you did me."

"No."

"I see. What did she have to say?"

Fiona sighed. "Plenty. I'm thoughtless. I've worried her nearly to death. Why have I done this to her? Oh, yes—and she loves me."

"You're charming, Fiona."

"Thank you." There was a pause. "I know she's hurt I didn't write. I did call her a few times. Not enough, I guess. But here's the interesting part of our conversation—Mom is going to Indiatlantic for a couple weeks' vacation. She's invited us to dinner, Friday, and suggested we spend the weekend. I told her you had to meet some clients in the office on Saturday."

"Oh, that's right. Rats!" Blythe doodled on her notepad. "Well, I'll just come back here in the morning. Did you tell her about...about what happened?"

"No," Fiona said, "not yet."

"I see."

"Stop saying that. She said to bring the wine and our handwork. For dinner it's spaghetti with meatballs. And for dessert—spumoni ice cream."

Blythe groaned. "That woman knows our weaknesses, doesn't she? Check the wine rack. I have a few nice reds. Do you have any favorites?"

"What I know about wine you could fit on the head of a pin."

Mentally Blythe went through her inventory. "I know just the one. Do you need anything for handwork?"

Fiona feigned indignation. "Of course not. Idle hands are tools of the devil."

"A stitch in time saves nine. I'll be home in about an hour."

So, their mother was coming to Florida. Over the past several years, Blythe could count on the fingers of one hand the number of times Madeline Rousseau had returned to her house in Indiatlantic. She only kept the place for her rare Florida vacations, and for her daughters to use for weekend getaways. After all, how could a small east Florida coastal town compete with the constant flash and sizzle of New York City? And, of course, there was her work in the world headquarters of Jonquil. The position of sales director for such an upscale cosmetics company had to provide no little excitement in itself.

Thirty minutes later, as Blythe scraped papers into a client's file, it occurred to her she had forgotten to ask her sister why their mother was coming back.

As always, when Madeline made one of her rare Florida appearances, Blythe found herself asking the same question: Was her mother preparing to marry again?

CHAPTER FOUR

"WHAT I WANT TO KNOW is how she got three consecutive men to live in the same house," Fiona said.

Blythe's gaze swept over the familiar used-brick and white-columned house. "Simple." She shut the Volvo's trunk. "She refused to move."

Fiona shifted her weight from one foot to the other. "Do you think she's planning to get married again?"

That, thought Blythe, *is what I'd like to know.* "The wallpaper should tell us something." Madeline changed it throughout the house whenever she was planning to marry. It was as if she hoped a different color and pattern would grant a fresh start.

The tightness in her sister's face remained. "That's right. The wallpaper."

"Come on." Blythe picked up her overnight bag and led the way to the front door, which swung open before she could knock.

"There you are," their mother exclaimed, ushering them into the house. "I thought I heard a car pull up."

Tall and trim, with stylishly tousled blond hair, Madeline Rousseau did not look her forty-nine years. She embraced each daughter.

Blythe glanced around. The wallpaper in the foyer was the same as she remembered from her last visit. The bands of tension squeezing Blythe's chest eased.

Why should she care if her mother remarried? She had her own life now.

Her gaze flicked across the small Queen Anne table. Daisies in a Waterford vase kept company with an antique silver frame. The latter housed a photograph of herself and Fiona, two smiling toddlers with chocolate-ringed mouths.

"Let's put the bags in your rooms," said Madeline, leading the way down the hall.

Blythe didn't follow her mother and sister immediately. Instead, she reached out and picked up the old photograph, absently running her thumb over the relief vine work on the side of the frame. Childish grins of long ago brought an echoing curve to her lips. Amazing how resilient kids are, Blythe thought as she set the picture back in its place.

The wallpaper might change, but this photo in its heirloom frame did not. Since the first day they'd moved here it had greeted every visitor, three stepfathers among them.

She carried her bag to her room and quickly unpacked.

Madeline peered around the edge of the door as Blythe finished up. "What about a glass of wine before dinner?"

Blythe smiled and hoisted the thermal wine carrier. "All set. Chardonnay sound good?"

"Perfect. And red wine for the marinara and meatballs?"

"Chianti Classico."

Madeline beamed her approval. "I knew there was a reason I married only men who knew wine."

Blythe stiffened, forcing her smile in place. "After you, Mom." She indicated the way to the kitchen.

Minutes later, the three women wandered across the patio and down the sloped lawn to the canal and the dock with bench seats.

Legs stretched out in front of her, Blythe sipped the cool, crisp wine. A breeze teased loose tendrils of her hair, tickling her jaws and nape. Faint, homey sounds of families at dinner drifted from the houses nearby.

"So," Madeline said, patting her younger daughter's leg, "tell me all about Alaska."

Fiona shifted restlessly. After a moment she answered, "It was okay."

Madeline laughed. "Okay? A woman goes off to the Yukon Territories, she's bound to have adventures."

Blythe felt sorry for her sister. "The Yukon Territory is part of Canada, Mom."

The older woman waved a hand in dismissal. "Alaska. Yukon. It's all cold. Fiona, you can't tell me you hibernated all that time."

Fiona cast a desperate glance at Blythe who shrugged. Hesitantly she began to recount the events of the past three years. This time there were no tears. Madeline listened quietly, but when Fiona spoke of living with Ethan, the older woman's spine stiffened. Her fingers drummed on the back of the bench. Blythe rolled the Chardonnay around on her tongue as she listened to Fiona and watched Madeline's slim fingers tapping the weathered wood.

She had known it would be like this.

Abruptly Blythe tossed back the last mouthful of her wine and stood. She paced the few steps to the other side of the dock and glared down at the water.

She remembered too vividly the cutting accusations, the bitter barbs hurled between Madeline and each husband when romance wore thin. Madeline had never failed to use her children as bludgeons to drive home the faults of every man she'd married. The last excuse had always been "poor father." Yet "good father" had never been a requirement when she chose her men.

Where did she get off judging Fiona? At least there had only been *one* man. At least Fiona hadn't had children to get chewed up in the crossfire. Again...and again...and again.

Blythe turned back to the other women just in time to see Madeline rise gracefully from the bench and shake out her full cotton skirt.

"Well. I must say, Fiona, your stay in Alaska was eventful."

Fiona nodded and looked away.

"I can't pretend I'm happy you lived with a man. If you were so much in love, I don't understand why you didn't just get married. He asked you, didn't he?"

"Yes." Fiona continued to gaze into the distance.

"Then why—"

"Maybe she didn't want to," Blythe said impatiently, cutting into Madeline's persistent questioning. "Did you know that in the last three years Fiona has built quite a reputation for herself as a potter?"

Madeline frowned. "And she couldn't have done it if she was married? I don't see why—"

Anger seared over half-healed wounds. "Maybe she didn't feel the *need* to be married," Blythe snapped.

Color drained from Madeline's face as she stared at her older daughter in shock. Her mouth quivered, and she quickly pressed her fingers to it. Blinking rapidly, she turned away as a tear slipped down her cheek.

The single droplet sliced a piece from Blythe's heart, flooding her with remorse. She'd promised herself this wouldn't happen. Certain subjects were best left untouched.

"Oh, Mom." She stepped forward and wrapped her arms around her mother who quickly dashed the tear away. "I'm sorry. Please." Blythe released a weary sigh. "Please, let's not do this."

`Madeline raised her hand to Blythe's cheek. "It's just—" She swallowed and tried again. "It's just that I worry about the both of you." She included Fiona in her gaze. The younger woman bit her lip. "Don't you think I know what I've done? How I've hurt you? I never intended to. I wish I could make you believe that."

"We believe it," Fiona said softly.

Easy for Fiona to say. She hadn't spent her days trying to shield a younger sister from the hurt of having yet another stepfather who didn't care a whit about children. Blythe had finally learned it was safest not to become attached to Madeline's men. None of them had ever wanted to be "Daddy." Not even her own father.

As she looked into those green eyes so like the color of Fiona's, Blythe knew she couldn't ask the questions that haunted her. Instead, she said, "Yes, Mom, we believe you." And she did. Madeline had given her daughters a legacy of doubt. She had also given them unconditional love.

Backing out of her daughter's embrace, Madeline took Blythe's hands between her own. She smiled. "I worry about the both of you. A mother's natural concern when she has two unmarried daughters. Someday I would like grandchildren, you know." She took a quick breath and released it. "Now, enough of living in the past. Who's hungry?"

They returned to the house and together they added the final touches to dinner. Once seated at Madeline's elegantly set table they dropped a curtain on the unhappiness of the past and reminisced about the good times. Their laughter sparkled.

"How will I have room for spumoni if you keep passing me the meatballs?" Fiona complained.

Madeline grinned. "You're a growing girl."

"If I grow anymore I'll be seven feet tall!"

"Or seven feet around," Blythe drawled, earning a peculiar look from her sister.

Madeline said firmly, "Nonsense. Neither of my girls will ever be anything other than beautiful."

Blythe got up from the table and walked into the kitchen to make coffee, followed by Fiona and Madeline, who joined her in the work of cleaning up and preparing dessert.

"How's your social life, Mom?" Blythe asked. The words were ritual, the understood meaning translating as: Are you serious about a particular man?

Madeline sliced the layered ice cream and lifted the slices onto gilt-edged plates. "You know, I'm beginning to think I got all the good ones. Until lately I've been very disappointed in the men I've met. They have no style, no sense of...of..."

"Romance?" supplied Blythe through clenched teeth.

Like a fairy godmother granting a wish, Madeline waved her cake server, apparently unaware of her daughter's reaction. "Exactly! They don't know how to *woo* a woman. I feel more as if I'm being *stalked*."

Blythe poured soap powder into the small receptacle on the dishwasher door. "You said 'until lately.' Does this mean you've met a man you're not disappointed in?" She closed the door more forcefully than she'd meant to.

Madeline frowned slightly. "Blythe, do be careful."

After they ate dessert they cleared the table and brought their handwork into the family room. As they talked, their fingers worked needles, fabric and yarn.

It had been too many years since they had spent an evening together like this, Blythe reflected. Husbands, father and stepfathers had come and gone but the three of them were a family.

Had their very closeness affected Madeline's marriages? Blythe wondered. The possibility had never occurred to her before.

"So, Blythe," said Fiona when the conversation had reached a companionable lull. "Do you plan to see Donald McKeon again?"

Caught off guard, Blythe blinked. "Duncan," she corrected. "Duncan McKeon." She glanced at her mother. Blythe could almost see her antennae go up.

"No one's mentioned a McKeon to me." Madeline leaned forward and poured them all more coffee.

"He's the nephew of new clients," said Blythe, casting a venomous glare at Fiona. "He thought I was churning their account when, in fact, it was their former broker who had done it. But Mr. McKeon apologized for his error like a gentleman." She shrugged. "That's all."

Fiona grinned and looked at her mother. "Ginny told me he's beautiful. And he owns a big software house in Atlanta."

Madeline's lips curved in a satisfied smile. "And he, of course, is interested in you," she said to her older daughter.

Blythe groaned inwardly. "No," she stated firmly.

Madeline stopped in the middle of a French knot. She looked over at Fiona who smiled broadly. Bending her head over the stitch again, Madeline said, "He's interested."

Just wait until I get Fiona home! Blythe thought furiously. "No, Mom. He's really *not* interested in me."

She recalled the way Duncan's eyes seemed to attract light and capture it, and felt a twinge of regret.

Madeline frowned. "Is he married?"

Here it came again: the pressure. "No."

"Engaged?"

Blythe lifted her shoulder in a half-shrug. "No." Martha and Amelia had made that quite clear on their first visit.

"Just stupid, then." Madeline sighed. "I've seen it so many times. Often they look perfectly normal. It's sad, really. And it happens even in the best of families."

Blythe, surprised her mother had given up so easily, glanced down at her knitting and smiled.

"He's probably just an incredibly handsome, *nice* man, Mom," Fiona suggested with a strangled quality to her voice. Her eyes gave her amusement away. "Besides, I wouldn't say our own pedigree is excessively pure."

Madeline sent her youngest a reproving stare. "Your fathers, I'll have you know, were from very good stock. *All* my husbands were. My own family came over shortly after the Mayflower."

"About a hundred years after. Not exactly the next ship," Fiona commented.

"Young lady, your forebears fought in the War for Independence. You qualify for membership in the Daughters of the American Revolution, as do your sister and I."

"I'm the envy of all my friends."

Blythe could see it there, shadowed in her sister's eyes, in the tight corners of her smile. Frustration and confusion, anger and sadness.

"There's something to be said for roots," Madeline stated firmly. Her fingers faltered in the execution of the next three stitches, as if she realized their ancestors might have had an unshakable sense of family but her daughters did not.

"How are things with your job, Mom?" Fiona asked.

At the mention of her position as North American marketing manager of Jonquil, Inc., their mother smiled.

Blythe knew Madeline realized how proud her daughters were of her. After her fifth divorce she had moved to New York and taken a job as a secretary with Jonquil, a once prestigious, but then skidding cosmetics company. In seven years, Madeline had been promoted to marketing manager. She had also increased market share, bringing the company's sales higher than ever.

"Oh, hectic. Stressful." Madeline's smile deepened. "Exciting."

"So you might stay a while longer?" Blythe took a sip of her cool coffee, and winked at her mother over the edge of her cup.

Madeline laughed. "You'd better believe it. If they ever want me to leave they'll have to drag me out of there, kicking and screaming. I love my work. I love being a part of Jonquil and I love living in New York. There's never a dull moment."

It was true, Blythe admitted. Life in New York had returned to Madeline the vitality she'd lost after the last divorce.

Again, Blythe longed to question her mother. Why had Madeline married again and again, only to discard her husbands? What was she looking for? What did she need?

But Blythe already knew the answer to her question: Romance. Her mother needed the narcotic of romance. Romance could conceal the rough edges of reality—for a while.

It seemed to Blythe the primary requisite for a prospective husband had always been skill in courtship rituals of a bygone era, mixed with a liberal touch of drama. The length of the marriage depended on his ability to maintain the fantasy after the wedding. When the romance was gone, so was the husband.

Eight years had passed since Madeline's last divorce. That was a record. Apparently romantic fools were harder to find in New York.

Had she finally found one? Was her mother back in Florida to rewallpaper the house? When Blythe had asked her, Madeline had neatly sidestepped giving an answer. Did that mean she planned to go for husband number six?

"Are you dating?" Fiona asked their mother.

"Yes, when I have time."

"Anyone special?" Fiona managed to make the question sound casual, though Blythe knew it was not by the jerking motions of her sister's fingers as she hemmed the skirt draped across her lap.

Madeline looked up from her embroidery. "Should there be?"

Fiona shrugged. "Oh, I don't know. Are you still hoping to find Mr. Right?"

A wistful smile touched Madeline's lips. "All my husbands were Mr. Right, at one time."

"I suppose we all have our moments," Blythe observed dryly. The comment won her a reproving glance from her mother.

THE SATURDAY MORNING appointment for which she'd returned to Winter Park went well, and Blythe came away from it with the satisfaction of knowing her expertise had helped insure her client's wealth and future security.

As she unlocked the door of her house she glanced at her watch. It was only eleven-thirty. Since Fiona had decided to stay the next two weeks with Madeline in Indiatlantic, Blythe had the rest of the day to herself.

She gazed out the window at the brilliant blue sky and wished for another luncheon appointment with Duncan. He was funny and charming and sexy. He'd listened intently when she'd spoken, as if what she'd said had been important to him.

But he'd shown no interest in further association with her, and that was that. It was better this way, she told herself firmly. She had plans for her life.

Instead of going to the health club for a workout as she normally did on Saturday afternoons, Blythe spent the day balancing her checkbook and answering her personal correspondence. By the time she sealed the last envelope it was late afternoon. She settled down on the couch with a much-anticipated mystery novel, and a bowl of buttery popcorn within easy reach.

The book turned out to be a page-turner. It was ten in the evening before she was willing to break for dinner.

Blythe stared into her refrigerator with dissatisfaction. Her stomach demanded food, but her appetite was being finicky. She finally grabbed her purse and drove to the supermarket.

Deciding on a root beer float, she wheeled her cart to the soft drinks. A six-pack of root beer went into the basket, and she headed toward the frozen section where she selected the richest, creamiest vanilla ice cream she could find. And what float was complete without an accompaniment of cookies? Blythe turned into the aisle lined with bags and boxes of cookies, cupcakes and cream-filled snacks.

And discovered Duncan McKeon.

He stood between the Ding Dongs and the Fudge Chewies, looking casually chic in pleated cotton trousers and a striped shirt. He appeared to be examining a package of butter cookies. Blythe noted the contents of his shopping cart: grapes and apples, carrots and bell peppers, brown rice and skim milk.

Dressed in a ratty coral sweatsuit, her hair in a tumbled-down ponytail and her cart burdened with a billion empty calories, Blythe decided now was not the time to renew their acquaintance. Quietly she backed out of the aisle, tugging at her resisting cart. She pulled harder and the wheels screeched like an angry owl.

Duncan looked up to find Blythe Summers with a white-knuckled grip on the handle of her push basket. Missing were her Italian leather pumps, her immaculate suit and sleek hairstyle. Tonight her dress was definitely casual. Bright color bloomed in her cheeks.

He found her irresistibly charming.

"Well, hello," he said. "Out for a little late-night foraging?"

"I got caught up in a book I was reading and time slipped away." She smiled. "Looks like you're doing your weekly shopping. Avoiding the crowds?"

He admired her smooth recovery from her obvious embarrassment. "Actually I had a snack attack, and just came for cookies."

Blythe eyed the contents of his shopping cart. Skim milk? Bell peppers? "Not exactly snack-attack ammunition."

Duncan followed her gaze. "No, it's not, is it? Usually, when I visit Martha and Amelia we eat out, so I haven't noticed what they eat while I'm gone. Tonight when I was going through the kitchen looking for cookies, I discovered they must still be eating the foods they grew up with—stuff high in fat, sodium and loaded with cholesterol. I thought I'd upgrade their pantry."

"You might get a little resistance," Blythe predicted, pleased to find Duncan so concerned about his aunts' well-being.

"Yeah," he agreed. "But it's worth a try. Maybe I'll buy them a new cookbook."

"If you like, I'll share some of my recipes with Martha and Amelia." She saw him glance at the items in her shopping basket. "I'm usually more health-conscious than this," she assured him.

"That would be great. They think a lot of you. Cooking tips and recipes from you would go a lot further than a cookbook from a mere male."

"A male they clearly adore."

"One they've raised to be innocent of the workings of a kitchen."

Blythe widened her eyes. "Oh? As a bachelor, how do you manage? Do you eat out every meal?"

Duncan grinned. "I'm not as innocent as they think."

No doubt. She nodded toward his selection of healthy food. "Where are the cookies you came for?"

"I want to try something new, but everything looks so good. Any suggestions?"

"Oh, yes." She walked to a section where the boxes displayed tempting pictures of chocolate-coated bars, and Duncan followed her. Every sensor in her body snapped alive at his proximity.

She reached up and plucked a package from the shelf. "The inside is peanut butter and more chocolate. They're sinfully good."

"Sounds like my kind of cookie." He reached out and took the package from her hand, his fingers brushing Blythe's. A delicious tremor raced through her.

"I . . . I have a weakness for sweets, too."

He looked at the ice cream and root beer in her cart. "So I see."

Blythe picked up another box of the cookies and placed it in her basket. "I'm having my own snack attack."

Duncan studied the package in his hand for a long moment. "I guess," he said reluctantly, "if I want

Aunt Martha and Aunt Amelia to eat healthier, bringing home cookies isn't the smart thing to do.''

With a small sigh, Duncan put the box back on the shelf. "Are you finished with your shopping?" he asked.

"Uh, not quite."

"Well, I'd better be going. It was good seeing you again."

Blythe was delighted he sounded so sincere. "Nice to see you, too." And she meant every word. How she wished . . . but that was silly.

Blythe waited until he'd disappeared down another aisle before she took off to return the ice cream and root beer. In the produce section she selected and bagged celery and a bunch of California carrots.

When she arrived at the front of the store, she discovered there were only two checkout lanes open. She stepped into line behind Duncan.

He grinned at her, his mouth curving wider as he noticed the change in her groceries. "Still have the cookies, I see."

She grinned back at him. "I couldn't quite bring myself to part with them."

They chatted about inconsequential things while they waited in line. Blythe enjoyed seeing this Duncan, relaxed and sociable, his cart filled with nutritious food for his aunts. The one thing he wanted he'd denied himself in the hopes of coaxing Amelia and Martha into eating more sensibly. She decided she liked Duncan McKeon very much.

He paid for his purchases, and with one final wave, disappeared out the front door. As soon as it was her turn, Blythe quickly paid for her items.

She managed to catch up with Duncan in the parking lot. "I'll share my cookies with you."

Duncan turned to look at her. "What?"

"My cookies." She reached into her bag and held up the package. "I'll share them with you. That way you won't have all that incriminating evidence at your aunts' house." She casually fanned her face with the box. "I wouldn't do it for just anyone, you know. Just self-sacrificing nephew-types."

His exotic features revealed his chagrin as he reached into his shopping bag and slowly withdrew a carton of peanut-butter-and-chocolate cookies. "Not so self-sacrificing, I'm afraid."

Blythe felt foolish for having made her offer. "Oh. Well. *Bon appétit.*" She took a step in the direction of her car, eager to be gone.

"Wait." He reached out and touched her arm, immediately withdrawing his hand as if uncertain of its welcome. "Didn't you say these were sinfully good?"

She paused. "Yes."

He hesitated. "Well, don't you think sin is better when it's shared?"

"I guess I've never thought of it that way."

"You were going to share your cookies with me. I'll share mine with you. Fair's fair." His smile coaxed one from her.

They went to Blythe's car and sat on the hood, under the night sky. The parking lot lamps provided a soft illumination, casting shadows, softening angles. They tore open their packages, and ate greedily. Looking at each other, their faces smudged with chocolate, they burst into laughter.

"Nature's most perfect food!"

"Do you have any mints with you? Martha and Amelia will be able to smell the peanut butter on your breath!"

"I'll say... I'll say I was attacked by a hoard of roasted peanuts. That's my story, and I'm sticking to it."

"But do you have any witnesses, Mr. McKeon?"

"Yes, officer. A blonde with chocolate on her face."

Blythe grinned. "You have chocolate on your face, too. I'll bet you looked a lot like this when you were a kid." *No wonder your aunts love you so much.*

"And you were the little girl with her hair in braids and dessert on her mouth and chin." He tugged gently on a lock of her hair.

Remembering, Blythe sobered. "No, not really. I was expected to be a proper little girl, and I had responsibilities. My sister... Well, I took my position as role model very seriously."

Duncan dug into his cookie box, found it empty and plucked a treat from hers. "Responsibilities. Mine began when I was ten and went to live with Aunt Martha and Aunt Amelia."

She didn't ask what had happened to his parents. The question was too personal.

"My parents were killed in a boating accident," he supplied, as if sensing her question. "My aunts were the only ones willing to take me. If they hadn't, I probably would have been placed in an orphanage."

Blythe tried to think of who would have stepped forward if something had happened to her mother. No one came to mind.

"I know it wasn't easy for them," Duncan continued. "The last thing they needed was a kid." He smiled. "Actually they did need a kid . . . or someone. And I needed them."

"Why did they need someone?" she asked.

"They were always sheltered. Their father believed women were delicate, simple creatures who needed protection from the world."

"Not up to the rigors of reality, eh?"

Duncan's mouth pulled up in a crooked smile. "Precisely. Husbands were expected to come along and take over guard duty, but only Martha married. Her husband, Horace, died a year after the wedding, and she moved back home. When my grandfather died, his daughters were suddenly on their own. Oh, he'd left them a very nice inheritance in a trust, but they had no idea how to balance a checkbook—or even how to write a check. I took over paying the bills and balancing their accounts when I was twelve."

"Not much of a childhood," Blythe murmured.

"I had a great childhood," he hastened to assure her. "It was just a little unorthodox. I had responsibilities, but Aunt Martha and Aunt Amelia were at every practice session and game I played. They cheered so loudly you'd have thought I was the star of the football team. Once they invited the team to our house after a game." His teeth flashed in a grin. "They served tea, and cakes, and little finger sandwiches."

"Really popular with the football players, I'll bet."

"Yeah. But my aunts are such ladies, the team members behaved impeccably."

"Did you get razzed about it afterward?"

The lopsided smile reappeared. "A little."

"Now you're Martha and Amelia's protective knight," Blythe said softly.

"They're doing quite well by themselves, these days."

"But you worry about them." It was a statement of fact. Blythe had seen his concern and was touched by it.

He offered her the last cookie. "Yeah. I do."

She enjoyed the confection, bite by bite.

Slowly he reached out a finger to the corner of her mouth and Blythe went still. She watched, mesmerized, as he brought his chocolate-smeared finger to his own lips, and slipped it between them, sucking.

Breath lodged in her throat.

"Mmm," he murmured, his gaze locked with hers. "Sweet."

He slid off the car and picked up his bag of groceries.

"Thanks for the cookies," he said and, with a rakish salute, turned and strode off across the parking lot, toward his car.

CHAPTER FIVE

FROM HER OFFICE WINDOW, Blythe could see the full moon cast silvery light over the tree-canopied streets of Winter Park. It was Monday night, two nights after her cookie encounter with Duncan. She knew this was the time when friends and lovers strolled Park Avenue. The ice-cream shops and restaurants would be filled with the cheerful murmur of conversation.

Here, the telephones had been silent for hours. Stewart Duke's doors were locked, and the inner offices were dark and empty. All but hers.

"You about finished?" Ginny leaned against the doorframe.

Blythe looked up from the portfolio she was analyzing. "Go home, Rodriguez. You have a husband and kids waiting for you."

Ginny shrugged. "I work late because there's a lot to do. Victor understands."

Blythe opened a drawer and scooped quarters from a glass ashtray full of change. "C'mon," she said, pushing up out of her chair. "Let's get something to drink."

In the employee lounge, which also served as a kitchen complete with microwave oven, sink and range, Blythe inserted the money into the soft drink machine and pushed the buttons for their selections. The women made themselves comfortable, Ginny on the sofa and Blythe in a chair, her feet propped on the seat of another.

"Did you know this stuff gives you cellulite?" Ginny pondered aloud as Blythe took a swig of her ginger ale.

"*Everything* gives you cellulite. Why do you always get orange? Every time you get a soda, it's orange."

"Probably for the same reason you eat so many of those microwave chicken dinners. I noticed when we nuked our meals this evening that's what you had."

"I don't like instant dinners," Blythe said. "I eat them because they save me time I can use to get my work done. I choose the chicken because it's the least revolting."

"Well, I drink orange soda because I like it."

"No kidding."

With a moan of relief, Ginny kicked off her shoes and put her stockinged feet up.

Blythe finally broke the comfortable silence. "I think it's time I hired another sales assistant."

"If we add another full-time sales assistant," Ginny said, "I can take some of the load from you, and we can all go home before nine o'clock at night."

"And what would I do if I didn't have to work thirteen hours a day?" Blythe asked, only half kidding.

"Start dating," the older woman answered promptly. "Maybe go so far as to develop a social life."

"I *have* a social life."

"Oh, sure. When you aren't working here you're working out at the spa. What about men? You don't date."

"I date." Blythe hadn't intended it to sound so feeble.

"I said *men,* not those simps you go out with. I take that back. Not all of them are simps."

"Thank you."

"Some of them are narcissists."

Blythe shifted in her chair. "Who died and left you the dictionary? The men I go out with are good company. They're well educated, with professions of their own. They understand the necessity of working long hours."

Ginny persisted, as if she were a dentist drilling a tooth the Novocaine has not quite numbed. "You're thirty years old and you've been avoiding relationships like a grieving widow. But I know better. I was working for Andrew before you even joined Stewart Duke. He was a crook and a creep."

"Why did you continue to work for him?"

"Victor was trying to get his engineering degree and we had three kids. We needed the money. I was looking for another job, though, until you married Andrew and became his partner."

"His stooge is more like it." Blythe's low chuckle was humorless, directed at the memory of her naiveté, of innocence lost.

Ginny reached out and grasped the younger woman's arm, giving it a little shake. "Hey, don't be so hard on yourself. You were young. You were so starstruck with a flashy senior broker you thought you were in love—"

"I was a blind fool. Why did you stay?"

"Because I thought you needed me." Ginny eased back into the sofa cushions. "You've been alone so long. Don't you think it's time for a relationship?"

Blythe gripped the arms of her chair. "I don't *want* a relationship." How could she trust another man? Too many had let her down too often. It was safer to keep them at a distance.

"Blythe, it's been two years since Andrew died. You can't hide forever. It isn't healthy. It isn't right. You deserve good things, like a husband and children. I know of at least four men in this office alone who would jump at the chance to take you out on a *real* date. Wouldn't you like a little romance?"

Romance! Blythe nearly vented her bitter laughter. Romance was just a pretty word used to cloak a refusal to face reality. It was the spinning of fantasies and dreams to the neglect of responsibilities—a neglect for which others often paid the price.

"Enough, Ginny." Blythe worked to moderate her tone. "I'm perfectly content with my social life."

Ginny scowled and took another sip of her orange soda.

Blythe examined her soft drink can as if its colorful lettering had transformed into a work of art. "The reason I want another sales assistant is to take over your work load, not just help you with it."

Ginny's head snapped up. Her eyes widened and the warm brown skin of her face grew greenish pale.

"Not to replace you," Blythe assured her hastily. "I want to free you up for something important. If you want to do it, that is."

"Do what?"

Dropping her feet to the floor, Blythe leaned forward in her chair. "You know how I've been talking about developing the retirement account business of small-to-medium-sized companies?"

"Yeah, for about two years."

"If I develop that business, my existing clients will get shortchanged. I need a partner, Ginny, and I'd like that partner to be you."

Ginny stared. Seconds slipped by. "Me?" she squeaked.

"I'll hire a sales assistant, now, so you'll be free to study for your licenses. That should take about three months. By the time you're on board, the new s.a. will know the ropes."

"Of course, I'll need to supervise her." Ginny frowned slightly.

Blythe could almost see the plans begin to unfold in her friend's mind. "At first, yes," she agreed. "If we can find someone good, that could be kept to a minimum."

Blythe already paid two-thirds of Ginny's salary. Stewart Duke's policy was one s.a. to three brokers. If a broker's business warranted full-time help, then he or she paid the difference. Blythe had also worked out a bonus system for her sales assistant and was confident she wouldn't have any trouble finding and keeping someone good.

"I can't let you do it."

Blythe stared at Ginny. "What do you mean, you can't let me do it? What's wrong?"

"You'd be paying for a sales assistant *and* me. The only person who would be working enough to warrant a salary would be the other s.a. You'd be supporting dead weight." Ginny looked miserable, but Blythe breathed a sigh of relief.

"Your nobility is misplaced, Rodriguez." Blythe grinned wickedly. "I'll get my money's worth out of your hide. Never fear."

"Why me?"

The edge of tears Blythe heard in her friend's voice told her she'd made the right decision. This would be as important to Ginny as it was to Blythe. "Why not you? You know all the clients and their accounts. You're too conscientious to give anything but your best. Besides, who else could put up with me?"

Ginny considered for a moment. "True," she finally agreed. "Who *would* put up with you?"

"Thanks a lot."

A WEEK LATER, as Blythe sat at her desk, scenes from last Saturday's encounter with Duncan still replayed in her mind. One moment he had been an angel, concerned about his aunts' health; the next he'd been a devil, stirring up a yearning in Blythe that refused to return to dormancy. If Duncan had been affected he hadn't shown it. And that made her feel foolish, which irritated her.

She told herself she was better off avoiding the man. It would be easy enough to do her grocery shopping at another store. Immediately her pride rose to reject that solution. This was *her* community. Let *him* find another supermarket. Preferably one in Atlanta.

The telephone rang.

"Hello? Blythe? This is Martha, dear."

"Yes, Martha. What can I do for you? Is there a problem with your account?"

"This is a social call, dear."

Blythe rested her elbows on the desk. "Oh?"

Martha chuckled. "For such a youngster you're terribly cautious. But I think you'll find my invitation painless. Today is Duncan's birthday, and Amelia and I would like to have a little party for him. A surprise. I know this is somewhat late, but we forgot to look at the calendar, you see. We can't bear the thought of letting the day go by without doing something for the dear boy. Will you come?''

A surprise party for Duncan. Blythe smiled evilly. Wouldn't he just love that? She was certain he wouldn't. In fact, she was sure he would be embarrassed. A tiny, yet delightful, revenge for his indifference...

''I wouldn't miss it for the world.''

''THIS POOR GUY must not have any friends at all,'' said the man in the ill-fitting coveralls standing next to Blythe. The name in the red oval above his right breast pocket proclaimed him Bob. The emblem under that indicated he worked at a gas station.

Blythe reluctantly donned the feathered paper hat Amelia had given her. ''Bob—''

''Herb. Bob quit, but I don't have my uniform yet so he loaned me this one.''

''Herb, he doesn't live here. The guest of honor lives in Atlanta, but his aunts wanted to do something nice for him on his birthday.''

''Nice!'' Herb snorted. ''I'd kill my wife if she did this to me. I bet no one here knows him. Makes him look like a reject or something.'' He straightened the cellophane derby perched atop his shaggy mane of brown hair. ''Nice spread, though. And who could say no to those sweet old ladies?''

Blythe looked around Amelia and Martha's screened-in pool area. The crowd waiting for Duncan to arrive was a mixed lot. It was clear the white-haired sisters had invited everyone they'd met in Florida, and had even convinced all their guests to wear party hats. How many actually knew Duncan?

HE DROPPED HIS BRIEFCASE on his bed with a sigh of relief. It hadn't been a bad day, Duncan thought, just a long one. The meeting at Central Florida Software had seemed to go on forever.

As he tugged his tie loose an image of Blythe Summers slipped into his mind. Wisps of pale hair, escaped from her ponytail, framed her face. She wore chocolate on her luscious lips. The pleasure he'd experienced, sitting on the hood of her car, eating cookies, flooded back. He smiled. She'd been on his mind quite a bit lately.

Martha walked into his room. "Come have a drink with us, dear."

"I'll be down as soon as I change, Aunt Martha," he assured her and leaned down to kiss her on the cheek.

"Oh, do come down now. You can change later." At his puzzled expression, Martha stood up on her tiptoes and tried to place on his head a party hat she'd kept hidden behind her back. "Happy birthday, dear."

Charmed and resigned, Duncan obliged his diminutive aunt and set the hat on his head, going so far as to fit the elastic band under his chin. He grinned.

"You didn't think we'd forget, did you?" she asked.

"*I* forgot. I guess the memory is the first thing to go."

"I wouldn't know. I'm not old yet."

"Aunt Martha, you will always be a breath of springtime," Duncan said as they walked down the curving staircase together.

"You're such a thoughtful boy." Martha smiled serenely and led him into the pool area.

"*Surprise!*"

From her place in the crowd, Blythe watched Duncan's face. Except for the widening of his eyes, his surprise would have been difficult to detect. His chagrin, however, was flagged by a crimson stain that washed up his neck to suffuse his features.

He stood tall and handsome, attired in a dark, conservatively cut suit, handmade Italian leather shoes and a pointed party hat.

Laughter bubbled up in Blythe's throat, but she managed to choke it down. The picture of the arrogant CEO as birthday boy was hilarious.

Duncan burned with embarrassment. He felt like an idiot standing there, wearing that stupid hat. He *hated* party hats.

Who were these people anyway? He looked around at unfamiliar faces, people dressed in an odd range of attire.

Inwardly he groaned as the truth occurred to him. Martha and Amelia had pulled these people off the street! Not one person here knew him. Everyone probably thought he was so pitiful his aunts were forced to coax passersby to his party.

His gaze stopped at the one familiar face in the crowd. Just when he thought things couldn't get any worse...

Once again, Blythe Summers witnessed his embarrassment. The one woman he wanted to impress, and it seemed as if she would forever find him looking like a fool.

It was too much. His aunts had really done it this time. He turned to the silver-haired ladies, anger igniting.

They looked up at him with anticipation in their eyes, their smiles tentative, hopeful. Duncan's anger sputtered and died. His aunts wanted to please him and they'd gone to considerable trouble.

As he thanked them for their surprise, and saw their joy, Duncan was reminded why he put up with being made to look like a jerk—why he'd always put up with it.

He hugged Martha and Amelia and kissed them on their flushed cheeks. While they led the guests in an enthusiastic, if unharmonious, "Happy Birthday to You" he stood smiling. Then Duncan thanked everyone for coming—wishing Blythe had not—and invited them to the buffet tables and the punch bowl.

With a deep sigh, Duncan glanced at Blythe. She had made no move to go to the tables. The smile on her lips looked odd. It wasn't until he walked closer that he realized the corners of her mouth were twitching.

"Go ahead and laugh," he told her morosely. "I think my apprenticeship as clown is about over. Next time you'll have to pay admission to see me in a situation like this."

Blythe laughed, then quickly smothered it. "It's not that bad," she sympathized. "Martha and Amelia just wanted to do something special for you."

"Yeah? I would have settled for an ice-cream cake."

She looked up at him. Suddenly Blythe felt there was no place on earth she would rather be at this moment than here. "May I say, you look especially cute in your hat."

"Allow me to return the compliment, madam. Feathers become you."

Blythe felt herself blush. Her fingers itched to snatch the wretched hat from her head. Instead, refusing to admit his score, she informed him, "Feathers, my good fellow, will take you anywhere."

A slow grin spread across Duncan's mouth. "I'll remember that." His smooth, deep voice made the promise an erotic avowal.

Duncan's proximity never failed to affect her. She found that a source of growing concern. "Is that so?"

"Oh, there you are." Martha walked up and took her nephew's arm. "Duncan, there's a gentleman over here who is most interested in computers, but I'm having difficulty explaining what it is your company does." She smiled at Blythe. "You don't mind if I take him away for a little while, do you dear?"

"Not a bit," Blythe assured her hostess brightly.

As soon as Duncan left, she located a bathroom in which to leave her party hat. Anyplace else might be too conspicuous. She noticed a number of guests were now bareheaded.

She headed for a buffet table where she selected a colorful pasta salad and barbecued chicken. Carefully she maneuvered through the crowd to a small table behind a bank of potted palms. A born people-watcher, she arranged her chair to allow the best advantage from which to observe her fellow guests.

A healthy-looking young man in a T-shirt emblazoned with Mel's Lawn Service and a silhouette of a lawn mower was talking to a couple who looked as if they had jogged off the trail, into the party—and maybe they had.

At the far buffet table a bald man in lime green polyester golf slacks and matching shirt piled his plate so high with food Blythe thought he might be preparing to feed a starving family of six. She watched with amazement as he found a seat and proceeded to wolf down the entire mountain by himself.

"Are you having fun, dear?" Amelia asked.

Blythe looked up to find Amelia and Martha smiling down at her. "This is a lovely party. I'm sure Duncan was completely surprised." She gestured to the empty chairs at the table. "Please."

"We're so glad you could come, Blythe dear," Martha said.

Amelia released a sigh. "Another year and still our Duncan is single. I could see it while his company was growing so fast, but now Macrocosm is quite big enough. It's time for him to get married and have children."

Martha patted her sister's hand. "We'll just have to be patient. Though it would be wonderful to bounce his little ones on our knees. He's such a handsome boy, he's bound to have beautiful babies."

Blythe didn't know what to say, so she smiled.

"Do your parents live in Florida?" Martha inquired.

"My mother has a house in Indiatlantic, but she lives in New York now. She's the North American marketing manager for Jonquil."

"Oh, my, how exciting." Martha exchanged glances with her sister. "She sounds like quite an accomplished woman."

Blythe nodded, longing for a bite of pasta salad.

"We would so like to meet her, wouldn't we?" Amelia looked to Martha for agreement.

"Oh, yes, indeed. She must be very talented to have such a gifted daughter. One who's so attractive." Martha smiled at Blythe. "You'll probably have lovely children."

"Uh . . ."

"You do want children someday, don't you?" Amelia asked.

"Definitely," Blythe agreed.

The sisters beamed at each other.

Blythe suspected where this was leading and tried to head it off. "Martha, do you still have the papers I gave you when you were at my office?" she asked.

The sisters nodded.

"If you'd like to take a few minutes, I'll quickly go over them again with you now."

Martha surveyed the party crowd. "I suppose it wouldn't hurt. We don't want to neglect our guests for too long. Let's go into the study."

Blythe followed her clients into the house and upstairs to the library, which contained a large mahogany desk with leather inlay on top. A solid-looking wing chair stood behind the desk. Such masculine furniture contrasted with the daintier Queen Anne chairs and side tables.

"The desk and leather chair were my dear Horace's," Martha said, solving the small mystery. "I couldn't bear to part with them."

They settled in the chintz-covered chairs, which had been arranged in a manner conducive to conversation.

From the desk, Martha retrieved the copies given them on their last visit to Stewart Duke. Blythe went through the list of investments, item by item, explaining what should be done with each, whether it was wiser to sell or hold.

DUNCAN CIRCULATED through the gathering, his worst suspicions confirmed. Almost everyone here was a stranger to his aunts. Each partygoer, however, commented on his aunts' charm.

He moved about the pool area until he finally felt he could return to his favorite guest. When he turned in the direction of her table, he discovered she wasn't there. He scanned the pool area.

A woman in toreador pants stopped him and asked about his company, what type of business it was, what kind of future it might have. He began to feel as though he was filling out a financial statement. Impatient as he was to find Blythe, he managed a polite facade for the inquisitor. When she began extolling the attributes of her unmarried daughter, he tuned the woman out. He smiled and nodded, trying to think of an escape.

It came in the form of a guest wearing work overalls with a gas station emblem. The man said, "I just wanted to shake the hand of a fellow who knows how to treat family. You keep that Cadillac of Martha's in mint condition. I'll bet that's even the original paint job, huh?"

"Yes—" Duncan darted a glance at the name patch stitched above the station emblem "—Bob. Yes, it is the original paint job. But you're the one who should take credit for keeping the car running. My aunts rest much easier knowing they can depend on you."

"Herb," Bob said.

"Herb?" *Bob Herb?*

Bob smiled and shook his head. "Never mind. I'm glad they feel they can depend on me. They can. But I've only been taking care of the Cadillac for a week. You're responsible for its prime condition."

"How very interesting," interrupted the woman, clearly irritated at the turn of conversation. "Are you married, Bob?"

"If you'll excuse me..." Duncan retreated, feeling guilty about leaving Bob in the clutches of Toreador Woman.

He decided his aunts would know if Blythe had left. When he couldn't find either Martha or Amelia among the guests, he went searching.

As he entered the hall from the second-floor landing, he heard voices coming from the library. Either his aunts or stray company, he concluded.

As he moved closer to the partially closed door, he recognized not only his aunts' voices, but Blythe's. She seemed to be going over their investments with them. He stopped short of pushing the door open and entering the library.

He listened as Blythe explained how the investments Raymond Fosker had sold his aunts worked, then made recommendations. When she finished, she said, "If you have questions, please ask. I want you to understand what we're talking about. You're women of the nineties, now." There was a pause, and he could imagine her flashing them a grin. "Knowledge is power."

To Duncan's amazement, Martha immediately asked Blythe to explain stock splits. For years he'd been trying to coax his aunts into taking an interest in investments, and now this woman, with a few words, had opened the gate.

Blythe answered Martha's question in a way that was easy to understand, yet there was no trace of condescension. As soon as she finished, Amelia inquired about Standard and Poor's rating system. Even Duncan found the answer educational.

"Thank you, dear," Martha said. "We feel much better now, don't we, Amelia?"

"Oh, my, yes. You've made it much easier to understand."

"We really must visit with our other guests now," Martha pointed out.

As Duncan entered the library, Martha was putting papers into one of the desk drawers. He heard her say to her sister, "I can imagine little girls wanting to grow up to be just like Blythe. I think I'll enjoy being a woman of the nineties."

"Yes," agreed Amelia. "Isn't it exciting? We must find out exactly what it is that nineties women do with their power."

Dread folded over Duncan like a musty wool cloak. His aunts' new interests always meant disaster for him. He'd be safer in Atlanta.

"Hi," he said, announcing his presence. "Everything okay?"

Martha looked up and smiled. "Oh, yes, dear. Blythe was just explaining our investments to us."

"We want to keep current, you know," Amelia told him.

Amazed to hear such a statement coming from one of his aunts, Duncan turned to look at Blythe.

"I'm sorry to have kept you from your guests," she said softly.

"Not at all, dear," Martha insisted. "You were so clear it didn't take long."

Together the four of them returned to the party.

Duncan carried with him an admiration for Blythe Summers he'd never expected to feel. He was glad he'd overheard her discussion with his aunts. She was sensitive and kind. She was also a professional who understood how business should be conducted.

Blythe watched Martha and Amelia move among their visitors. They charmed and confused with their naiveté and slightly off-kilter logic. She sighed. Being their broker would probably never be an easy job.

"There's a table over there."

For the first time Blythe noticed Duncan's paper hat was gone. She smiled. "Let's grab it."

He pulled out a white wrought-iron chair for her, and when she was seated, took his place opposite her.

"So. Have you met everyone?" Did she sound as breathless as she felt?

"There are some interesting people here. For instance, see that man in the purple shorts, the one Martha wanted me to talk to?" Duncan leaned closer to her, looking in the direction of the subject. "He's a computer programmer who keeps bees."

His closeness sent a small shiver skimming under the surface of her skin. "That would have been my guess."

"The lady over there in the skirt with the frog painted on it? She paints frogs on skirts."

Blythe widened her eyes. "No kidding?"

"Would I lie to you? She sells entire frog outfits to expensive boutiques. Says it's the rage with lady golfers."

"What do men golfers get? Frogs on their pants?" It seemed logical to Blythe.

"Certainly not. They get frog shirts and caps."

"Definitely more masculine."

He chuckled. "A little too precious for me, I'm afraid. See that couple—the ones in their jogging shorts?"

"Yes?"

"They were shanghaied as they jogged down the street. They were nice enough to humor two little old ladies."

Blythe laughed. "Your aunts are hard to resist, aren't they?"

Duncan leaned his forearms on the table, grinning as he looked down at the acrylic surface, then up at her. "*I've* never succeeded."

Blythe wished she was immune to Duncan. It would make everything easier. Maybe, if she could dislike him...

"Even when they put you through this?" she asked. "Martha and Amelia have embarrassed you in front of a large audience. Aren't you angry?"

He shrugged. "I'm not exactly delighted about looking foolish. But they're very special ladies, and they were trying to do something nice for me. I can see they worked hard on this party. I know it was difficult for them to approach strangers and invite them into their home." His smile returned, warmer than before. "Though obviously not everyone they invited was a stranger."

Blythe quickly turned her attention to the dainty flower arrangement that stood between them, in the center of the table. "Obviously not," she agreed with an attempt at lightness. As she traced the tip of a fern frond she considered this facet of Duncan.

He had created one of the largest software houses in the United States. It took a certain ruthlessness to build such an enterprise, the instincts of a predator.

Yet she'd witnessed a side of him that was woven of abiding affection and deep devotion. He put up with the embarrassing situations Martha and Amelia created because he loved his aunts. It was as simple, as selfless as that.

A few stones fell from the wall she'd built around her heart.

"Should I get you a microscope?"

Startled, Blythe looked up at Duncan. "What?"

"You're studying that fern so closely, I thought you were looking for amoebas. Is there a bug on it?" Duncan leaned forward and peered down into the arrangement. "Did you find something that doesn't belong there?"

His nearness had the power to block out sound and movement in the rest of the enclosure.

His forearm rested on the table next to hers. His was longer, larger. It spoke of strength and disciplined power.

Duncan followed Blythe's gaze down to his arm, and smiled inwardly. She didn't seem to be offended by his closeness. That was a good sign. That day at lunch Duncan had twice sensed her withdrawal.

Clearly this woman wasn't on the prowl. Duncan guessed Blythe would be selective about the man she chose, and that pleased him. He'd already seen evidence of her loyalty, and that pleased him, too. Duncan regarded faithlessness as another form of dishonesty. He despised dishonesty.

No, he thought, Blythe Summers was a lady in the finest sense of the word. She was intelligent, able to hold her own in a duel of wits, and gracious, even under fire. It didn't hurt that she was beautiful, of course, but beauty was an easily obtainable commodity if that's all one was interested in.

Over the years, Duncan had learned he needed the stimulation and challenge only an equal could provide. To his disappointment and disgust, he'd learned equals were rare. Too rare.

Not to take advantage of finding such a woman would be similar to passing over a faceted diamond discovered among smooth river pebbles.

When Blythe looked up she found Duncan studying her. She wondered what thoughts flowed through his mind. When he wasn't infuriated, or devoting himself to being charming, Duncan McKeon was difficult to read.

"Would you like to do something together?" he asked.

"What did you have in mind?"

"A movie." He grinned, and his eyes told her he was amused by her caution. "I'm trying to impress you, so I'll even spring for the popcorn."

How could she resist this man? He was a challenge, he was fun, he was beyond a doubt the most gorgeous male she had ever met. Why was she even trying to resist him?

Because she had her life under control now, she reasoned. Because she had everything exactly as she wanted it. After she had her retirement fund business rolling she would look for a mate, one who lived here in Central Florida.

"What do you say?" he coaxed.

"I say—"

"We'll find something really off-the-wall."

Who could pass up an off-the-wall movie?

"When?" Blythe asked.

"What about next Saturday?"

"Saturday is fine." She smiled. "I'll even buy the sodas, since you're picking up the tab for the popcorn."

Duncan laughed, and Blythe felt a corresponding flutter in her middle. "A woman after my own heart," he said.

He looked over his shoulder at the rest of the party, then back at Blythe. "I guess I'd better spend a little more time with my birthday guests," he said.

Her smile grew as her struggle to tamp down the pleasure bubbling inside her failed. "I guess."

"I'll talk with you before Saturday." With a grin and a wink, Duncan left to mingle.

One evening, she reasoned silently as she watched him stop to talk to the couple in jogging attire. It would be fun, and that would be the end of it. She wasn't about to mess up all her carefully laid plans.

Just a movie. How complicated could things get?

CHAPTER SIX

TUESDAY Blythe closed the heavy directory and looked at the list she'd made of pension fund prospects. It was shorter than she'd expected, but it would keep her busy for a while. Competition would be brutal. Blythe knew she wasn't the only one who thought the rewards were worth the struggle.

First she must get her foot in the door. If she couldn't convince anyone to listen to her she was dead in the water. With that thought in mind, she picked up the telephone receiver and started dialing.

Call after call she received put-offs or outright rejection. She feared if she allowed herself to think about it, she might become discouraged. So, without pause, she went from one number to the next, concentrating on the information she gleaned, the possibilities.

Finally she received a spark of interest. Martin Chasen, controller of Chasen and Sons, Inc., a company specializing in chemical fertilizers, agreed to a meeting in a few weeks' time.

As soon as she hung up, Blythe rushed out of her office to Ginny. "I did it!" she bubbled. "I got an appointment with the controller of Chasen and Sons!" Blythe felt like dancing a jig. "Well, don't just sit there. Tell me I'm terrific!"

Ginny's somber expression finally penetrated Blythe's elation.

"What?" Blythe demanded. "What is it?"

"Ada Kernfelder just closed her account."

Blythe stared at her sales assistant. "*Ada?* Why?"

Ginny shook her head. "When I asked that, she told me just to close the account."

"Where is she moving it?"

"She wouldn't say. You know how paranoid she is."

Blythe chewed the inside of her lip as she tried to think of a reason the elderly woman, a longtime client, would insist on withdrawing her substantial account. "Paranoid, yes, but she's always eventually listened to reason. It's not like Ada to do this."

Her earlier excitement forgotten, she walked back into her office and called the seventy-three-year-old widow.

What if some fast-talking con man had convinced Ada to invest her money in a scam? Such occurrences weren't uncommon in Florida with its large population of retirees. And it wouldn't be the first time Ada had been tempted to trust all her money with a smooth operator whose office, as well as his credentials, proved nonexistent.

"Ada? This is Blythe Summers. Ginny tells me you want to close your account. Is there something wrong?"

There was a long pause before the quavering voice of the ancient New Englander answered. "I just want to close my account."

Blythe palmed her paperweight. "You didn't tell me you were thinking of taking your business elsewhere. Ada, this worries me. Won't you tell me why you're closing your account?"

"It's my money," snapped Ada. "If I see fit to close the account, I can."

"That's true," Blythe agreed. "But you have to admit I've been a good broker. Your investments have increased in value. You have a better, more secure income today than when you came to see me six years ago. I can take credit for that, can't I?"

Seconds ticked by, then Ada said grudgingly, "Yes."

"Are you sure you want to close the account?"

"Yes."

Blythe set the paperweight back in its place, and leaned her forearms on her desk. "All right. But would you do me the courtesy of telling me why?"

Again silence filled the telephone line. "I...I...my grandson is a broker now and he wants me to put my account with him."

Last year Ada had said her only grandson was a successful veterinarian. It seemed unlikely to Blythe he would want to quit his lucrative practice and become a stockbroker. She sighed. "Bring a letter when you come, Ada, setting out your instructions. Your money market shares have to be sold—give them two days to clear. You'll receive your stock certificates in about six weeks, and you already have your other papers. I enjoyed having you as a client, Ada. I'm sorry to lose you."

Leaning back in her chair, Blythe mulled over Ada's sudden insistence on closing her account. Over the past six years Ada Kernfelder had found Blythe's guidance profitable, so profitable she had even sent several of her friends to Blythe.

True, the elderly woman had sometimes needed reassurance—Ginny called it paranoia—but Blythe had given it willingly. Who didn't get a little paranoid where their life savings were concerned?

It was not a rare thing to have a client close or transfer her or his account. People's circumstances changed. Blythe accepted that. But it was rare to have an established client call out of the blue and demand her securities and funds.

What was Ada's true reason for closing her account?

"IT WAS *AWFUL!*"

Duncan laughed as he took the cup of espresso Blythe offered. "It was pretty bad, wasn't it?" he agreed. "Well, we were looking for an off-the-wall movie."

She held out the plate of cookies to him: "*Planet of the Ninja Amazons* certainly filled the bill. I can't think of one redeeming feature about it, can you?"

Duncan shook his head. "No. The script was terrible and the special effects were an embarrassment. It was as bad as those old Japanese science fiction flicks."

"I disagree. At least *they* were funny."

"But they weren't supposed to be."

"That's what made them so hilarious."

Duncan grinned. "You're cruel."

Blythe excused herself for a moment, going to the kitchen for a spoon. While he waited for her, Duncan's gaze roamed her great room.

It was eclectic. Arranged around the room were an antique brass cash register, an ancient Greek amphora and a modern sculpture in black marble, each on its own mahogany pedestal. Vanilla walls were hung with watercolors by Florida artists, and throughout the room thriving green plants sat in pots that ranged from delicate to bizarre. The furniture was simple in line and color: oak end tables, brass lamps, wheat-hued couch and wing chair.

The focal point of the room was the fireplace. Large, with a generous hearth, the dark wood of its mantelpiece was carved with the figures of medieval dragons, damsels and knights.

Duncan liked the room. It reflected the woman who had created it, and he found her more fascinating with each hour he spent in her company.

Now, as Blythe sat down across the coffee table from him, Duncan admitted to himself she had piqued something in him. Curiosity, a sense of kindred spirit—he wasn't certain. He only knew she was impossible to forget.

He studied Blythe as she reached for a cookie. Soft lamplight highlighted the curves of classic cheekbones. Her mouth was accentuated by shadow. Mesmerized, he watched as she bit a piece from her cookie. Tiny crumbs clung to her lower lip. As the tip of her tongue darted out to capture the sweet morsels, Duncan's body responded sharply.

He shifted in his chair. She seemed unaware of her effect on him. At the party, Duncan had sensed her reluctance to agree to go out with him tonight. Until he learned why she was so hesitant, it seemed wise to take things slowly.

Again, Duncan looked around the room. A bronze jar caught his eye. It shared a shelf with an oriental arrangement of silk flowers.

"Interesting piece," he commented, indicating the jar.

"It's a funerary urn."

This room certainly was filled with the unusual. Duncan chuckled. "Uh-huh. What dynasty?"

"It dates a little more recent than that."

"How recent?" he asked.

"About two years."

Hadn't Martha said Blythe's husband had died two years ago? An unpleasant thought formed in Duncan's mind.

He took a swallow of hot espresso. A mental image came to him: Blythe, dressed in black, her face concealed by a long veil. She was weeping inconsolably as a funeral director presented her with the urn.

"Duncan?" Blythe thought he looked strange.

"Anyone I know?"

She took the urn from the shelf and brought it over to him. He stared as she lifted the plain lid.

"Would you like a candy?" she asked, holding the urn out to Duncan.

"Candy?" he croaked.

She picked out a cellophane-wrapped peppermint and handed it to him. "Yes." With a forefinger, she stirred through the confections. "There are other kinds, here, if you don't like peppermint."

He leaned forward to peer into the bronze jar. "The urn looks real."

"Oh, it is. It was a gift from a client who owns a funeral home. The market had gone down for three consecutive days and he presented it to me, tied with a big black bow. It had candies in it." She replaced the lid, and set the vessel back in its place. "I've got a lot of nice clients."

"You think an urn is nice?"

"I was depressed," she explained. "He took the time to try to cheer me up."

"I take it he wasn't heavily invested in stocks," Duncan observed dryly.

"No. His money was in other things."

"If I ever want to impress you I now know what gift to buy." His gaze traveled to the shelf.

"No, thanks. One urn is enough."

"I'm relieved to hear it." Duncan picked up his cup and took a sip of strong, tepid coffee. Reluctantly he swallowed the nasty stuff, hating cool coffee more than ever. He set the tiny cup back in its saucer. "If you keep peppermints in a funerary urn, what do you keep in the amphora?"

Blythe laughed. "*I'll* never tell."

Slow and sensuous, a smile moved over Duncan's lips. "Never?"

Her heartbeat tripped. How could anyone imbue that negative, little word with so much promise?

Eyes the color of wood smoke met hers.

Blythe tried to remember his question. "I . . . I . . . meant that figuratively."

Duncan's smile widened into a wicked grin. "I'd be happy to go over figures with you, anytime."

"The only kinds of figures I discuss are things like price/earnings ratios, trading highs and lows, dividends and yields."

"Pity."

Heat percolated in Blythe's veins. She tried to remember when last a man had affected her this way—stroking her without a touch.

"It's late." Duncan rose from the couch and walked around the table, taking her hands and drawing her to her feet. "For me, tomorrow's another workday," he said, leading her to the foyer.

Blythe stood facing him, looking up into his eyes, simmering with anticipation.

Duncan gently drew her into his arms. His warm breath sent shivers through her. From this perspective his shoulders seemed wider than ever.

Lowering his head, Duncan brushed his lips once across hers, then back again. He slanted his mouth to best advantage, then took complete possession.

Blythe closed her eyes, swamped by the realization that she'd been waiting for this moment. She clutched at his shoulders as her inner balance swept into flight.

He brought her more firmly against him and she worried dimly he might be able to feel her nipples through the light cotton of her blouse, the thin satin of her bra. That thought vanished as he slid his tongue coaxingly across her teeth. She opened to Duncan, receiving his seeking tongue as her blood sang through her veins. An intoxicating dizziness swirled through her, her only anchor their points of contact.

She could feel the pounding of his heart. Its accelerated rhythm seemed to connect directly to her own.

Duncan loosened his hold. Gently he brushed back a tendril of hair that had escaped from her chignon. "I want to see you again, Blythe," he said, his voice low, deep, rough.

Blythe knew, given a chance, what they had at the moment could, *would,* grow and intensify. For a while.

Should she give that spark a chance?

In her life Blythe had already known so much uncertainty. So much hurt. She was safer without Duncan. When the differences and distances between their lives inevitably grew intolerable there would be a price to pay. If she said no now, she could go on as before. Safe. Alone.

Duncan studied her face, waiting for her answer.

"Yes," she whispered, spurred by a recklessness new to her. "Yes."

Smiling, he opened the door and kissed her again.

Expect the affair to end. Enjoy it while it lasts, whispered the voice of common sense.

As Blythe watched him walk to his car and get in, she wondered what the future held for them. She was so used to taking the secure path; the way before her suddenly loomed unknown and frightening.

Blythe watched until the twin red lights of Duncan's car finally disappeared into the night, then turned and went inside.

After she cleared the dishes and put them in the dishwasher, she walked through the house, checking locks and turning out lights.

In the bedroom, she changed into her nightgown, then went into the bathroom where she washed her face. When she tried to squeeze toothpaste onto her toothbrush, it fell to the floor, smearing the pale paste. Blythe picked up the brush. Particles of lint and dust stuck to it. She stared down at the small glob on the carpet and burst into tears.

THE FOLLOWING DAY, Blythe drove over to the coast to pick her sister up. All the way back from Indiatlantic Fiona was unusually quiet. Initially she resisted Blythe's gentle probing, but finally snapped at her older sister.

"*Nothing's* wrong, okay? I just don't feel like talking. That's allowed, isn't it?"

Blythe glanced in surprise at Fiona, who sat frowning straight ahead, her arms clasped over her chest. "Sorry. I guess any fool could see everything is just peachy with you."

"Stuff it, Blythe."

"Have it your own way, Ms. Charm. Stew in silence." Blythe worked the tension out of her fingers clenching the steering wheel. Clearly whatever was bothering Fiona would remain a mystery.

Fine. If Fiona wanted to brood, it was her privilege.

They had just entered the city limits of Winter Park when Fiona turned to her sister.

"I'm sorry I snapped at you. I—I'm not feeling well."

Blythe noticed the younger woman's pallor.

"Do you need me to pull over?"

Fiona swallowed. "No. Just get me home, please."

As soon as they pulled into the garage Fiona was out of the car and into the house. The door of the guest bathroom slammed. Blythe could hear her sister retching.

When the sounds of sickness finally stopped, she tapped on the door. "Fiona? Are you all right?"

"Yes." The word was a broken sob.

Alarmed, Blythe tried the door. It was locked. "Fiona, baby, please let me in. You need help."

Seconds dragged, then the door to the bathroom opened. Fiona stood there looking miserable.

Blythe felt Fiona's forehead for fever, but found no unusual warmth. Worried, she smoothed stray strands of hair away from her sister's face.

Fiona tried to smile, but it wavered and disappeared.

Blythe fussed over the younger woman until Fiona was settled in the wing chair in the great room. Then Blythe went to the kitchen where she prepared chamomile tea to soothe her sister's stomach.

The water seemed to take forever to heat. As soon as she heard it bubble in the kettle, she removed it. Minutes later she set the tray with the teapot and two cups on the coffee table.

Blythe sat on the couch and poured them each a cup of herbal tea. "This should help."

Fiona took a sip and swallowed hard, as if having difficulty getting it down. "I have something to tell you, Blythe," she said, "and I don't know how."

"Just say it," Blythe encouraged. "Whatever it is that's worrying you—"

"I'm pregnant," Fiona stated in a flat voice.

"Pregnant?"

Fiona nodded heavily. Her hand trembled slightly, clattering cup against saucer.

"How long have you known?" Blythe asked, staring at her sister's downcast face.

Fiona mumbled a reply.

"Speak up."

"Since before I left Alaska."

"Oh." Questions raced through Blythe's mind, but she refused to voice them. Fiona had a right to privacy—even from her older sister. Certain things needed to be discussed, but for now, Blythe decided there was only one question Fiona needed to hear.

"What can I do to help?" she asked softly.

The look of profound relief that played over her sister's features touched Blythe.

"Ethan...Ethan doesn't know." Fiona darted a glance up at her sister, then returned her gaze to the clenched hands in her lap. "If I had told him he...it would have been even harder to leave."

"Fiona." Blythe took one of her sister's tight fists and gently pried it open. The hand was cold. She clasped it in her own. "Why don't you call Ethan? Don't you think he deserves to know he's going to be a father?"

"No!" Fiona's eyes grew large and she tried to jerk free of her sister. "No. He'll try to make me change my mind. He knows how." Her attempt to pull away from Blythe unsuccessful, Fiona now clutched the hand that held her. "Promise me you won't call him," the younger woman implored. "Please, Blythe. Promise me."

Blythe searched her sister's face. "Has he hurt you?"

Fiona shook her head. "Not Ethan. Never Ethan. No, I've hurt *him.*"

"Then why won't you call him?"

The ponderous ticking of the grandfather clock in the foyer filled the silence. Blythe waited.

"I'm not ready to talk to him," Fiona finally said. "I have to be strong to do it, and I'm not. He'll try to change my mind about getting married."

"And you're still not sure." *You always run and hide, little sister. If you use that tactic this time, I'm afraid you may regret it the rest of your life.*

"I'm still not sure," Fiona agreed.

Blythe looked down at their joined hands. Fiona was vulnerable. She needed protection.

"All right," Blythe said slowly, and raised her gaze to her sister's. "You're my sister and that baby of yours is my niece or nephew. Maybe you'd both like a little company. I'd feel better if you planned to stay

with me, at least during the pregnancy." She paused.
"Did you tell Mom?"

"No. But I think she's guessed. I got . . . sick a couple of times."

With her long, russet hair pushed behind her ears, Fiona looked curiously vulnerable and young, like the pale portrait of a French schoolgirl. Blythe ached for her.

"Blythe?"

"Yes?"

"When I start my Lamaze classes, would you be my coach?"

With an effort, Blythe swallowed around the lump in her throat. "You bet."

"I'D FEEL LIKE a fifth wheel," moaned Fiona. "I'm sure Duncan didn't mean for me to tag along."

"You're not 'tagging along.' You're coming by invitation from both of us. This is going to be *fun*," Blythe coaxed. "Duncan's aunts are coming, too. You haven't met them or Duncan, and I want them to meet you. We've been over this before. You agreed to go. We'll all have a good time, and I'll get to show off my beautiful sister."

"You all know one another. I'd only be in the way." Fiona's classic features pulled down into a sullen expression.

"What?" Blythe demanded, flinging her arms up in exasperation. "What's the real reason? Is it morning sickness?"

"No."

"Are your feet swelling?"

"No."

"Then what is it?" Blythe realized her voice was gaining volume. "What is it?" she repeated more quietly. "What's your reason this time?"

Fiona glared at her older sister. "I—I don't feel good, that's all."

Blythe glared back. "Well, I should think not! Ever since you got back from Indiatlantic you've hidden in this house like some damned troglodyte. A week is long enough. Look, if you really don't feel good you need to see the doctor. But he'll probably tell you to get some fresh air."

"Oh, and riding over to Cape Kennedy in an air-conditioned car is going to provide me with lots of fresh air and sunshine."

"All right," Blythe conceded, "we'll roll the windows down. The weather's too pretty to turn the air on anyway. And don't forget, there's the walk from the parking lot to the Space Center."

Fiona sighed. "All right. You win."

Blythe gave the younger woman a hug. "Good. We'll pace this to your comfort. If you get tired, let us know and we'll rest a while. I'm certain Martha and Amelia will benefit from a leisurely pace, too."

"Thanks," Fiona said dryly as she pulled on her athletic shoes. "I appreciate being put in the same category as eighty-year-old ladies."

"You're a pregnant person. You probably have a lot in common with the aged." Blythe grinned wickedly. "Aches and pains, tire easily, weak blood."

"I'm staying home!" wailed Fiona. She looked at Blythe. "Did you tell Duncan or his aunts that I'm pregnant?"

Slowly Blythe shook her head. "No. I won't say anything to anyone until you're ready for people to know."

Fiona heaved a sigh and offered a weak smile. "I guess it's okay. I mean, it'll be pretty hard to miss before too long. I... It's just... Well, in these liberated times I didn't think being an unwed mother would bother me as much as it does."

Blythe pressed her lips together, refusing to say what she thought—that Ethan wanted to marry Fiona, and it seemed obvious to Blythe that Fiona loved him. No, if Fiona's doubts were strong enough to drive her back to Florida, there was a definite problem. But without Ethan to speak in his defense, it might be difficult for Fiona to resolve anything.

"I know, baby." Blythe believed it would get harder for Fiona. She hated being so powerless to protect her sister from misery.

The sound of a car pulling into the driveway alerted them.

Blythe grabbed her purse. "C'mon. They're here."

She hustled Fiona out of the house, and locked the door behind them.

Duncan stepped out of Martha's old, baby blue Cadillac to meet them. Blythe introduced him to Fiona.

"Beauty, I see, runs in the family," he said.

A round of introductions were made at the car.

"Oh, do sit back here with us, Fiona, dear," offered Martha. "You'll be quite comfortable, I assure you."

Fiona smiled and slid onto the back seat. "Thank you."

During the drive to the Space Center, Martha and Amelia kept up a steady stream of questions to the younger members of the group and told stories of life in a bygone era in a moneyed community on the north side of Atlanta. Blythe was pleased to see they had captured Fiona's attention. Her sister listened raptly, occasionally asking questions.

Duncan glanced over at Blythe. He'd been looking forward to seeing her all week. They hadn't had a chance to get together since they'd seen *Planet of the Ninja Amazons* the previous weekend. Tuesday Martha had suggested they all go to the Space Center. As impatient as he was to have Blythe to himself, he'd agreed, not wanting to hurt his aunts' feelings.

Duncan glanced into the rearview mirror and wondered if Blythe and her sister had quarreled. It didn't take a behavioral scientist to see Fiona had been initially less than enthusiastic about this trip. She seemed more relaxed now, though.

"I'll bet you haven't been on many dates as hot as this one," he told Blythe in a low-pitched voice. Out of the corner of his eye he caught the smile below her sunglasses.

"You might be right."

Duncan turned his head and looked at her, then back at the road. Was she kidding? Or did it bother her he'd made it a group outing? Her dark glasses made it difficult to read her expression.

"I'm teasing, Duncan," Blythe assured him in a quiet voice. "This'll be fun."

He breathed an inner sigh of relief. "Yeah. It will be fun, won't it?"

Blythe served as navigator, and soon Duncan piloted them into the vast lot where cars from all over North America were parked.

As they walked into the first building, Spaceport Central, a sign suspended from the ceiling informed them tour tickets were available outside at the ticket pavilion. "Do you want to take the tour?" Duncan asked.

"What is the tour, dear?" Martha inquired.

"A bus takes us out to the Vertical Assembly Building and the crawler path."

"Oh, yes!" exclaimed Amelia. "Let's do."

Duncan turned to his older aunt. "Martha?"

"Of course, dear. I wouldn't want to miss anything."

"Fiona?"

"Yes. I'd like that."

He and Blythe went to get the tickets while Fiona, Martha and Amelia viewed the exhibits in the main area of Spaceport Central.

The ticket counter was in the courtyard midway between Spaceport Central and Galaxy Center, which housed the IMAX theater. Duncan examined a brochure. "What do you think? Should we live dangerously and buy tickets for the theater without taking a poll first?"

Blythe raised her eyebrows. "What? Bypass the democratic process? It's a risk."

"One I'm willing to take. I can't imagine Amelia or Martha not wanting to see this. The screen's seven-and-a-half stories tall."

Lately Fiona became irritated easily, and Blythe suspected she might bristle if she was not consulted.

For the sake of group harmony, however, Blythe decided to take a chance. "Count us in."

After buying the tickets, Duncan and Blythe rounded up their relatives and went to the boarding area. They took seats on the bus and waited while the other tourists found places.

This tour had been a good idea, Duncan thought, easing his arm onto the back of the seat, brushing Blythe's shoulders. She turned to him with a questioning look, and he smiled.

"Am I disturbing you?" he asked.

"No."

He sighed heavily. "Darn."

Her eyes sparkled, and that luscious mouth curved up.

Duncan wanted to pull Blythe into his arms. He wanted to press her back against the seat and feel her against him. He wanted to kiss her senseless.

A masculine tightening prompted Duncan to shut down the steamy images so clear in his mind. He sat very still for a moment.

His relationship with Blythe was new, fragile, and Duncan sensed in her an uncertainty bordering on reluctance. It unsettled him.

"Blythe, dear," Amelia warbled as she leaned forward in the seat behind, "a friend gave Martha and me a hot stock tip."

A stone sank in Blythe's stomach as she managed a smile for the older woman. "Hot" stock tips usually spelled trouble.

The low murmur of voices that had filled the bus ceased instantly and Blythe was conscious of the other passengers fastening their attention on Amelia and her. A dropped pin would have clanged in the silence.

"Maybe you'd like to tell me later, Amelia, when we get off the bus," Blythe suggested.

"Oh, no, dear," Amelia insisted. "If I wait, I'll forget. The name of this company is Carter-Something. They make deodorant."

"Carter-Wallace. They make Arrid. It's a good stock. Solid."

"They make something else. Something very popular. Now what was it?" Amelia frowned in concentration as she tried to recall. "I remember when Eunice told me.... It has something to do with a war, an ancient war."

Blythe was certain the bus was getting warmer. She shifted uneasily under the scrutiny of her co-passengers. Duncan's interested gaze seemed to intensify into a laserlike beam. She fervently wished Amelia would lose interest in the stock tip until they got off the bus.

Duncan lifted an eyebrow. "Ancient war?"

"Trojans!" Amelia crowed in triumph. "They make Trojans. What is a Trojan? Some sort of toy?"

Blythe cleared her throat. "Sort of."

Duncan's grin turned wicked. "Is that what you think a condom is? A toy?"

Oh, God. "No." Her voice cracked. "They're serious business, all right."

She caught a glimpse of Fiona's amused smile from the corner of her eye. Across the aisle, an enormous bald man with a naked woman tattooed on his arm winked at Blythe.

"Condom?" Amelia looked at Martha. "What's a condom?"

"I don't know, dear. Ask Duncan," Martha advised.

"Yes," Blythe urged. "Ask Duncan." She smirked.

"Uh ... yes." Suddenly Duncan seemed to realize their discussion continued to hold the undivided attention of everyone on the bus. Several seats down a youth tittered.

"Inquiring minds want to know, Duncan," Blythe prodded in a low voice.

Duncan smiled at his aunt. "I'll explain it to you later. Now is not the time."

His aunt blinked. "Very well, dear. If you think it best."

"Trust me."

Gradually the drone of other conversation filled the void.

"That was sneaky, McKeon," Blythe informed him.

Duncan chuckled. "She would have been embarrassed."

"Oh, I see," Blythe muttered indignantly. "It was okay if *I* was embarrassed."

"I wouldn't have dreamed of interrupting your explanation. You were so smooth." He gently tugged a lock of her hair.

"Thanks a lot." Blythe found his touch distracting. Her thoughts skittered to an image of Duncan, framed by a partially open door, silhouetted in the bathroom's light; naked Duncan opening the foil of a condom.

Blythe swallowed hard. It was difficult to meet his eyes without blushing.

After a small eternity, the bus stopped at the crawler path. Tourists squinted down the three miles of track and marveled at the size of the gargantuan crawler, which conveyed shuttles to the launching site. They went on to view the colossal Vertical Assembly Building from afar, yet close enough to feel dwarfed. Ordinarily Blythe would have found these things fascinating. With Duncan so close, so attentive, these wonders were relegated to background color.

As they reboarded the bus at the VAB stop, Duncan told Fiona and his aunts about the movie tickets. Blythe saw the slight stiffening in her sister's carriage and received a cutting glare from green eyes.

Martha and Amelia, on the other hand, were delighted.

"Oh, my," Martha marveled. "Seven-and-an-half stories high! Fiona, dear, isn't that exciting?"

Fiona's rigid posture relaxed slightly. "I guess."

"It will be the next best thing to being there, standing close to all those shuttles and rockets," Amelia assured Fiona. "This is the opportunity of a lifetime!"

A smile fought for control of Fiona's lips, finally taking hold. "I wouldn't want to miss that. Bring on those shuttles and rockets."

Blythe breathed a small sigh of relief when they finally entered the theater. She and Duncan chose their seats and waited for the others, but Martha and Amelia towed Fiona to seats several rows away.

"Why are you sitting there?" Duncan called to Martha.

"We can see better, dear," Martha replied, looking pleased with herself.

"The screen is over seven stories high. You'll be able to see no matter where you sit."

"No, no," Martha insisted, "we can see much better from here. You forget our age. Fiona understands, don't you, dear?"

Fiona smiled knowingly. "Oh, indeed I do."

"There, you see?" Martha turned around and took her seat.

Tall Fiona sat between the two petite aristocrats. She waved at Duncan and Blythe, who waved back.

"I've never seen my aunts do that," Duncan said. "I didn't think they had a matchmaking bone in their bodies."

Blythe smiled, not knowing what else to do. She found the situation a little awkward. The last thing she and Duncan needed was a pair of determined matchmakers. This relationship was destined to be temporary. It would be too difficult for it to be anything else.

Duncan studied Blythe as she looked around the inside of the theater. He'd watched her with his aunts again today. They responded to her attention like day lilies opening to the sun.

Fiona also got along well with Amelia and Martha. Since they'd left Winter Park this morning he'd witnessed the beginning of friendship among the three. He had also noticed instances of friction between Fiona and Blythe, sensed fleeting anger and distress.

He laced his fingers with Blythe's, and smiled when she looked at him. She didn't ease her hand from his, as he'd anticipated, and he felt unexpectedly relieved. "Wanna neck?" he asked.

Blythe laughed. It was a light, lilting sound that encircled his heart, making him feel youthful and clever.

"I thought we were supposed to sneak off to the balcony for that," she pointed out.

He turned and looked behind him, then at Blythe. "There is no balcony."

"They just don't build movie theaters like they used to."

Duncan leaned back into his chair. "Well, they won't get any more of my trade. Their choice of architecture has put a damper on my social life."

A pale eyebrow lifted. *"Social?"*

"I couldn't very well neck by myself, could I?"

Her mouth curved up. "Point taken."

The movie proved to be a high point of the excursion. The realistic sound system and the towering screen combined to enthrall the audience. Only the lack of a balcony kept Duncan from finding it perfect.

CHAPTER SEVEN

THE FOLLOWING WEDNESDAY morning brought a large order from a client, and the resolution of a contested entry time for a stock purchase, settled in Blythe's favor. She hummed as she went about her work.

"Life's just a bowl of cherries for you today, isn't it?" Ginny teased.

"Into each life a little sunshine must fall. I do believe today is a ray."

"Speaking of sunshine, I notice Duncan McKeon has been calling you or dropping by to take you to lunch every day for a week. Are you getting serious?" asked Ginny hopefully.

"Nope. We're just havin' fun." Blythe took the typed letters Ginny handed her and signed them.

"That's how it always starts."

Ginny's smile was altogether too satisfied for Blythe's comfort. "Well, here's a news bulletin, my friend. That's all either of us wants out of this. We live too far apart, and we're both too wrapped up in our work for things to get serious."

Ginny's smile faded a little. "Then why all this attention?" she persisted.

Blythe rolled her eyes in exasperation. "Because we enjoy talking business. Because he's one of the few people I can talk to about my work. He understands.

And he likes talking to me about Macrocosm. I find it fascinating." *And because he's intelligent, funny and sexy, and because the sparks are incredible.*

"Business!" Ginny echoed incredulously. "You talk about business? A man who is too good-looking to be a movie star and you can't find anything better to talk about?" She narrowed her eyes. "I don't believe you."

Blythe toyed with the corners of the papers she held. "Well, maybe we don't talk about business exclusively."

Triumphant, Ginny gloated. "I thought as much."

"We discuss our families—his aunts, my sister." Blythe grinned.

Ginny shot her a withering stare. "Don't you have something better to do than to stand around annoying me?"

"Yes, ma'am." Blythe ducked back into her office.

This was shaping up to be one of those rare, near-perfect days. All she needed to make it complete was Duncan's telephone call.

When Ginny buzzed her, Blythe quickly picked up the handset, expecting her sales assistant to announce Duncan.

"It's someone named Ethan Dodd."

Blythe's anticipation evaporated, leaving a lump of ash in the pit of her stomach. "Thanks, Ginny." When the other woman hung up, Blythe drew a fortifying breath and pressed the flashing button.

"Hello, this is Blythe Summers."

"Hello, Ms. Summers. This is Ethan Dodd. You are Fiona Burnett's sister, aren't you?" The question rang with urgency.

If only there wasn't such desperate emotion in his voice. Then it would be easier to be impersonal. "Yes, Mr. Dodd. Fiona is my sister."

"Please, I'm looking for Fiona. I've got to find her. You're my only lead. Your home number is unlisted. All I had to go on was that you're a stockbroker in Central Florida."

This area of the state was studded with cities and towns, and Blythe couldn't even estimate the number of brokerage firms located here. His accomplishment astonished her. Ethan Dodd was a determined man.

"Please tell me where Fiona is," he said.

Damn Fiona! She should be talking to this man, not me. Blythe felt trapped. Once again, Fiona had run away from a problem. *And look who's left holding the bag.*

Again, she drew in a deep breath and eased it out. "Ethan, I'm afraid Fiona isn't ready to talk to you." Why had she said that? Fiona hadn't committed herself to *ever* talking to Ethan again. But Blythe couldn't bring herself to tell him that. Not when he was going to such lengths to find the woman he loved.

Silence from the other end of the telephone line clawed Blythe's nerves. The faint hiss of the long-distance connection reminded her time was not the only thing this man had spent in his search for her sister.

"When do you think she'll be ready to talk to me?" Pain saturated his voice.

Blythe winced. "I—I don't know. I . . . really don't know."

She heard his sharply drawn breath and its unsteady release. "Where is she?"

Leaning her elbows on the rosewood desk, Blythe rested her forehead against the heel of her hand. "I can't tell you that."

"Can't or *won't?*"

"Can't. I gave her my word, Ethan. She wants time to think."

"Can you tell me...is there—" His voice broke. "Is there someone else?"

Fiona's abrupt departure had left Ethan hanging on tenterhooks of uncertainty. Pity for Ethan twisted in Blythe's chest. "No. No one else."

"I see," he said raggedly.

Again, silence filled the line.

"Please," he pleaded, his voice filled with anguish. "Please tell me where she is. I have to talk to her. Don't you understand? *I love her.*"

Blythe's throat tightened. Moisture welled in her eyes. "I'm sorry, but I just can't help you. Goodbye, Ethan." She moved to hang up the telephone.

"Wait!" His shout rang clearly, though the handset was almost to the cradle.

She lifted it back to her ear. "Yes?"

"Take my telephone number. I'll give you the one for my office and the one for my apartment." He dictated them to her. "Please don't lose them. She might...forget."

"I'll make certain the numbers are safe."

"Thank you," he said unevenly. "Goodbye."

After she hung up, Blythe stared out the glass wall to the bull pen where new brokers attempted to cold call their way to success. She rolled the cool glass paperweight between her palms.

Fiona wasn't happy, Blythe knew, and as time passed the young woman drifted deeper into irritable depression. Evidently Ethan wasn't faring any better.

Blythe had come close to admitting Fiona was staying with her. It would have been the best thing to do, she was sure. But she'd made a promise to her sister. A sister, she reminded herself, who had the right to make her own decisions, even if Blythe thought them unwise.

BY THE TIME Fiona and she cleared away the dinner dishes that evening, Blythe had given up ever finding the perfect opening to introduce the subject of Ethan. There didn't seem to be any graceful way of broaching the matter of his call. Fiona hadn't mentioned a word about him or their life together. Blythe decided she'd have to bring it up herself.

She shot her sister a sidelong glance, noticing again the circles under the younger woman's eyes. Fiona needed to know.

"Ethan called today."

Fiona's head snapped around, her eyes wide. "H-he called? At your office?"

"He's trying to find you, Fiona." Blythe reached out to gently lay her hand on her sister's arm.

Fiona stepped back. "How did he find you? I swear, Blythe, I never gave him your number. I didn't want you mixed up in this."

Blythe sighed, remembering how she'd felt during that telephone conversation. "You told him I was a stockbroker in Central Florida. The man called one brokerage firm after another until he found me. He's desperate to talk to you."

Long seconds passed as Fiona stared down at the floor, chewing her lip. Finally she asked, "What did he say?"

"He said he loves you."

Fiona blanched. "No." She shook her head. "How could he, after the way I ran off? He'd never be able to forget. If I went back, he'd always wonder when he left for work in the morning if I'd be there when he got home."

When Blythe curved her arm around Fiona's shoulders, her sister made no move to draw away.

"And would you?" Blythe asked softly. "Remember you won't be alone. You'll have your and Ethan's child. Now that you've had a little time apart, time to consider, would you still be there when Ethan got home?"

Fiona raised green eyes filled with doubt. "I honestly don't know."

"Do you regret leaving?"

"I regret everything. My whole life is a regret. Isn't everyone's?"

Blythe thought of Andrew. She knew she should have reported his unethical activities. She'd known then. He'd lied to his clients, *their* clients, and even though she'd worked frantically to undo the damage he'd done, he'd been a senior, more experienced broker. His word had carried more weight.

In the end, they'd been ready to accuse her as well as Andrew. Her name had been blazoned across the papers along with his. Her photograph had been shown on television news, alongside her husband-partner's. Only the clients who'd remembered her counsel had saved her.

Shame still seared her soul.

Yes, she had regrets.

Maybe it wasn't too late for Fiona. Blythe rested her temple against her sister's. "He gave me his telephone numbers—work and home. I put them in the kitchen address book." She gave Fiona a reassuring squeeze, and was pleased when the younger woman squeezed her back.

"Thanks, but I need more time," Fiona murmured.

Sadness touched Blythe. "Your choice."

THE SUN GLOWED in a perfect blue sky. A good omen for the weekend, Blythe thought as she sipped her coffee Saturday morning. Duncan had told her they were going someplace unusual today. He'd said it was a surprise.

She sat in the kitchen, gazing out the garden window, waiting for him. Her surprise for him was a picnic lunch. She'd packed a loaf of freshly baked dark rye bread, a chunk of Havarti cheese, thick slices of ham, crisp Delicious apples and a chilled bottle of Riesling in a picturesque basket. If his plans held no place for the lunch, they could always eat it later.

When a knock sounded at the front door, Blythe smiled. Ten o'clock on the dot. She grabbed the basket and hurried to meet him before he knocked again. Fiona was still asleep.

"Hi," she welcomed him in a low voice.

He greeted her with a slow, sweet kiss that stole her breath. "Hi, yourself," he murmured.

"I packed a picnic lunch for us. Can we use it?"

He dropped a kiss on the tip of her nose. "You bet."

When they were settled in the car, with lunch in the trunk, Blythe asked, "What's the surprise? Where are we going?"

Duncan backed out of the driveway. "If I tell you, it won't be a surprise."

"But if I know, I can enjoy the anticipation," she reasoned.

"True." He glanced at her and grinned. "All right. We're going to a winery. I've found one in Lake County and it's open to the public."

"A winery? I love touring wineries!" She recalled her visit to Napa Valley, California, three years ago. It had been an adventure in the ancient romance of wine. Rolling hills, carefully tended vineyards, swirling wine in elegantly simple goblets. Age-old techniques had been explained. Blythe treasured the memories of that experience.

"I thought you'd enjoy a visit."

"Oh, yes. I knew there was a winery up near Tallahassee, but I didn't know there was one in the next county."

Duncan turned in the direction of Interstate Four. "Oakmont Winery and Vineyards. Actually I'm surprised there's not a thriving wine industry in Florida."

"There used to be, back in the early 1900s. Pierce's disease wiped out the vines. Only the native muscadine survived. I'd heard the University of Florida has been working for years to develop disease-resistant grape varieties, but I didn't know how successful they'd been."

"Successful enough, it seems."

"This is exciting," Blythe declared with obvious delight. "I'll bet Oakmont uses the new hybrids.

They talked about the wines produced in California and compared them with European wines as they drove from Orange County to its neighbor.

Lake County was aptly named, Duncan thought as they drove through the rolling hills. Here and there, small lakes studded the green-and-gold landscape like azure jewels. But his thoughts didn't center on water or wine. They were merely the setting he wanted when he broke the news to Blythe.

Tomorrow he left for Atlanta, his business in Florida finished. Negotiations with Central Florida Software had ground to a halt. They hadn't been able to reach an agreement on Macrocosm. CFS wanted an entrance into the Atlanta Market, but they didn't seem willing to pay for it. Their latest proposal had convinced Duncan he was wasting his time. He'd been away for a month and he had a company to run. As much as he wanted to be with Blythe, he couldn't afford to delay his return any longer.

In previous relationships, his leave-taking would have been a simple matter. No regrets and no ties to complicate life. Brief and understood.

From the very beginning, though, his experience with Blythe had been beyond the bounds of his usual alliances with women. This was...this was more complex. Yet more elemental. Infinitely more profound. Duncan shook his head. Everything about their interaction was just... *more.*

Which puzzled him, because there had also been less. With Blythe he had never crossed the line into physical intimacy, even though she was a beautiful, desirable woman. And it wasn't because he didn't want her badly enough. God, he detested every one of those cold showers! No, he'd reined back because...

well, because with Blythe, everything was special. And somehow, he'd sensed she would never settle for a casual affair.

Initially he'd been reluctant to sully what they had with the stress the distance between Atlanta and Winter Park would inevitably impose. They'd always have their sweet memories. But now, faced with leaving, he found that wasn't enough. He wanted to explore what was between them. He wanted . . . more.

He turned off the Turnpike. It wasn't long before they saw a sign announcing the entrance to Oakmont Winery, and they turned into the driveway.

The architecture of the winery made Blythe think of old Spanish missions and grand ranchos, though this oak-tree-shaded building had been built only a few years ago. It sat on top of a hill, surrounded by the neat rows of its young vineyard.

Duncan swept his arm out in an expansive gesture, encompassing the property. "The rebirth of viticulture in Central Florida."

He escorted her inside, into a large room featuring a wine-tasting bar and displays of various Oakmont wines. A woman in a colorful apron bearing the winery's logo greeted them, and offered to guide them on the tour.

They went upstairs, into a small auditorium, where they were the only viewers. The guide lowered the lights, turned on the slide show and quietly withdrew.

Blythe's attention to the history and science of winemaking in Florida dwindled rapidly when Duncan began nibbling behind her ear.

"Intoxicating," he murmured.

Blythe moved her head to make it easier for him. If he'd seemed distracted earlier, his attention was firmly focused on her now. Shivers of pleasure went down her neck.

"You have no respect for education," she complained breathlessly.

He lifted her hair, and dropped soft kisses along her nape. "That's not true," he objected in a low voice. "I'm all for expanding one's horizons."

"For instance . . . ?"

"Well, for instance, I've just learned you have a tiny mole here." He pressed his lips to it. "And I've just discovered I like how your hair feels against the back of my hand."

"A scholar," Blythe breathed, and was just turning her mouth to his for a proper kiss when, through the window in the door, she saw the guide approaching.

Quickly she straightened in her seat. "The show's over," she whispered to Duncan. "Guide's here."

Duncan released Blythe's hair, but left his arm resting behind her, along the back of the bench.

The woman in the apron led them out of the theater onto a walkway overlooking the machinery, the large wooden wine casks and the turning racks for the bottles of sparkling wine. Blythe noted there was a lot of empty space. The owners had built for the future, the guide assured them.

They proceeded onto the balcony, outside, which overlooked the lake and the vineyard, and the hills in the distance.

Duncan decided this was the place he would tell Blythe. Turning to the guide he said, "Would you mind if we just enjoyed the view for a while?"

The woman smiled. "No. When you're ready, go through that door—" she indicated one at the end of the balcony "—then down the stairs, and we'll conduct your wine tasting."

When they were alone, Duncan and Blythe stood looking out over the serene landscape. Duncan curved his arm around Blythe's waist and drew her close. Neither broke the peaceful silence for minutes.

"I have something to tell you," he finally said.

She looked at him, quietly waiting.

He gently brushed a stray lock of hair behind her shoulder. "My business in Florida is concluded. I leave for Atlanta tomorrow morning."

She paled, but her composure didn't waver.

"Well," she said after a minute, and drew a deep breath. "We both knew this time would come."

"Yes, we did, but we never talked about it."

She didn't meet his eyes, and he felt a stone sink in his stomach. "What's there to talk about?" she asked. "You live in Atlanta. Macrocosm is there." She turned to face the broad acres of grapevines. "I live in Winter Park. It's where my business is. You have to go back." When Duncan didn't respond, she asked uncertainly, "Don't you?"

Blythe had feared this moment, knowing all along it would eventually come. She just hadn't seen at what point their budding relationship would end. Logically it made sense to end it here, but she'd hoped . . .

It would have been kinder to tell her at the end of the day, she thought. Disconsolate, she stared out at the vineyards. Duncan stared at her profile. He realized Blythe might not say a word to close the distance yawning between them. But her posture, her movements conveyed distress. He guessed she must be as uncertain as he was. Maybe she didn't want to call it quits. Not now. Not when there was still so much between them yet to explore.

He took the first step. "It's only about an hour and a half by air from Atlanta to Orlando International."

She turned to face him. "Yeah?"

"Yeah." He reached out and cautiously placed his hand on her shoulder. Her muscles were rigid.

"I've always liked flying," she said hesitantly. "How about you?"

"Crazy about it," he answered promptly. Her shoulders relaxed a little.

"We must both be crazy." She offered him a tentative smile.

"As loons." He took her into his arms.

"I'd say—"

"No more talk," he muttered, and sealed her mouth with the best kiss he could give her. He tried to share everything he was feeling in that moment.

Blythe twined her arms around his neck and clung to him.

Finally he took her hand, and led her to the door. "C'mon. I want to see how your lips taste when they're wearing Florida wine."

"HOW ARE THE TESTS coming?" Blythe asked Monday when she came across Ginny studying.

Ginny beamed. "Great! My scores are good and I'm on schedule to finish in time for the series seven exam, just like we planned."

"You're amazing, Rodriguez," Blythe said admiringly. She offered Ginny a can of orange soda. "My treat. Maybe we ought to pour it on your tracks to douse the flames."

The future broker accepted the soft drink. "I am amazing, aren't I?"

Blythe laughed. "Too amazing for words." She took a swallow of her cola.

"Think of it," Ginny said. "With our brains and good looks, we could be two rich women."

"Now you're catching on. All we have to do is work fourteen-hour days for the rest of our lives and we might make money past our dreams of avarice."

Ginny leaned back in her secretarial chair, and stared consideringly at the ceiling. "I don't know. I can dream pretty big."

"If we don't get back to work, dreams are going to be the only thing we retire with." Blythe swallowed the last of her soda and tossed the can into the recycling bin.

"Spoilsport," Ginny muttered as she reopened her book.

As Blythe walked toward her office Leonard Brock sauntered up. "I hear you're having a little run of bad luck, Blythe."

She turned and faced Leonard. "Oh?"

He brushed at a speck of lint on his immaculately tailored lapel. "Word is that you've had two accounts close recently. Two large accounts."

Blythe froze. *Two?* She knew better than to underestimate Leonard's sources. The man might be a gossip-monger, but his initial information was usually accurate. It maddened her he knew about one of her accounts before she did.

"You know how it is, Leonard. Sometimes these things go in streaks. It's inexplicable." Blythe refused to give him the satisfaction of admitting her ignorance of the second account. Just wait until she found the person in operations who'd been chatty with the office rumor king!

The broker looked up from his grooming, and smiled. "Let's just hope *three* isn't a charm for you, Blythe. People talk, you know."

A bad taste seeped into her mouth. "What do you mean by that?"

Leonard's smile took on a feral quality. "You are, after all, the former wife and partner of the infamous Andrew Summers."

Fear, cold and clenching, uncoiled its too-familiar tentacles. She stared at Brock.

"I was just afraid," he continued, "losing those important accounts might have something to do with your past." His smile was quick, fleeting. "If I can help you, let me know." Leonard Brock walked away.

Trembling, Blythe walked unevenly to her office and collapsed into her chair. She held her hand in front of her face. It shook. "Damn him," she whispered fiercely. "Damn him to hell." She wasn't sure, at that moment, who was more deserving of the curse—Leonard or Andrew.

Ginny appeared at her side. "What is it? What's wrong?"

"Oh, nothing. I shouldn't let Leonard get to me like that." Blythe looked into her friend's brown eyes. "No, that's not true. It is something. Leonard rushed over to tell me I've lost another big account. Then he implied it might have something to do with my partnership with Andrew. All those people testified on my behalf. Ginny, I was judged innocent!"

"Leonard is a creep. We both know that. Listen, Blythe. Who is it that wanted this office when Arnold Serliff retired?"

"Everyone," Blythe said dully.

"Leonard was the most insistent. Even though his numbers weren't as good as yours, he declared it his by right of seniority. But who did Tom decide to give it to? This big office with the picture window and the great view?"

"Me."

"Right. Because you earned it. You're a top producer. Leonard Brock is petty and malicious and hates being stuck in his cubbyhole at the end of the hall. I'm afraid he doesn't love you, Blythe."

"The feeling's mutual."

"Even his sales assistant despises him. Maybe the guy deserves a little pity."

Blythe looked at Ginny. Ginny looked at Blythe. "Naaah," they chorused.

After Ginny returned to her desk, Blythe walked over to operations, where she found another of her important clients had indeed closed an account.

Blythe spoke to the operations manager. Divulging the business of one broker to another was a breach of ethics and Stewart Duke policy. What bothered her more, at the moment, was having her loss thrown in her face by Leonard before she even knew about it. Blythe found it embarrassing, infuriating, and she made her sentiments known to the operations manager, who earnestly promised such an occurrence wouldn't happen again.

"Why did the client come to operations, anyway?" Blythe asked.

"You were at lunch, and the client wanted the account closed immediately. He even scribbled out a letter instructing us to do it, while he stood here."

"Did he say why he wanted the account closed?" asked Blythe.

"No. Just that he wanted it closed, pronto."

Back in her office, Blythe dialed the client. "Donald," she said, "this is Blythe Summers at Stewart Duke."

"Oh!" came his startled reply.

You didn't expect me to call, did you? After working with him all those years, he hadn't had the courtesy, or the guts, to talk to her. "I've been advised you closed your account while I was at lunch." The man was retired, for God's sake. He didn't need to take care of his business on a lunch hour. Unless he was avoiding Blythe.

"That's right. Uh, that's right, I did."

"May I ask why you want to close your account?"

"I don't think it's any of your business."

"Your account, Donald, was my business for six years. I made money for you, talked you into diversifying for safety. If you're unhappy about something, talk to me. If I come out to see you and Louisa, I'm certain we can work everything out. Say, one-thirty?"

"No. Don't bother to come. We have nothing to say to you. Good day." Donald Hanlon hung up.

Blythe stared at her handset as if she could discern some sense from the scatter of tiny holes over the receiver. Finally she set it back in the cradle.

Hanlon had sometimes been difficult and sometimes brusque, but he'd never refused to hear what she had to say, and he certainly had never been rude. Why had he changed?

Her stomach churned and twisted, and acid rose in her throat. The air seemed to have been sucked out of her office. Blythe found it hard to breathe. Only the knowledge that she was visible through the plate-glass walls kept her straight in her chair, her head up, her face set.

Why was this happening to her? Was Andrew's larcenous behavior, and her failure to report it, resurfacing to taint her again? *God, no, not again!* Too clearly she remembered the sly, covert snubs, the silent, accusing looks. The humiliation. The guilt. It could all be rekindled by a well-placed whisper.

"It's here," called Ginny from outside Blythe's office door.

Slowly Blythe levered herself out of her chair and joined Ginny to look at the brown cardboard box resting on the calendar blotter.

"It's a box," Blythe observed, still struggling to swallow her latest defeat.

"Not just any box." Ginny touched a cardboard side reverently. "It's the newest batch of test materials," she explained.

Blythe nodded.

Ginny studied Blythe's face. "What did you find out?

"It was the Hanlon account."

Breath hissed through Ginny's teeth. "Lordy-mama. That account was worth over a million."

Blythe couldn't bring herself to speak. Why had Donald Hanlon done such an about-face? She tried to think of something she might have done. His investments were doing well.

"It wasn't worth that much when Hanlon started working with you," Ginny stated hotly.

"Nope." Blythe jammed her hands into her skirt pockets.

Ginny frowned. "What's going on? Why is this happening?"

"I wish I knew." Blythe's throat tightened. She dragged in air to help relieve the tautness. "Do you . . . still want to be a broker?"

Ginny blinked. "Well, of course I want to be a broker." She took Blythe's elbow and hustled her into the glass-walled office. "You're helping me leave a dead-end job. You're opening a whole new career for me. And when I grow up, I want to be just like you."

"Bankrupt?"

"Okay, so maybe not exactly like you." Ginny pinned Blythe with a stern gaze. "Losing the Hanlon account is certainly *not* going to break you. You've got a number of accounts even bigger."

Blythe heaved a sigh. "Oh, I know that. It's just . . . I want to know *why*. Ginny, it's all getting too familiar. I went through this before with Andrew—the withdrawn accounts, the innuendo, the rudeness. Then one man finally came out and said what was on his mind, but only because Andrew had been fooling around with the guy's girlfriend. That's when the house of cards collapsed. And I'm afraid that's somehow connected with what's happening now, the loss of these accounts."

Inside she still bore the brands of shame and guilt. Blythe locked her gaze with Ginny's. "I never want to go through that again."

WEDNESDAY AFTERNOON the following week, Blythe picked up the receiver expecting to hear the voice of one of her clients.

"Come to Atlanta for dinner," Duncan murmured.

Electric shivers played up and down Blythe's spine in response to the resonance of his masculine voice. "When?"

"Now. Tonight."

"Isn't this a little sudden?"

"I don't care. It's been two weeks and I want to see you."

Blythe blinked. This assertiveness revealed a side of Duncan she had never witnessed before. He wanted to be with her and that, apparently, was that. She smiled, her feminine ego thoroughly gratified.

"All right. You make the reservations and I'll make flight arrangements."

"We can dine at Chez McKeon. A very exclusive place."

She knew where that could lead, and she wasn't ready, wasn't certain. "Please extend my regrets to the chef. Another restaurant would be preferable."

Duncan saw his very romantic, very intimate evening vanish. He wanted time alone with her. He needed time to woo her. It had been so long since he'd indulged in romance he'd almost forgotten how exciting it could be. The titillation. The tension. The miracle of fulfillment.

"Have you been to the Priory?" Duncan asked.

"No."

"You'll love it. I'll make reservations."

"What time?"

"It will depend on when you can get here. I'll call the airlines to see what flights there are and make arrangements to have a ticket ready at the counter. Then I'll make the restaurant reservations and call you."

Blythe hesitated. There was an implied intimacy, an unspoken commitment involved with Duncan rendering such a service. "I'd rather make my own plane reservations." The thought of him performing the courtesy made Blythe uneasy, as if he threatened to trespass on jealously guarded territory. "If you would take care of the restaurant, that's more than enough."

"My invitation, my responsibility. Besides, if you order your own tickets, you have to call me back, then I have to see if we can get reservations, then *I'd* have to call *you* back. It's easier my way." He spoke low in his throat, his tone amused.

Blythe could envision him clearly. High-planed cheekbones under slanting, silver gray eyes. Finely sculptured mouth smiling, one side cocked slightly higher.

"Humor me, please," she coaxed.

He sighed. "All right. Call me."

She smiled. "I will."

Three hours later she walked down the jetway and boarded the seven-twenty-seven bound for Atlanta.

Blythe took her seat in first class—coach had been booked full. Men and women in business suits predominated here, and she felt conspicuous in her strapless, black velvet evening dress and black taffeta wrap with its deep violet ruffle, her patterned black stockings and black high heels. She knew the glitter of *faux* diamonds at her ears, throat and wrist contrasted stunningly with the black velvet of the dress and the silver gold of her hair, which was smoothed into its customary chignon.

Duncan had told her to dress formally. If this didn't impress him, nothing she did would.

Blythe enjoyed the satins, silks and laces generally considered the prerogative of a woman, but that pleasure was usually curtailed since she worked in a male-dominated industry, with tradition-oriented investors. Conservative suits and dresses were the order of the day. Blythe smiled to herself. What she wore under those severe garments was anything but conservative.

As the plane lifted from the runway into the darkening sky, Blythe took off her wrap and settled comfortably into her seat. When the flight attendant offered her a drink, Blythe declined.

Oddly, at that moment, she felt confident. She had no unsteady nerves to calm. Blythe experienced only the excited anticipation of seeing Duncan.

Alone.

In Atlanta. Her confidence suddenly seeped away. What did she know about Atlanta? It was big, the hub of the South. Blythe had been to New York—what was so intimidating about Atlanta?

You're entering his territory, whispered logic. *Up until now, you've been in your own. You advance into an unknown area.*

Unknown. It equated with risk.

Blythe shifted restlessly in her seat. Somehow, it seemed easier to face the possibility of future hurt when standing in her own house, her own office, or even the Space Center, which was at least in Florida.

Here she was, dressed to kill, on her way to a strange city to meet a man whose intentions she wasn't quite sure of. Everything familiar to her was thousands of feet below, hundreds of miles behind.

What had she gotten herself into? This whole idea of dinner in Atlanta on the spur of the moment was madness! It was...it was...*romantic.*

The coil of panic that had been tightening in her stomach instantly turned to ice. Romance. Why hadn't she seen it earlier? She should have made the connection as soon as Duncan suggested it. This was exactly the sort of thing her mother would do. Blythe closed her eyes. She was taking another step down the road her mother had paved with her numerous marriages and her inevitable divorces. A road slick with the tears of innocent victims.

The attentive flight attendant approached Blythe a second time. "Are you sure you wouldn't like some champagne?" he asked.

Blythe smiled weakly. "Yes, please. I've changed my mind."

CHAPTER EIGHT

IMPATIENTLY Duncan strode back to the gate waiting area. He looked down at the plastic cup of orange juice he clutched in one hand and frowned. He didn't really want the stuff, but it had seemed hours since he'd arrived, and he was restless. He downed it in three deep draughts and tossed the container into the trash receptacle without taking his eyes from the gate door.

Minutes later, passengers emerged.

It wasn't difficult to spot Blythe. Tall, with moonlight hair, she was clothed in black velvet. He could see her searching the waiting area, and he started walking toward her. Then her eyes met his, and her mouth—that delectable mouth for which he had great plans—smiled.

As if sensing his determination, the others surrounding the gate made way for him, and Duncan strode directly to Blythe.

As soon as he reached her he took her into his arms and kissed her with the deep, lingering passion of lovers long parted.

The elation at seeing Duncan overrode Blythe's caution. It wasn't simply that he looked splendid in a tuxedo. There was something more, a feeling that bubbled up inside of her. She wanted to laugh and hug him. At the same time, she wanted to draw away—only for a moment, just long enough to examine her emotions and adjust them to leave her back in control, less affected.

The touch of his lips blew that wish out of her mind. Duncan moved his mouth over hers with such yearning it sent her world spinning. He held her close, pressing her against the solidness of his body with starved urgency.

Blythe twined her arms around his neck.

Finally he relaxed his hold, allowing a little distance between them. Duncan grinned. "Welcome to Atlanta, darlin'. You look more beautiful than ever."

If only her heart would slow down, Blythe thought, maybe this giddiness would stop. "My, my, but you do know how to make a body feel at home."

Duncan rested his hand at the small of her back, and leered down at her, wiggling his dark winged eyebrows. "I have you in my clutches now, me proud beauty. The ways of the big city are wicked and wonderful."

She widened her eyes in feigned innocence. "Can we go with the wonderful, tonight?"

"Sometimes," Duncan drawled, locking his gaze with hers, "they're one and the same."

Blythe shivered, but before she could form a suitable retort, he guided her toward the exit.

At the departure area, Duncan directed her to a black limousine. A uniformed chauffeur stepped up to open the door.

Inside, Blythe found polished mahogany paneling, and leather upholstery the deep garnet of a fine Bordeaux. As the driver moved into the flow of traffic leaving the airport, Blythe smiled. "I'm impressed. Is this how you get to work every day?"

"Borrowed finery, I'm afraid. Courtesy of the rental company."

Dark and elegant in his satin-lapeled tuxedo, Duncan moved across the compartment, from his seat to hers, in one fluid motion. He sat close. Very close.

Blythe was aware of his breath stirring her hair near her temple. She tensed, faintly nervous at being confined in such close proximity with someone so physically different from herself, so alien in thought, so overpoweringly...masculine.

Duncan sensed her unease. Maybe he had come on too strongly. But he had missed her. He wanted to touch her, to feel the warm softness of her against him. He studied the curve of her ear. If he teased the inner whorl with the tip of his tongue would she shiver—or shudder? Reluctantly Duncan decided to wait.

He stretched out his legs and rested his arm across the back of the seat behind her. Blythe found herself relaxing, but there was still that fine hum of tension. Like the crackling static that heralds an electric storm, nervous tautness permeated the air between them.

"I'm glad you came," Duncan said after countless heartbeats. His voice, deep and smooth, flowed over her, soothing, exciting.

Blythe smiled. "So am I."

"Have you heard about the Priory?" he asked.

"It's in an old church, isn't it?"

"That's right. An old stone church."

Blythe felt faintly relieved at the less intimate turn of their conversation. She glanced at Duncan, hoping to catch a clue to his thoughts.

His face was unreadable. In the low light of the limousine, his hooded eyes were dark. There was no tension in his mouth—it curved neither up nor down.

She had wanted space and he'd given it to her, here in this closed compartment. Yet the very air she breathed was warm with his presence.

"Did I tell you how smashing you look in a tuxedo?" she asked.

Slowly Duncan turned his head. His mouth curved slightly. "No, I don't believe you did."

"Well, you do. And I like the tucks of your shirt." She moved a lacquered fingernail to the perfectly stitched folds over his chest, but lost her nerve to touch. "There's something chilling about a man wearing ruffles."

Duncan laughed. "I'll remember that." His appreciative gaze roamed over her, warming Blythe down to her coral-tinted toenails.

She blushed, and felt ridiculous for doing so, causing herself to blush more vividly.

Finally the car stopped in front of a stone church. The limousine door opened, and the driver assisted her out. Blythe waited a moment while Duncan dismissed the chauffeur. Then, his hand resting again at the small of her back, they entered the Priory through its tall Gothic door.

A white-robed woman welcomed them and ushered them to their table, which was located in what had once been the nave of the church. Soaring arches converged into a series of Gothic groined vaults and windows that had held stained glass now revealed the night through etched, beveled panes. Above, in what had formerly been a choir loft, a harpist played.

"You're right," Blythe whispered over her menu. "This place is unique."

Duncan grinned. "What are you whispering for? It's a restaurant now."

"Oh." Blythe smiled. "We don't have anything like this in Winter Park."

"I don't doubt it."

"What's that supposed to mean?"

"Only that Winter Park, even Orlando, is small compared to Atlanta. There are a lot of things this city has that a smaller town can't offer."

"Like traffic, crime, pollution."

Duncan looked down at his menu. Without looking up, he said, "Everything is relative."

Blythe turned her attention to the list of Priory's offerings of continental fare. "What do you suggest?"

"Their quail stuffed with sage and porcini is good."

"Is that what you're ordering?"

"Yes."

She scanned the offerings and their descriptions. Finally Blythe closed the menu. "I'll have the quail."

"I think you'll like it."

"I'm sure I will. Besides, if I ordered something different, yours might look better."

They placed their orders for food and wine, and lapsed into silence, listening to the music of the harp.

Duncan cleared his throat. "Well. Have you seen my aunts, lately?"

"No, I haven't." Blythe could think of nothing to add to her reply. Frantically she searched her mind for another subject. Why was she so ill at ease?

"Uh, how's business?" *Very clever, Summers,* she thought disgustedly. *You'd wow them at diplomatic cocktail parties.*

"Fine. Great. Business is really...great." The expression that could only have been relief changed to desperation. "Have you seen...no... How's the market?"

Blythe pounced. "The market closed six up on the Dow."

Duncan stopped their server and spoke to him in a low voice, passing something into his hand. The young man left in the direction of the musician's loft.

A minute later, the harpist began to play "The First Time Ever I Saw Your Face." Poetic and poignant, the love song was imbued with an ethereal otherworldliness by the skill of the harpist.

The song was a favorite of Blythe's but she'd never told Duncan. It had the power to evoke in her a sense of an innocence, now lost. She met his gaze and he smiled. He reached out his long-fingered hand and covered hers. "A new start to the evening."

She returned his smile. "A new start."

At that moment their salads arrived, accompanied by a bottle of wine. When the robed server left, silence returned to their table, sitting between them as if an unwelcome guest.

Blythe ate each elegant dish served to her with all the appreciation of a robot, as a rabble of butterflies fluttered in her stomach. Conversation sputtered and faded.

Since before she'd arrived at the Atlanta airport, she'd been on edge. Maybe coming to Atlanta hadn't been wise.

Blythe glanced up into Duncan's eyes. He winked.

Then, again, maybe it was the smartest thing she'd ever done.

Finally the last plate was taken away, and the coffee poured.

"I haven't been to Atlanta before," she offered.

"Your first time. I'm honored." Duncan slipped his hand next to hers, and lightly stroked the back of her wrist with his thumb.

That whisper touch erected a tingling bridge to her breast. Blythe stared down at their hands and swallowed. Heat rose in her.

She lifted her gaze. It collided with his with unnerving force. Tremors reverberated along what she had always thought were perfectly steady nerves.

Duncan smiled. It was a slow, confident curving of his mouth. "You feel it, too."

Blythe couldn't force the short affirmative word out of her mouth. It refused to come. To speak it aloud was to commit herself. Duncan would know his power.

"Say it." His voice was at once command and plea.

"I—"

"Blythe."

She lowered her eyes to his hand, which now covered hers. "Yes," Blythe whispered.

He placed a finger under her chin and raised her face. She met his eyes . . . read the imperative in them.

"Yes," she told him. "I feel it, too."

"It frightens you."

Blythe drew a deep breath and let it out. "A little."

Duncan nodded. It was not difficult to see that Blythe was caught in an internal battle. Did she fear she would lose a fraction of her independence? Hadn't she learned no one can be completely independent and expect a relationship to flourish? *You're a good one to philosophize about independence and relationships,* he thought wryly.

"I admit, it is a little terrifying." He lifted her hand and gently uncurled her fingers to expose her soft, unprotected palm. With a feather stroke, he traced his fingertip along her lifeline, and felt a tremor pass through her. "I think what we feel is something very special." His light touch moved to her inner wrist. "Tell me—is this an everyday experience for you?"

Blythe wanted to close her eyes, to concentrate on her body's tingling, flushed, achy response to Duncan's simple touch. Andrew had never elicited this reaction. None of her male companions had even dared to try.

Duncan's question burned in her mind like a hot coal. Everyday experience? The feelings she held for him defied such a mundane description.

Blythe raised her eyes to his. "I think you know better."

His eyes darkened. His mouth slowly curved. "If you're finished with your meal, I have something at my office I'd like you to see."

She eyed him speculatively. "Not etchings, I hope."

"I keep those at my condo."

"Ah."

Minutes later, outside on the street, the limousine appeared. Again, the uniformed chauffeur assisted Blythe in, and again she sank into the leather seat. This time, however, Duncan took the seat across from her.

She'd expected him to slide close to her, to rest his arm across the back of the seat, close to her shoulders, maybe even over her shoulders. Instead, he kept his distance. Blythe felt relieved and disappointed at the same time. Her ambivalence disturbed her.

The driver delivered them to a bronzed-glass skyscraper. With a nod to the security men, Duncan whisked Blythe through the lobby to an elevator, their steps echoing. Together they waited, both staring above the door, silently ticking off the stories as the elevator carried them up, level after level.

Blythe's senses were irresistibly focused on Duncan's hand cupping her elbow. His skin was warm against hers. At a slight flexing of his fingers, Blythe looked at him, but he continued to study the digital counter.

Finally they arrived at their destination, and stepped out of the elevator into a reception area. Cold elegance in the form of crystalline gray marble, glass blocks and chrome greeted them. Blythe couldn't imagine Duncan being responsible for this room.

"Did you do this?" she asked.

Duncan chuckled. "God, no. I hate it. The damage was done by the time I discovered what was going on."

"Did heads roll?" If it were *her* reception area, there would have been blood on the walls when she'd located the individual responsible.

"Yes." He leaned back against the high marble reception counter, his elbows resting behind him on the polished surface. "I like what you did with your house. Any suggestions on how to give this some life?"

Blythe studied the room for a moment. She indicated the low table in front of the couch. "A bold arrangement of colorful flowers would help."

He pushed himself away from the counter and walked toward her. "You have a fine sense of color and texture. Very sensuous."

Blythe stood still, uncertain yet expectant, uneasy yet hopeful.

Duncan simply reached for her hand. "Come. I have something I want you to see." He led her down a corridor, through another, slightly smaller, reception area with a secretary's desk, and into a large office.

Through the enormous picture window, Atlanta spread below them like a treasure of jewels strewn across black velvet. Shadowed shapes of buildings varied in size and configuration, crowding in on glittering streets. Even though, from this height, the scale was minuscule, Atlanta's vitality and dynamism was apparent to Blythe.

She stepped nearer the glass and its panorama. "Oh, Duncan," she breathed. "This is magnificent."

He came to stand beside her, sharing the view. "From ashes trampled under Union boots to this in little more than a century. I wish we had time to explore it tonight. I want to show you my city."

The twinkling lights beckoned her. Blythe wanted to investigate this metropolis, learn what made it special to Duncan. Reluctantly she recalled her responsibilities. "My plane leaves soon."

Duncan turned to face her. "Next time, then."

His voice was soft and low. Less than an inch separated them, but he made no move to close that distance. His male presence dominated the room. He held her gaze, compelling her to think of nothing but him, nothing but them. Together. The air vibrated with the tension of an electric wire.

She wasn't certain who moved first. Blythe only knew the satisfaction of finally being in his arms. She clung to him, hungry for contact. His lips took hers with ravenous intensity, sweeping aside any vestiges of doubt and caution. Then Duncan's tongue entered her mouth. He swirled and caressed, pursuing her. Hesitantly, she stroked his tongue with hers.

Fever ignited between them. Their breathing accelerated, establishing a labored, shallow, syncopated rhythm. Duncan's hands tightened on her, pressing her against him. His readiness was unmistakable, hard against her.

His arousal sent silent alarms clanging. If she didn't stop this now, in a minute he would lean her back against his desk, and she would accommodate him, welcome him.

And afterward she would pay the price in self-reproach and uncertainty. It would spell the end of any chance the two of them might have for more than this night.

She struggled to clear her mind of the searing smoke, aching with thwarted desire. "Duncan." It was little more than a whisper, yet it took all her willpower, all her strength.

Gradually his hold on her loosened. He leaned his forehead against hers, his breathing still rapid, but slowing. "Damn, woman. It's like wildfire when I'm with you."

It was like wildfire, Blythe realized, still dazed. Exactly like wildfire: unexpected, hot, out of control.

Duncan straightened slightly, maintaining his embrace. He caught and held her reluctant gaze. "I want you, Blythe. I want your heart, your soul, but at this moment I especially want your body." Lightly he drew a fingertip from her shoulder, down the creamy expanse of skin to the top of her bodice. Blythe shivered.

Duncan chuckled softly, then groaned. "Misery loves company."

"You're miserable, all right," she agreed weakly.

"I'm also patient."

Blythe could think of nothing to say. She couldn't promise to resolve her anxieties. They'd had a lifetime to grow.

His eyes narrowed. "I want more with you than just sex. But eventually, I want it all. I want *you* to want it all."

She wondered what "all" was, if it included love and trust. She regarded Duncan, looking for her answers and finding none. His face was unreadable.

Wordlessly he directed her to the door with a sweep of his arm. It was time for her to go home.

Duncan recalled the limousine, and they glided through the night with few words spoken between them. He saw Blythe to her gate just in time for her to board.

He tenderly brushed her cheek with his hand. He touched his lips to hers, then drew away. Duncan gazed at her a moment longer, then turned and walked back to his own world.

Blythe almost called out to him to stop. So badly did she want to know his real feelings she would have gladly begged for the truth. Only pride, bleak and unrelenting, kept her to the path through the gate, through the jetway and down the isle to her assigned seat. With numb fingers she buckled her seat belt and ignored the aircraft's ascent.

She sat alone, the only passenger in first class. In that dark and early hour Blythe rested her head against the frigid windowpane.

I want more with you than just sex. But eventually I want it all. I want you to want it all. Duncan's words replayed through her brain until they echoed.

Blythe did want it all. Oh, she did. She ached with her need, trembled with it. She wanted love, trust and intimacy with Duncan, sanctified by those emotions. But she couldn't let herself expect these things, not with the lessons she'd learned in her life.

She was drawn to him, and she desired him—there was no denying that. An element was missing, however. Something essential.

Trust.

Though, intellectually, she knew he'd done nothing to warrant her wariness, Blythe did not wholly trust Duncan. She was gun-shy.

In quiet, tearful rage Blythe damned her mother's need for something as unreliable as romance.

Duncan. How she wanted him to be the exception. She wanted to love him so badly it clawed at her heart. What had happened to her resolution to accept the temporary nature of her relationship with Duncan?

She wanted the real thing. The thought of settling for less brought clenched fists and more tears. Everything came back to trust. How did one have faith when there was that persistent doubt learned from repeated, painful lessons? What could she do to make it go away?

Blythe shifted in her seat, rolling her head back against the rest, closing her eyes. She drew the wrap closer around her to ward off the growing chill.

Would trust ever come? she wondered in despair. And if it did, would she recognize it?

"THAT'S RIGHT, Blythe. I want you and Fiona to come to the house for brunch this Saturday."

The long-distance connection from New York was clear and Madeline's Virginia breeding-will-tell accent came through unimpaired. How it remained unaffected by the more clipped pronunciation of her mother's adopted city Blythe didn't know, but she was glad.

"Unless of course," Madeline continued, "you have something more important to do."

Blythe massaged the bridge of her nose. She'd had little sleep last night. After her experience with Duncan in Atlanta, the last thing she needed was her mother trying to manipulate her through guilt. Madeline seldom resorted to that maternal tactic, using it only when something was important to her.

"What's going on, Mom? Usually you only get to Florida once or twice a year. There's a man, isn't there?"

Madeline's drawn breath was audible. "A special man."

Blythe's middle tightened.

"He lives in Indiatlantic," her mother continued. "I met him on a visit home about six months ago. We've been seeing each other. He flies up to New York. He's become important in my life, Blythe. I didn't want to say anything to you or Fiona prematurely, but now it's time. I want you both to meet him."

"Are you—" the words lodged in her throat "—getting married?"

"The subject of marriage hasn't come up."

Yet.

"We'll be there Saturday, Mom. What time?" Since Fiona left the house only to buy potting supplies or groceries, it seemed unlikely she would have other plans to prevent her visiting on Saturday. Blythe felt safe in accepting their mother's invitation on her behalf.

"Eleven would be fine." There was a pause, then Madeline added, "I haven't told you about him before this because...well, Spencer is different from the others. He's wonderful. I wish you could be happy for me."

Her mother's hurt stabbed at Blythe. She did her best to cover her anxiety. "What makes you think I'm not happy for you? I'm always happy for you."

"You try," Madeline conceded. "I know you have no reason to be excited. All I ask is that you withhold judgment until you meet him. His name is Spencer Devon. He's a retired air force colonel. It's like we were made for each other."

Blythe winced. Madeline and every one of her previous husbands had been "made for each other."

"Great. We'll be there to meet Mr. Wonderful day after tomorrow."

Again Madeline sighed. "All right. Remember—an open mind."

"You know me. Open and accepting."

Two mornings later found Blythe and Fiona on their way to Indiatlantic.

"I still don't see why you thought you had the right to tell Mom I'd come," Fiona snapped, her arms folded rigidly under her breasts. She sat on her side of the Volvo's front seat, as far from Blythe as possible.

Blythe fumed as she drove. Her sister had stormed through the house when Blythe had told her about the conversation with Madeline. "You didn't even ask me!" she'd shouted, just before she'd slammed her bedroom door.

It must be the pregnancy, Blythe thought. And right now that unborn child was Fiona's best protection. If her sister wasn't pregnant, Blythe was sure she'd have wrung that milk white neck by now.

"Should I have said no? Maybe I should have told her, 'I'm sorry, Mom. Fiona may not want to come. You'll have to talk to her directly'? Your social schedule isn't exactly booked up. I assumed you'd want to see our mother when she's in town and asks us to come over. If you didn't want to come, why didn't you call and tell her yourself?"

"That's not the point!"

"Oh? Then tell me, just what *is* the point?"

Fiona's emerald eyes blazed. "The point is, you think you can answer for me. Like what I want doesn't matter. I want to be consulted. I'm an adult, not a kid!"

Blythe pulled her gaze from the road ahead, and looked at her sister. She restrained herself from saying what she was thinking—that Fiona had certainly been acting like a kid lately.

Fiona quieted immediately, as if she realized how pettish she sounded.

The rest of the trip passed in silence.

When they entered their mother's front door Madeline greeted them with hugs and a kiss on each daughter's cheek, her lovely face illuminated by a beatific smile.

Blythe eyed the wallpaper in the foyer. It had not changed since her last visit.

A man walked out of the kitchen and smiled at them. He joined them in the foyer, and Madeline introduced the latest love of her life, Spencer Devon.

He was tall and trim and distinguished looking. There was gray at the temples of his conservatively cut brown hair. Rugged, tanned handsomeness triggered mental images of pack horses and wide mountain vistas, campfires and flannel shirts. Blythe guessed him to be in his mid-fifties.

Spencer took Blythe's hand in a firm, warm shake. Brown eyes measured her as she assessed him.

"Your mother tells me you're a stockbroker," he said, his voice deep and clear.

"Yes, I am."

He turned to Fiona and shook her hand. "And you're a potter."

"Yes, sir," Fiona replied.

"I'm a writer," he offered.

Blythe's growing hope that Spencer was a different breed from Madeline's usual deflated considerably. Husband number three had been a writer. Or, rather, had said he was. He hadn't spent much time writing.

As if reading her daughter's mind, Madeline stepped close to Devon and slipped her arm through his. "Spencer writes mysteries. He's quite good at it, and his books are immensely popular."

Blythe read mysteries, but she couldn't recall ever seeing a book by Spencer Devon. She wondered if her mother had actually *seen* one of these immensely popular novels.

Grudgingly she decided to give him the benefit of the doubt. "Do you use a pen name?"

"You read mysteries, I take it, and haven't seen anything under my name. I write as Richard Hawkesbury. I started writing while I was still in the air force, and wanted to keep my two professions separate. Besides, Richard Hawkesbury sounds more like a mystery writer than Spencer Devon, don't you think?"

"*You're* Richard Hawkesbury?" Blythe had read his latest, *Pen and Blood,* and found it impossible to put down. "I enjoy your books."

Madeline tugged gently on Spencer's arm, towing him toward the country kitchen-family room. "Come along, everyone. The food is getting cold."

Over the meal the four of them relaxed. Conversation opened doors that allowed each a look at the other. Halfway through Blythe's second cup of coffee, she found herself exchanging an approving glance with Madeline.

Just how serious was her mother's relationship with Spencer? Were they considering marriage? Blythe looked at Spencer Devon. Madeline had never before sought her daughters' approval of a man, but it seemed to Blythe that's what her mother was doing now.

The man who now sat sipping his coffee across the table did not bombard them with charm, nor did he seem overtly romantic. He struck Blythe as practical, down-to-earth. The retired air force colonel did not typify the bon vivant fellows or the sensitive-poet types Madeline had been so drawn to in the past. He wasn't witty, but he had a pleasant, dry sense of humor. Almost against her will, Blythe found herself liking Spencer Devon. A glimpse told her Fiona, too, seemed to have lost some of her doubt.

Hours later, when Spencer and Madeline walked them out to the car, both Blythe and Fiona fished for clues as to whether or not their mother was thinking of marrying the mystery writer. Their probes were gracefully eluded.

Before they'd even turned off Madeline's street, Fiona asked, "Well, what do you think?"

"I'm not sure." Blythe slowed to a stop at a red light. "Everything I've seen tells me I should like him, but it's as if I'm afraid to believe."

Fiona nodded. "I know. I *want* to like him—if he had nothing to do with Mom I *would* like him. It's just that she's never picked a winner before, and it seems almost impossible this time would be different. Still," she turned to face her sister, "I think Spencer is going to be it." She sighed deeply, the sigh of a woman whose uncertainties clung to the bedrock of her past. "At least this time we won't be there to watch him leave, if everything doesn't work out."

As Blythe drove west she tried to analyze her feeling of relief, of hesitant satisfaction. Maybe it was easier to like Spencer because she was no longer dependent on her mother's good sense—or lack of it—in choosing a mate.

Maybe he was easier to accept because he was a nice man; intelligent, accomplished, sensible. The others had been intelligent, some had even been accomplished. None had been sensible where Madeline had been concerned, and her children had always fallen by the wayside. Spencer Devon, she thought, would probably have made an excellent father.

It was obvious to Blythe her mother was in love with him. Judging from Spencer's looks and gestures, it seemed he reciprocated Madeline's feelings. Since neither seemed inclined to discuss with Blythe or Fiona the subject of matrimony, maybe that was enough for the time being.

CHAPTER NINE

GINNY'S EXPRESSION promised trouble. As Blythe returned from the operations department, she viewed her worried future partner with sickening dread.

"What's the matter?" she demanded.

Ginny hurried Blythe into the office, where the older woman shut the door and turned to face her friend.

"Another account was withdrawn," Ginny said quietly.

Blood drained, leaving Blythe slightly dizzy. Abruptly she sat down in a client chair. "Oh, no," she managed, barely able to move her lips. "No."

Ginny folded her arms and stared at the toes of her shoes. She looked up, met Blythe's gaze. "Tom wants to see you."

So, Blythe thought numbly, her account losses had finally drawn the attention of Stewart Duke's branch manager. What now?

"He asked that you stop by his office when you came back."

Blythe nodded and stood. Without another word, she turned and walked down the hall.

When she entered Tom Jarzabek's office, he took one look at her and immediately ordered her to sit. "You look shell-shocked, Blythe. I take it you saw no warning this account would be withdrawn?"

She shook her head. "Who is the client?"

He glanced down at a notepad in front of him. "Helen Mabry. Widow. The account was worth about two thousand dollars a year in commissions." Tom paused a moment, allowing time for the information to sink in. "This is the third large account that's closed. What's the cause?"

Blythe struggled to swallow around the knot in her throat. "I don't know. I can't get a straight answer. Ada Kernfelder avoided an answer, then lied. Donald Hanlon told me it was none of my business. Did Helen say why she was withdrawing her account?"

"No. In fact, she was distinctly quiet about it. But I strongly suggest you try to find out." He tapped the eraser end of his pencil against the notepad in front of him. "You know I stuck by you during that scandal over Andrew's practices. He was my responsibility. You're my responsibility. But I'm also responsible for this office. I don't want to see another such affair attached to your name, Blythe. We all survived intact the first time, but I'm not certain we could a second. I can't risk Stewart Duke's reputation again, especially not with the same party accused." Tom Jarzabek studied his pencil, then glanced up to lock gazes with Blythe. "I don't like it, but that's the way it's got to be. Take care of this. Find out what's causing your clients' defections and put a stop to it."

"You're—" Blythe halted, waited until she had absolute control of her voice. "You're assuming this is more than coincidence."

At his lifted eyebrow her face burned with humiliation.

"Do *you* think it's coincidence?" he asked.

She stared at him bleakly. "No."

Blythe stood, suddenly weary of the turns her life had been taking.

"I'll help you if I can, Blythe," Tom said. "But I won't put the office in jeopardy."

Blythe gave him a tired nod. "I understand."

The walk back to her office was interrupted by the unwelcome presence of Leonard Brock.

"Did you have a nice lunch today?" he asked.

Blythe shrugged with forced casualness. "It was okay. Nothing to write home about."

"Too bad you couldn't have enjoyed it more. It might have softened the blow about that account." He shook his head and clucked in patently false sympathy. "All your hard work, going right down the tube."

Blythe's dislike of Brock sharpened. "If you'll excuse me, I have work to do." Without waiting for a response, she hastened her step just enough to give him her back. *Bastard,* she seethed silently. *He's enjoying every minute of this.*

Ginny showed the good sense to give her friend some breathing space when Blythe returned. She offered Blythe an encouraging smile, and went back to supervising the conscientious new sales assistant, Wendy Luo.

Blythe pulled the account book containing Helen Mabry's address. She jotted down the information on a sheet of memo paper and tucked it into her purse.

Determined to find out what was behind the closed accounts, she decided not to call the client. So far, calling hadn't gotten her anywhere. Maybe face-to-face with Blythe, Helen would find it harder to evade questions, harder to lie.

Ten minutes later, Blythe pulled her car into the driveway of a large yellow house surrounded by azalea bushes. She got out and climbed the steps to the front porch, where she knocked on the door.

A tiny, wizened woman dressed in slacks and a long overtunic answered. Immediately her wrinkled face clouded. "I closed my account," she snapped, and stepped back to close the door.

Hating to do it, Blythe took advantage of her greater height and strength, and held the portal open. "Helen, please tell me why you closed your account. All I want to know is *why*."

"Get away from my door!" quavered the old woman. "Leave me alone!"

Blythe recognized the fear in the widow's voice and withdrew her arm. The door slammed, followed closely by the thud of a dead bolt being shot into place.

Desperate, Blythe rapped the door knocker. "Mrs. Mabry, please. Tell me what you think I've done. *Why* did you close your account? We've worked together for years. Why are you acting like this?"

"You know why," shrilled Mrs. Mabry from the safety of her home. "Now go away before I call the police!"

Rage, helpless and potent, seized Blythe. This harridan knew the secret, held the key. Without it, Blythe's career—the only constant in her life—would bleed away into nothing.

She struck the door with her fist. *"Tell me why!"*

Mrs. Mabry began to sob, dry, whispering, frightened sobs.

The elderly woman's distress pierced Blythe's anger, shriveling it until Blythe felt small and mean. For a moment she stood, tired, listening to the pitiful sounds of weeping on the other side of the door.

She sighed heavily. "I'm leaving now, Mrs. Mabry."

Feeling like crying herself, Blythe walked down the steps, back to her car and returned to the office.

At her desk, Blythe picked up the telephone receiver, then put it back down. She stared at it. Everything seemed to be pulling at her. Her sister, her mother, her work.

Her work. It was more than that to Blythe. It was the only thing that had always been there, ready to welcome her. It allowed escape when the need arose, repaying her long hours and dedication with self-esteem, recognition, and security.

Blythe needed to talk to Duncan. They'd spoken twice since their dinner last week, though neither had mentioned getting together again. But for reasons she didn't want to think about, at this moment the comfort only he could offer was important. She dialed his work number, and after a few delays, was connected.

"Blythe?" He sounded surprised.

Panic gripped her. *This is a mistake!* She couldn't possibly tell Duncan what was bothering her. What if the loss of these latest accounts *was* connected to the ordeal of three years ago? The past would be dredged up.

Blythe wanted Duncan's good opinion. She wanted him to respect her. How could he if he knew she'd been accused of *fraud?*

"Blythe, are you there?"

She wouldn't tell him. It was too shameful. Blythe couldn't bear for him to know.

She was unable to think of another reason for calling him. "I—is this a bad time to call? I mean, if you're busy I'll understand. I wouldn't want to interrupt something important. Are you in the middle of something important? Just tell me if you are. This was a bad idea, wasn't it? Why don't I just call back another time? That would be better, wouldn't it? Yes, another time is better—''

"Blythe—" There was amusement in his voice.

"Oh, God, I'm babbling, aren't I? I never babble, but you wouldn't believe it to hear me now, would you? Please believe me. I just hate it when people babble."

"I believe you. In fact, I never thought I'd see the day when Blythe Summers babbled. Life's strange, isn't it?"

She found his voice unutterably soothing. It was similar to being enfolded in a cloak of silk and sable while inhaling the aroma of freshly baked bread.

Blythe's mouth curved in a slight smile. "Yes, it is." She was glad she'd called him.

"How's your day been?" he asked.

She couldn't tell him. She just couldn't. What could she say? *Well, Duncan, I'm worried about these withdrawn accounts because I'm familiar with the signs of client panic. I saw a lot of it when I was publicly accused of lying and cheating?* What would the avenging archangel of ethics think of that? Blythe had seen suspicion in his eyes once. She couldn't bear to see it again and know this time he had cause.

"Pretty crummy," she replied with forced lightness. "It's been one of those days when things seem to be going smoothly, then someone drops a load of bricks on your head, you know?"

His low chuckle in her ear firmed her tenuous smile and sent delicious tingles down her back.

"Unfortunately I do," he said "But this must have been a doozie to set you dialing my number."

Her face heated. "I—I—"

"I'm glad you called. Now I have someone I can gripe to about how rotten yesterday was. It looked like we were going to lose a big account, so I spent hours in an emergency meeting and the rest of the day putting out fires."

Blythe relaxed, relieved that he had changed the subject. "Did you save the account?"

Duncan's sigh signaled resignation, and a hint of the frustration he must have felt earlier. "No. We may get them back in a few years—after they've had a chance to regret spending their money on brand x's system. But for now, the deal is dead."

He'd built Macrocosm through innovation, and long, grueling hours, Blythe thought. She knew how important the company was to him. "Oh, Duncan. I'm so sorry. Will this hurt Macrocosm?"

"It won't help, but it won't do any real damage. Macrocosm has a diverse base. No one account can sink us. This ship is built to last."

That's what they said about the Titanic. "So you've not sustained damage to the structure?"

"No." A grin came through in that one word.

"Now you're off to conquer new hotel chains and time-share resorts."

"Onward and upward. Actually I received some good news today. One of my salesmen landed Premier."

"Even I've heard of Premier. The largest property management company in North America, right?"

"Right. They wanted quality and dependability, and they liked the idea of working with an industry leader."

"So of course they came to you."

"Of course." Again she could feel that grin.

Blythe's mental imagery of Duncan's crooked, sexy smile quickened her breath. The memory of the kiss they'd shared in his office assailed her.

"Why don't you tell me what ruined your day," Duncan coaxed. "So far, you've just listened to me. I feel better. Let me make you feel better."

Her palms grew damp. In her mind she could see a darkened room, illuminated by a single candle. On a rumpled bed Duncan poised, ready to make her feel better. Much better.

"Blythe." His voice was strangely husky.

Jerking her thoughts back to their conversation, Blythe cleared her throat. "Uh, well, I guess my experience was something like yours yesterday. A client closed an account. It was a big account, and I'd worked with this particular client for years. I know that comes with the territory, but it still hurts." *She slammed her door in my face, and wept in fear of me.*

"Did she say why she closed her account?"

"No. But I've learned people's reasons don't always make sense." The occasional peculiar client was a fact of life. This recent rash of lost accounts, she was certain, had nothing to do with client peculiarities.

"Boy, don't I know *that.*"

Was he thinking about his aunts? Or her?

"Listen," she began hesitantly, feeling her way, "about last week . . ."

"We've discussed this already."

No, they hadn't, she thought. Not really. During the two telephone conversations they'd had since the night they'd dined at the Priory, they'd both skirted the subject of what had really happened later at Duncan's office. Both had accepted responsibility for things not going smoother during her first trip to Atlanta, but they had avoided the reasons. It left her with a vague feeling of dissatisfaction.

"Duncan, I think it was mostly my fault. I'm not used to doing things impromptu, and suddenly I was someplace strange, out of my territory—maybe even out of my league, I don't know."

There was a pause on the other end of the telephone line. Then he said, "No, darlin', not out of your league, but definitely out of your territory. I wanted to show you mine, but we didn't get much of a chance for that, did we? It probably didn't help that I came on so strongly. It's just that I...missed you." Pause. "I'm not being totally honest with you. I *did* miss you, Blythe. I also wanted you—so badly it was all I could do not to make love to you right there in the limousine."

A full body blush scorched Blythe. She was torn between embarrassment and excitement at the prospect of him fantasizing about her as vividly as she did about him. Remembering how on edge she'd been in the limousine at the airport, embarrassment won out.

"Blythe? Are you still talking to me?"

"Yes, Duncan. I—I'm still talking to you." *And fantasizing about you.*

"I didn't think my wanting you would come as any news."

She tried to collect her thoughts. "It doesn't. Not really."

That was it. The real reason they had both been so edgy.

Blythe sensed they were reaching a turning point in their relationship. She wasn't sure she was ready for it. Moments passed in silence, as she desperately tried to sort her chaotic emotions.

Duncan was at least honest. At this point Blythe wasn't certain if she was capable of being so candid with herself, much less with someone as intricately involved with her as Duncan.

It was all getting too complicated. She needed time to think.

Blythe raked her fingers through her hair, tearing locks from her chignon. "Can we...can we maybe not talk about this right now?"

In the quiet that followed, Blythe could see in her mind's eye Duncan's face shuttering, taking on that inscrutable, unreadable nonexpression.

"Certainly."

Blythe drew in a deep breath hoping oxygen would activate her brain.

"Duncan?"

"Yes."

"Duncan, don't go blank on me. It's irritating as hell—and it scares me."

"Pick a subject, any subject, as long as it has nothing to do with us. Is that it?"

"Yes. No! I mean..."

"What?" he asked softly. "What do you mean?"

Blythe hesitated. "I'm not sure I know what I mean. Discussing how we feel about one another—it makes me uncomfortable."

"Uncomfortable?" Sarcasm colored his voice. "Just when do you expect to get comfortable? Another couple of months? A year? Never? Blythe, I think there's something special between us. A spark that can grow to warm us both. If I'm mistaken, tell me.''

"You said you'd be patient," she cried.

In the responding silence, Blythe chewed her lip, afraid something precious might be slipping through her cursedly hesitant fingers.

Finally Duncan released a heavy sigh. "I did say that, didn't I? What an idiot."

Blythe tried to smile and found her lips trembled. "Not an idiot. A wise man. And brave."

"Right. That's me. Duncan McKeon, brave guy."

"It has a certain ring to it." Blythe blotted unshed tears of relief from her eyes.

"Let's get together again, Blythe. I'll try to make it down there the weekend after next, but I'll talk to you before then."

"All right. And thank you, Duncan." She stared down at her desk.

"For what?"

"Just for being there when I called."

"Anytime, darlin'. It works both ways."

A WEEK LATER, Martin Chasen regarded Blythe evenly from the other side of his mahogany-veneered desk. Through small gestures and turns of phrase, the short, stocky, middle-aged man with the crown of thinning red hair had tested her since she'd arrived for her long-awaited appointment with him. All were subtle power plays well-known in the business world. Blythe had been through the trial countless times before, and her responses were almost automatic.

She'd managed to glean a good deal of information from the controller of Chasen and Sons, Inc., between all his power probes. As they conducted their verbal fencing Blythe gradually sensed she had gained his cautious approval.

Like an Arabian rug merchant, Blythe first spread her more tantalizing plans before him, to whet his appetite. She knew everyone at Chasen and Sons would benefit from what she could do, but how much they would benefit depended on what she uncovered in her survey.

"All right, Ms. Summers," Chasen finally said over steepled fingers, "you've piqued my curiosity. What do you need from me?"

She slid a list across his desk to him, noting again the company spent a minimum on office furniture, and wondering if such frugality could be traced to the controller. "If you could provide me with copies of these items I'll work up a proposal."

They set a time to meet again in two weeks, and Blythe took her leave.

When she returned to the office, Ginny was ready for her.

"Well?" she demanded as Blythe swept by, into the glass-walled sanctum.

Blythe beckoned with a crooked finger.

As soon as Ginny followed her in, Blythe reached behind her friend and gently shut the office door.

Instantly Blythe shed her composure.

She whooped joyfully and grabbed Ginny in a fierce hug. "He wants a survey!"

Ginny's face lit up. "Hot damn! He's interested!"

Blythe straightened her jacket. "We're women who are going places," she announced.

Ginny grinned. "That's right. Just before you came in, I sent in the results of my latest and last test before the big one. I passed with flying colors! I'm scheduled to take the series seven, week after next." She gave Blythe a brief hug and walked to the door. "Nothing can stop us now!"

BLYTHE'S INTERCOM buzzed. "Duncan McKeon is on line one."

"Thanks, Wendy."

Happily she lifted the handset and pressed the button to connect.

"Hello, Duncan."

"Is that the best you can do? A man wants to think his woman is yearning for his call."

His voice flowed like cream over her senses and left her wanting more than words.

"I didn't know I was your woman." Like no one else, he had the power to catch her offguard. Blythe found it unnerving. She also found it exhilarating.

"Whose woman are you, then?" There was a smile in his voice.

She smiled back. "I'm my own woman, McKeon."

"Can we share?"

"You big city boys are such slick talkers."

"That's why our cities are so big."

She laughed. "I wouldn't touch that line with a ten-foot pole."

"Aw, you're no fun."

"Just shallow and cowardly."

Duncan clucked reprovingly. "You're much too hard on yourself. You're not shallow."

"Now that you've overwhelmed me with flattery, are we still on for Saturday?" They'd made plans to see the play at Edith Bush Theater, Saturday evening, then go out to dinner.

"That's why I called. I've got the possibility of good news and the certainty of bad news."

She had an idea of what the bad news was. "You can't make it."

"I'm sorry, darlin'. We're getting ready to release a new package, something revolutionary in the industry, and a few things have come up unexpectedly. I don't dare leave now. No telling what else might happen."

Disappointment flattened Blythe's pleasure. Two weeks since she'd last seen him. Two long weeks. Oh, she understood, Blythe told herself. Really she did. Business often didn't keep convenient hours. She knew that from her own experience. "A man's gotta do what a man's gotta do."

"You understand, then?"

"Of course."

"I thought you would."

Blythe rose from her chair and picked up her paperweight. "You said there was a possibility of good news," she pointed out.

"Since I can't go there, why don't you come here? Spend the weekend. My condo's big, more than enough room for both of us. I'll show you Atlanta. It'll be fun."

"I thought you couldn't be too far from your office."

"I can carry a pager. At least we can be together."

She stopped rolling the glass ball between her palms. "Duncan—"

"It's autumn, now. If we wait too much longer the weather might be too cold to really enjoy doing it," he reasoned.

"Doing what?" She just wanted to make sure.

"Touring Atlanta. Why?" he asked so innocently she didn't know whether to be suspicious or ashamed of herself for entertaining doubt. "What did you think I meant?"

"It's the connection," she said. "Have you had trouble with static on your line today?"

There was a pause. "No, darlin'," Duncan drawled. "The static is strictly from your end."

Blythe felt her face warm.

"Why don't you fly in Friday, after work, and I'll pick you up?" he suggested.

Blythe felt as if she stood on a precipice, facing a chasm of uncertain breadth. Beyond lay a beckoning land of plenty. One leap...

She backed away. "I—no, I can't. I've got so much work to do, and—and I just...can't."

Silence greeted her lie. Blythe immediately wished she could take it back and substitute something more convincing.

"What are you afraid of, Blythe? We don't have to sleep together if you don't want to." His words were softly spoken.

"I'm not afraid of anything." Another lie. "I'm just busy now, that's all."

"I see. But not too busy for me to come to Winter Park."

Blythe didn't have an answer to that.

"Am I wasting my time?" he asked. "Do you want me to go away and leave you alone?"

"No," she whispered, unable to do more. Her throat tightened and her heart hammered painfully.

Duncan paused, then said only, "If you change your mind, call me."

Blythe nodded, caught herself and managed a credible, "Yes. I will. Goodbye, Duncan."

Her hands shook and she carefully set down the paperweight before she dropped it.

Send him away? Did Duncan really think she could? In the second following his question, Blythe had seen the truth: If he left, she would never get over the hurt.

She fumbled with a file, opening it and sifting blindly through the contents with trembling fingers. Finally abandoning her effort, Blythe propped her elbows on the desk and pressed her forehead against her clenched hands.

Was she in love with Duncan? Was he in love with her? He'd never mentioned the word. For all she knew he might have no interest in commitment.

If only he weren't so charming. If only she didn't know the destructive power of charm. But she did. Every one of her mother's husbands had taught her that lesson.

It couldn't be love, that was all there was to it. Infatuation, maybe. Still, how could she be certain?

Blythe forced herself to examine all the facets, to inspect every plane of her existence. Slowly she came to the conclusion that left her shaken.

Duncan was the best thing in her life.

He brought laughter, warmth and excitement. He made her feel things she'd never felt before. She found she desperately wanted that to continue.

A man as dedicated to his family as Duncan couldn't be like her stepfathers, like her father. Martha and Amelia depended on him, and he never let them down. Here was a man to whom family ties were important.

Quickly, before she could change her mind, Blythe made reservations with the airline. Then she called Duncan.

"Is your offer still good?"

CHAPTER TEN

FIONA picked up an envelope from the pile of mail and grinned. She pulled out a check and handed it to Blythe. "My biggest yet. I'm getting there."

Blythe was still nervous about accepting the invitation Duncan had extended that afternoon, but not so nervous she failed to notice the open fly of her sister's jeans peeping out from under the edge of the T-shirt. "I'll say."

Impatiently Fiona tugged on the hem of the cotton knit top. "Not *that*. This!" She pointed to the check in Blythe's fingers.

Blythe read the numbers. The amount suggested Fiona might be able to support herself and her child in comfort, if not luxury.

That knowledge eased Blythe's growing concern somewhat. Her own income had been affected by the loss of so many important clients. Again fear squeezed her chest. Why were her clients leaving her? What had she done? Their defections dredged up painful memories, created a new threat that hung over her like a shroud.

She managed enthusiasm. "A very nice check indeed. My sister, the famous potter."

Fiona blushed. "Maybe not famous, exactly, but no longer unknown—at least in some corners."

"The corners that count." Blythe hugged her sister. "Let's celebrate."

"That sounds like fun. What should we do?"

Fiona's pleased smile pulled at Blythe's heart.

"Well, the evening's young. It's only—" she glanced at her watch "—six o'clock. It's a weekday. Why don't we go to the Comedy Fair?" Blythe wondered which comedians were playing the club.

"I could use some laughs."

"I know, baby. I think we both could. I'll call for the reservations, and you go shower and change." Blythe was elated her sister was finally showing a willingness to leave the house for something social.

"Wait a minute. I can't go." Fiona sighed sharply. "I don't have anything to wear that fits."

Blythe immediately took advantage of the opening. "No problem. You need some comfortable clothes. Now is as good a time as any to get them. We'll go to the mall first. Go shower and I'll call."

"But..."

Patiently Blythe waited, ready for excuses.

"I don't want to buy any new clothes."

Blythe raised an eyebrow. "I don't think you'll have a choice much longer. You won't be able to get into those jeans. Maybe you shouldn't even be wearing them now. What if it's squashing the baby?"

Fiona hesitantly lifted her hands to lay them on her swelling abdomen. She raised a worried gaze to her sister. "Do you really think so?"

What do I know about babies? "You can't go around with your fly open for five more months, and wearing tight clothes can't be good for Fiona, Jr."

A soft smile curved Fiona's lips. "Fiona, Jr. I guess I haven't given much thought to the sex of it. Or choosing a name."

Blythe noticed her sister's use of "it" in referring to her baby. No thought of the child she carried, especially not a name. Ignore the condition and it won't exist. *Run and hide, little sister.* Blythe said nothing. There was time yet. Maybe things would work out.

"Go ahead and call," said Fiona. "I'll get ready. Surely we can find something at the mall a human dirigible can wear."

As Blythe hung up from her call to the Comedy Fair, she released a weary sigh. Reservations were made, but she wouldn't have time to change out of the suit she'd put on that morning; not if Fiona was to have any time to pick out clothes.

Fiona emerged from her bedroom in record time wearing another long, faded T-shirt and jeans, which Blythe guessed were open. "Ta-ta!" Fiona sang. "Squeaky clean and ready to go."

"Amazing!" Blythe picked up her purse and keys. "Let's hit the road."

"Around here, all roads lead to a mall!" Fiona crowed.

Blythe headed for the garage. She planned to take advantage of her sister's buoyant mood. These days, it was too rare.

At the shopping center, Fiona balked at entering the maternity shop. "That's for . . . for . . ."

"For what?" demanded Blythe impatiently. She wanted the old Fiona back. The sweet, cheerful sister who was probably still living somewhere in Alaska.

"Pregnant women."

"Are you telling me you think you just have a bad case of gas, Fiona? Because I'll be happy to enlighten you. Bicarbonate of soda will not make it go away."

"Blythe," whispered Fiona unevenly. "I'm scared."

Instantly Blythe softened. "That's allowed. Being scared is definitely allowed." She steered her sister over to an unoccupied bench not far from the shop. "Don't you see? By refusing to admit you're pregnant you're cheating yourself. You're denying yourself the pleasure of growing with your baby. A baby conceived in love."

"What...what if she looks like Eth-Ethan?"

Blythe noted the change from "it" to "she" and smiled. "Wouldn't that be wonderful? You love Ethan, don't you?"

Fiona choked off a sob and Blythe wrapped a protective arm around her sister's shoulders, hugging Fiona to her side.

"It's not too late to call him."

Fiona took the tissue Blythe handed her, and wiped her cheeks and eyes. "Yes, it is. Ethan would never forget what I put him through. I know he wouldn't. He'd try, but he'd never be able to forgive me."

It was obviously pointless to argue. They sat there a few minutes more.

"Are you up to going to the Comedy Fair?" Blythe finally asked.

"Yes." Fiona expelled her breath in a rush. "I want to go."

"Then we'd better buy you some clothes."

Fiona nodded then blew her nose on the damp tissue.

"C'mon, rich potter lady." Blythe slipped her arm through Fiona's and led her back to the maternity shop where two pregnant women were shopping. Outside the door, in the mall, stood a man trying to keep a small boy entertained. The child waved vigorously to one of the women in the store, who smiled and waved back. A wistful longing for children of her own seized Blythe. She turned away to help her sister.

Her dismay grew with every article Fiona selected. Each was designed to conceal the new roundness of her body.

As if Fiona could read her sister's mind, she explained, "I'll be able to wear these after...afterward."

Blythe looked at the stack of garments, studied the marigold-colored cotton sweater, and brown skirt the tall redhead wore. It looked good on Fiona. And no one would ever know she was pregnant. Oh, eventually they would, when she grew so large a waddle replaced her lithe sway. But not now. Not for a while.

Run and hide, little sister, Blythe thought again sadly.

FRIDAY EVENING, in Atlanta, Duncan put Blythe's suitcase in the trunk of his Mercedes and came around to slide behind the steering wheel. He grinned at her as she sat next to him, worrying a crease of her camel-colored slacks between forefinger and thumb.

"This is going to be great!" he exclaimed. "I've already made a tentative agenda you can check when we get to the condo. See if you want to make any changes." He started the car and headed it toward the airport exit. "It's going to be great!"

Duncan's obvious pleasure touched Blythe. His welcoming kiss at the gate had quelled some of her anxiety, but had set something else simmering in its place. She wanted to reach out and touch him, to give physicality to their strengthening bond. Instead, she smiled at him.

For some reason, on a fundamental level, Duncan's potently masculine presence always made her feel secure. Safe. Intellectually, however, she knew her emotional safety was far from secure with this man.

Blythe decided thinking about it only made her nervous. "Where are we going tomorrow?" she asked abruptly.

"Grant Park, High Museum. Do you like historical homes?"

Blythe nodded. "I love old, restored houses."

"If we have time, we'll tour Tullie Smith House and Swan House. Sunday I thought we'd play it by ear, since we'll have only half a day."

"I'm looking forward to seeing it all. Are you going to show me where you grew up?"

He glanced over at her. "Do you want me to?" Pleased surprise colored his question. Duncan turned his eyes back to the highway.

"Yes. I do."

His grin returned. He drew her closer to him. "Then I guess we'll go to Buckhead."

Blythe allowed herself a tiny sigh of contentment. Snuggled against Duncan's side, in the curve of his arm, it was so easy just to rest her head on his shoulder.

The next thing she knew the car was stopped and Duncan was brushing his lips against her temple. "Wake up, darlin'," he murmured. "We're home."

Sleepily Blythe tried to orient herself with her surroundings. "Home?"

"My condo."

Blythe sat up and looked around. They were in a parking garage.

Duncan took her suitcase from the trunk, then helped her from the car. "You went out like a light. You must've been dead tired."

"I'm okay," she mumbled, swaying. "Really."

Duncan helped her out and shut the passenger door. He curved his arm around her, shepherding her toward an elevator, where he punched the button.

Blythe spotted the coral smudges on his shirt. "I've ruined your shirt with my lipstick," she lamented.

"That's what cleaners are for."

As soon as the doors rolled open Duncan drew her inside and punched a number. That done, he lowered his face to hers and kissed her parted lips.

How such a soft touch could send her pulse into triple time Blythe couldn't guess, but she found she didn't much care. It did. That was enough.

She wanted to be closer, and snuggled against him. Duncan moved to compensate for the shift in weight but the suitcase foiled his effort. He stumbled, fell back against the wall with a grunt and landed sharply sitting down with Blythe piled on top of him.

The doors opened.

"Don't look, Francine!" thundered the voice of a stout matron as she stepped sideways to block the view of a teenage girl. Angry eyes directed their fire-and-brimstone gaze at the couple on the elevator floor. "Mr. McKeon, I expected better of you. Clearly I was mistaken!"

Mortified, Blythe struggled to lift herself from atop Duncan. Her face burned. If there'd been a mouse hole close by she'd have crawled inside.

Duncan stood and brushed himself off. He picked up the suitcase in one hand and, cupping Blythe's elbow with the other, escorted her off the elevator. "Mrs. Farnham," he said evenly, "everything was quite innocent, I assure you. Your accusation is unfounded."

Mrs. Farnham looked at Duncan's lipstick-smeared shirt and harrumphed. "I don't think so," she declared, and marched into the elevator, Francine firmly in tow.

Blythe groaned in an agony of humiliation, and Duncan grinned. "Don't let that old biddy upset you. We've probably given her life a little spice."

"How very consoling."

They walked down a carpeted corridor.

Duncan unlocked the door of his condominium and led the way in, switching on the lights.

Blythe looked around, stunned. White-stucco walls, soaring ceilings and large, plentiful windows gave the place an airy cheerfulness. Or would have, had it not been for the cacophony of styles of furniture—all employing an overabundance of wood, leather and black wrought iron. *Sort of Johnny Appleseed meets El Cid.*

"You hate it as much as you did the lobby of my office," Duncan observed morosely.

Blythe couldn't deny it, so she diplomatically chose silence.

"I know. It's god-awful. I'm not crazy about it, either. I told the interior designer the *feel* I wanted, and this is what I got." He sighed. "I'm sure I'm more articulate than, than..." Duncan swept his arm out to indicate the results.

"It's . . . well . . . It certainly makes a statement." *In gibberish.* Blythe walked farther into the living room and wished she hadn't. She eyed an ugly wagon-wheel coffee table.

Duncan came to stand close behind her, and all thought of his decor vanished from her mind. She could hear him breathing. She could feel the warmth of him down the length of her body. A wave of longing rolled through her. She waited for his touch.

"You're tired," he muttered. "I'll show you the rest of the condo tomorrow." With that, he picked up her suitcase, climbed the stairs and disappeared onto the second floor, leaving Blythe to follow.

She hurried after him, down a hall, past a large room. This must be the master bedroom. With the master's bed. Duncan was nowhere in sight. Blythe hastened her step and found Duncan waited for her one door down.

Blythe regarded the guest room. She didn't know if she felt relief or hurt at automatically being placed here. It certainly did nothing for her ego to know she was so resistible he hadn't even tried to coax her into sharing his room. Of course, she told herself hastily, she really was relieved. No doubt about it, she was darned . . . relieved. "Thank you, Duncan. I'm certain I'll be quite comfortable. A good night's sleep, then we'll see Atlanta." The heartiness sounded false even to her.

Duncan looked around the room, his face unreadable. Jaw muscles bunched. His gaze settled on the bed. "Goodnight, Blythe," he said, and strode from the room, closing the door softly behind him.

Blythe discovered she'd been holding her breath, and released it in a discouraged sigh. Good night's sleep—who was she trying to kid? The answer was simple: Duncan. She wanted him to believe she'd close her eyes and quickly fall asleep. Fat chance.

She unpacked, undressed and slipped on her nightgown. The sheets were cool and fresh and normally she would have taken a bit of comfort from that. Tonight they just reminded her she was safe. Utterly, damnably safe.

She lay staring into the dark, reminding herself this was what she wanted. Duncan had been a perfect gentleman. He'd put her in this guest room decorated by some weirdo with a wrought-iron fetish and had left her without so much as a good-night kiss. She pounded her pillow, and flopped onto her side. What had the manufacturers used in this mattress? Bricks?

Finally, despairing of ever finding sleep, Blythe slipped out of bed and went to the window, lifting the shade far enough to see out.

The full moon hung in the night sky like a disk of white jade, reigning over diamond-dust stars. Blythe eased the shade back into place. That was obviously the answer, she told herself. It was a documented fact that incidents of strange behavior escalated during full moon.

If she could only get some sleep, tomorrow it would be easier to see things in perspective. Maybe some warm milk would help. Blythe pulled on her satin robe and padded downstairs to the kitchen. The vertical blinds were open, and pale celestial light illuminated the great room, spilling into the kitchen.

"Trouble sleeping?"

The silken baritone sounded directly behind Blythe. She jumped, nearly dropping the carton of milk. Whirling around, she came eye to throat with Duncan. "What are you doing here?" she demanded breathlessly, pressing her hand to her chest, as if the pressure would calm her thumping heart.

Duncan shrugged one shoulder. "I live here."

Blythe raised her eyes. His face was inscrutable, sculpted planes of moonlight and night shadow. What was he thinking?

"Here." He placed a snifter in her hands. "This will work better than milk."

A biting fragrance pierced her nostrils. "Cognac." She looked pointedly at his own snifter. Only a sip remained. "Has it helped you?"

His quicksilver eyes glinted. Duncan grinned wolfishly. "Only one thing can help me."

Her fingers tightened involuntarily on her glass, but she remained silent.

"Do you like your room?" He finished the contents of his snifter.

"Yes. It's very nice." She hated the room, hated lying in its bed alone, knowing Duncan was only a door away. But more than that she hated knowing she'd brought it on herself. And still, she was uncertain enough to hesitate over that first step onto the swaying bridge.

"Good. I aim to please." He turned and walked out of the kitchen, to the bar in the great room where he poured himself another cognac.

Hesitantly Blythe followed to the doorway. She watched as he lowered himself into a chair in front of the enormous picture window.

"Duncan?"

He gave no indication he'd heard her soft call.

She moved toward him, step by cautious step, across the plush carpet plain that separated them, until she stood beside him. "Duncan?"

He didn't look at her, but continued to stare out the window. "Why aren't you in your bed, little girl, all tucked up and safe for the night?"

Uncertain if his question was rhetorical, Blythe answered. "I couldn't sleep."

"Drink your cognac."

A few sips might help her relax, she thought, and raised the glass to her lips. Mellow fire rolled down her throat, leaving a pleasant aftertaste on her tongue. She sipped again. And again.

Blythe decided to take the remaining contents of her snifter back to her room. Everything would be clearer tomorrow. "I'll see you in the morning, Duncan," she murmured and turned to leave.

His hand shot out and captured her wrist. "You wouldn't want to go without kissing me good-night, would you, darlin'?" Duncan rose and turned to Blythe in one controlled movement. He took the glass from her and set it on the small table next to the chair. Slowly he gathered her into his arms and bent his head over hers, his face so close Blythe could see the striations in the narrow, smoky bands of his irises.

Almost involuntarily, she reached up and touched her fingers to the thick midnight of his hair. As if her move was a silent signal, Duncan bent his head and took her mouth with erupting passion. His lips moved against hers with an urgent hunger that left her breathless. His hands roamed up and down her back. They ventured farther and glided over her buttocks, cupping them, drawing her hips snugly against his, leaving no doubt as to the state of his arousal. A small sound, part whimper, part moan, made its way up her throat.

Something filtered through Duncan's fogged awareness. Different. He frowned, working to drag his concentration from the drugging effects of Blythe, so sweet and pliable in his arms. Change. It was that which had triggered the alert. So pliable. Too pliable.

He had promised her he would be patient. Since then, there had been moments—many moments— when he'd regretted binding himself so, but it was up to her to make a clear declaration when she was ready for deeper intimacy. He had given his word.

Duncan, cursing himself for a fool, withdrew his arms from around Blythe and moved away. Blythe blinked. She stared at him, dazed.

"Good night, Blythe." His words were strained, hoarse.

Why had he pulled away, she wondered, her body still warm from his touch and aching for more. She knew he wanted her.

Confusion and frustration battled within her. Pride won out. She drew herself up to her full height, chin up. "Good night, Duncan. Sleep well." She turned on her heel and swept from the room.

BLYTHE WOKE at eight in the morning, her body clock unaffected by Atlanta's higher elevation. She showered, and pulled on navy twill slacks and a silk, ivory-colored T-shirt. Leaning close to the bathroom mirror, she scrutinized her hair and makeup. They had to be perfect before she went downstairs and did *not* bring up the subject of last night.

In the great room, Duncan, clad only in a pair of faded jeans, slouched in a leather-and-pine chair, his long, lean legs stretched out in front of him, crossed at his bare ankles. He glanced up from the newspaper he was reading, and grinned. "Morning', darlin'." With masculine grace, he stood and stretched. "Want some coffee?"

Blythe tried not to stare at her first glimpse of Duncan's beautifully molded torso, of his broad shoulders and long-muscled arms.

Nervousness made her smile too brightly. "Coffee sounds good." Ice water sounded better.

"What about breakfast?" He crossed the room, narrow hips rolling in a panther-like stroll. His cocky half smile reflected in silver eyes.

"None for me, thanks."

He gave her a soft, brief, infuriatingly innocent kiss. Surreptitiously she drew a deep breath. He smelled of warm, recently scrubbed skin.

"Bad news," he told her, moving on into the kitchen.

She trailed behind him. "What?"

Duncan poured a cup of coffee and held it out to her. She accepted the steaming mug. "Emergency. I have to go into the office today. I got a call from production this morning." He touched her cheek. "I'm sorry, darlin'."

Blythe stared into the cup cradled in her hands. She sighed and looked up at him. "Well, you did say you might have to go in."

Duncan looked relieved that she was being so understanding. "Why don't you go ahead and take a look at the agenda I made. It's on the table in the living room. Do some sight-seeing on your own, till I get back."

"Do you know when that will be?" She sipped her coffee.

"Not yet. This may take a while. I'd guesstimate around five or six."

"Why don't you call when you have a definite answer, and leave a message on your answering machine. Give me your code, and I'll periodically check the machine to see when you'll be back here, and plan to meet you. If that's okay? Meanwhile, I'll expect to see you about six."

"Great." Duncan gave her his code number. The Macrocosm switchboards were closed on the weekend, and even with his direct line, she'd have difficulty contacting him. He'd be moving around the production department, in and out of meetings.

He put his arms around Blythe and slanted his mouth across hers with pent-up promise, careful to offer no more than she might be willing to receive. When he felt the muscles in her back tighten, he reluctantly eased away. "I'll make it up to you," he said huskily.

Blythe struggled to cover her shortness of breath and the faint dizziness that were familiar side effects of Duncan's kisses. Unable to gather her wits sufficiently to respond with anything sensible, she smiled. She was still standing there with the same expression when she heard him mount the stairs and close his bedroom door.

Coffee. She needed coffee. The stuff in her cup had cooled, so she warmed it in the microwave.

He wanted her. She wanted him. That was simple enough. Why did he stop? The timer went off and she withdrew her cup from the microwave. She sipped thoughtfully, analyzing and sorting suspicions and clues. Why was she ready to go to bed with Duncan? What was different now? Slowly her lips curved.

She loved Duncan. Honorable Duncan. A man who kept the promises he made. One promise was patience. Blythe laughed, delighted. He'd kept his word.

He must be waiting for a sign, she reasoned, or a statement from her before he moved to deepen their physical intimacy. Blythe hugged herself. She craved that intimacy, that fusing of their souls. She needed the melding of their bodies. Her smile widened. She'd give him his sign.

Minutes later, Blythe kissed Duncan quickly as he dashed out the door. She waited to make certain he was truly gone, then found a telephone book and began making arrangements.

SIX HOURS LATER, Blythe walked around Duncan's dining table, inspecting the settings for flaws.

A white linen tablecloth covered the polished surface. In the center she had placed a silver candelabrum bearing two tapered candles of palest pink. An arrangement of pink and yellow roses worked with fern tips and baby's breath encircled the base of the candle holder. China, silver and crystal caught the glow of the overhead lights. Satisfied with the dining room, she retraced her steps to the mirror in the first-floor bathroom and once again checked her appearance.

Her hair was in its customary chignon. The classic style suited the midnight violet gown Blythe had scoured Lenox Square to find. The slit skirt fell in a straight, narrow column to the floor. As she walked or sat, long legs clad in fine black hose could be glimpsed. The neckline of the dress, with its soft notched collar was almost demure—until she moved. Clusters of pearls covered each earlobe. Elegantly sexy.

Again, Blythe returned to the kitchen to make certain all was prepared and neatly in its place.

The sound of keys in the front door lock paralyzed her.

This is it, she thought, swallowing hard. Blythe stepped into the foyer.

Duncan opened the door. He held his briefcase and a clear plastic box of flowers.

Blythe thought again how handsome this man was. The classic lines of his body provided a perfect foil for the exotic features of his face.

He surveyed her, his expression unreadable.

She remembered her plans. "Home at last. Here, let me take these things. Would you like a drink?"

Without a word, Duncan stepped closer to her, lowered his head and kissed her, cutting off further conversation.

When he raised his mouth a full minute later, he observed her from hooded eyes. "'She was a Phantom of delight when first she gleamed upon my sight...'"

"Byron?"

"Wordsworth. But mere poetry can't do justice to your beauty tonight, Blythe." His voice was low and sensuous.

Romance artifice, of course, but he looked as if he believed every word. If Duncan wanted romance, he had come to the right address.

A wicked playfulness took hold of her. If this evening was to go as planned, Blythe determined she must take control now.

Her mouth curved in a sultry smile. She lowered her eyes and raised them, slightly, looking up at Duncan through her lashes. In her best throaty voice she said, "I've prepared dinner. Are you hungry?" She turned and walked away a short distance, then stopped and looked back over her shoulder to find his expression one of alert interest. "Coming?" she purred.

Duncan studied the exquisite woman in front of him as they walked into the living room. Here was a new facet of Blythe—romantic, mysterious. He was intrigued.

Blythe iced down the wine and turned to find Duncan leaning against the doorframe, watching her. Silently he approached her with the flowers. Giving them more attention, now, she saw they were a delicate spray of pink moth orchids.

To her surprise, Duncan didn't hand them to her. Instead, he took them out of the container and placed them in her hair, over her temple.

"Orchids become you," he told her in a low voice that seemed to be more vibration than sound. He leaned forward and pressed a soft kiss behind her ear. His warm breath sent a shiver through her.

With one finger, she lightly traced the outline of his ear and a path down the side of his throat. She opened her hand to smooth her palm over the width of his shoulder. His eyes followed her hand as it continued down his arm.

"Thank you." She parted her lips slightly, pausing. "Won't you come into the dining room now?" she continued. "I'd like you to see the result of my labors."

"I thought I was."

Blythe cast him a coy glance. "You haven't seen anything yet."

She looked on, suppressing her nervousness, as he inspected the understated richness of the set table. What was he thinking? Was he even the slightest bit impressed?

Or had he already given up on her? With terrified resolution, Blythe forced the thought back. Now was not the time for such doubts.

"Very nice, Blythe."

"I thought we might dine now," she suggested, and suddenly felt the word "dine" might sound too pretentious. In the next second she corrected herself. With the dinner she had created, they would indeed dine.

"If your cooking is as good as you look, I'm going to set you up in business."

"I have a business, remember? I'm a stockbroker who preys on the accounts of sweet old ladies."

Duncan winced. "Damn, woman, won't you let a man forget? I'll still be hearing about that on my deathbed."

Blythe's heart fluttered. *Is he implying we'll grow old together?* she wondered, caught between extremes of joy and caution.

"Please sit here," she said, indicating the chair at which she stood. Obligingly he did so.

Halfway to the kitchen, Blythe heard his objection. He was not about to sit there while she waited on him. She turned and walked back to him, pressing his shoulders down to seat him again. As he looked up at her there was protest in his handsome face.

With the tips of her fingers she stroked the dark hair at his temples. She leaned closer and lightly nuzzled his ear, breathing, "We could have gone out, but I wanted to be alone with you. All I want you to do is light the candles and relax." Blythe moved slightly away and looked at his face expecting to see assent.

His eyes were almost closed and his breathing had grown shallow. He made no move to leave his chair.

When she returned to the dining room with their Crab Louis, the candles had been lit and the white wine she'd left in the ice bucket had been poured. To give the soft glow of candle flames maximum benefit, she lowered the overhead lights. As she turned the dial, Blythe watched Duncan's features move into relief.

Leaning slightly to one side, she set one plate in front of him. She was close, and it was difficult not to allow her hands to touch him. He smelled of soap and skin. Duncan never wore cologne, and she was glad. His personal scent was much more sensuous.

"I think you'll like this," she told him as she leaned over to center the dish in front of him.

Duncan caught a tantalizing glimpse of creamy white cleavage and straightened in his chair. He watched her walk around the table and sit. The dark violet silk clung to her hips and the enticing curve of her buttocks. That damned dress had flashed him promises of long, svelte legs, and full, ripe breasts since he'd arrived home, and it was working him into madness. The glances and touches only served to stoke the fire that had already been raging these past two months.

It wasn't like Blythe to tease, he told himself as he shifted uncomfortably. And he didn't want this meal! Duncan glared at the food before him. He'd force himself to eat. After all, she had gone to considerable trouble, by the looks of it. Grudgingly he took a bite of the Crab Louis. It was good.

As he chewed, his eyes strayed to Blythe's. They were lowered, her attention on her plate. The long, curling lashes almost touched her cheek. He looked at her mouth. God, what a kissable mouth. What other, wonderful, things could it do? How would it feel if she... At his body's instant, tightening response to his vivid mental imagery, Duncan abandoned that line of thought and dragged his gaze up. Blythe slowly lifted her eyes and jolted him with a high-voltage aqua stare.

The rich seafood turned to sawdust in his mouth.

By the final course, Blythe knew she need not have taken such pains with the meal. Neither one of them had eaten much. When Duncan still seemed disinclined toward conversation, she cleared the dishes away.

"Coffee?" Blythe asked as she dispatched the last plates into the dishwasher.

Duncan came up behind her and when she straightened, she could feel his breath stirring the tiny hairs at her nape. He was close, so close. She shivered nervously, as if she were a mare being crowded by a stallion.

Strong, tapered fingers brushed silver-silk tendrils back from her cheek. Lips pressed softly behind her ear. "Let's have the champagne," he whispered.

In the great room, Duncan wrapped the chilled bottle in a towel and removed the cork with a full-bodied *pop*. Blythe inserted a compact disc into the player. As soft violin music floated into the air, she turned to watch him fill two champagne flutes with wine. Smiling, he held one out to her. Minute bubbles effervesced through the crisp dry aroma, tickling her nose.

"I have a toast." Duncan raised his glass and she followed suit. The light caught a crystal prism-cut and flashed a spray of rainbow. "To love. A risky investment but one that yields rich returns." He grinned and moved to touch his glass to hers, but stopped at a motion of her free hand.

"To love." She gave a toast of her own. "A long-term investment."

Blythe watched for hesitation as Duncan completed the toast. She found none. A pure musical note chimed as the glasses met. Satisfied, she sipped her champagne.

Duncan gently removed the drink she held, setting it on an occasional table. He took her into his arms, holding her close. Blythe twined her arms around Duncan's neck and allowed her fingers the sensual freedom of his hair, black, heavy, luxuriant.

His arm pressed her more tightly against him, at the same time his mouth descended onto hers. He kissed her with the raw hunger of a man who has fasted too long. She parted her lips, granting his probing tongue access to wine-sweet inner crevices. After a moment of breath-stealing exploration, he lifted his head. No longer were his eyes pale gray. Now they were darkened with desire, and Blythe knew there was no turning back.

CHAPTER ELEVEN

HIS KISSES were like opium and Blythe wanted more. She offered up her mouth to him.

Duncan accepted her gift. As lightly as the breath of a butterfly, he brushed his parted lips across hers. Back and forth, barely touching.

Tentatively Blythe touched her tongue to the inside of his lower lip and she felt him tighten his embrace. His breath quickened. His response pleased her, fueled her growing excitement. Emboldened, she slid her tongue tip across the sensitive underside of his lip. His tongue met hers and she stroked it.

He pulled the pins from her hair, and a shimmering mantle of gilt silver cascaded down Blythe's back. With possessive satisfaction, he entangled his hand in the silken fall. The orchid dropped to the carpet, unheeded.

Duncan rushed his hands down her back to cup her derriere, pressing her hips to his.

He was hard. He was hot. She could feel the strength and heat of his male arousal through the fabric that separated them.

With a groan that originated deep in the center of his body, Duncan rubbed himself against her. "Ah, Blythe. That feels good. So...good..." He buried his face in the curve of her neck.

Shocked at precisely how good it felt, Blythe closed her eyes. All consciousness, all sensation centered at that potent point of contact. But it was not enough, not nearly enough to satisfy the heated ache, the *want*. Passion rose in her with relentless tidal pull. "Yes," she whispered, letting her head fall back loosely on her neck, exposing the pale arc of her throat to his fevered mouth. "Yes."

The dinner, the dress, this melting, willing response; Duncan finally accepted it as Blythe's signal to him.

Holding her in his arms, reaching around her back, he attacked the long row of tiny covered buttons that closed her gown. Her fingers adroitly unfastened his tie and tossed it away.

Their kisses multiplied, blazing over face and neck as they moved through the living room to the stairs.

She pushed the jacket off his shoulders, and he impatiently jerked his arms out of the sleeves. Blythe threw the garment over the banister.

When her hands moved to the top button of his shirt, Duncan snarled and swore.

"Damn these little buttons! Is this a plot? Some fiendish torture hatched in that woman's brain of yours?"

A feline smile curved her lips as she backed him up another stair step and pushed his button through its buttonhole. With long, lacquered nails Blythe opened that bit of shirt. She touched her tongue to the patch of warm skin it exposed at the base of his throat. "Perhaps." Unvented laughter bubbled deep. "Hurry, Duncan." Another button, another moist touch.

"I'll buy you another dress," he promised huskily, and grasped handfuls of fabric at her back.

"No! Duncan, no, I like this dress. It's special." In her attempt to escape the intended destruction, Blythe found herself wriggling against him. It felt good. She did it again.

Duncan grunted, hands paralyzed. "Blythe..." he croaked.

The next button she opened had him struggling with the dainty fastenings again.

His rumpled white shirt went down onto the carpeted stairs. As they moved along the hall, the doorknob of a room they passed received a belt.

Then they were standing in the master suite.

The large room was illuminated with row upon row of oil lamps the size and shape of votive candles. Two tall beveled mirrors picked up the lights and increased their number tenfold. The chamber's soft glow danced to the silent music of the tiny flames, but the dark at the towering ceiling remained undisturbed. The aura of an ancient shrine, where timeless rites celebrated eternal mysteries, pervaded the room.

Duncan froze, his arms still embracing Blythe, his hands on the stubborn buttons.

She held her breath.

"This looks like a setup," he muttered.

"It is."

"Good." His eyes were smoky, his kiss heart-stealingly tender. Blythe clung to him, wanting the moment to last.

Finally, in unspoken assent, she swept her hair forward over her shoulder and presented Duncan her back. From this more advantageous position he made quick work of the remaining fastenings.

When he would have slipped the silk off her shoulders Blythe stilled his hands. She swallowed, seized by unexpected nervousness. Slowly she turned. With unsteady fingers she worked the hook and button of his trousers free. The rasp of the zipper sawed through the silence.

Abruptly Blythe turned away, fumbling with the buttons at her wrists. She strained to hear the rustle of clothes as he undressed, knowing after all her planning she was a coward, praying he would not be disappointed with her. Blythe turned to face him. Her breath stuck in her throat.

Duncan was marvelously formed, with long-sinewed leanness that testified to strength and agility. Muscles rippled beneath supple skin as he approached her. Blythe lowered her gaze. He was a most impressive man.

She closed her eyes, drawing on the rumbling currents of the storm that built within the room.

"Blythe."

Her eyes opened to meet his and between them leaped a concussive current—the slash of lightning across the heavens.

She wanted him. They were here, this night, by her design. A small smile curved her lips as she drew her eyes down his body, witnessing her success. Blythe's desire for Duncan whirled into a vortex of long denial now released, blending with the heady intoxicant of a female's sexual power over a male.

She was Seductress and he was hers.

Duncan witnessed the transformation. The woman standing before him now wore a knowing smile. This time when he moved to slide the gown from her shoulders she did not stop him. Silk glided down Blythe to settle like a shadow at her feet.

She wore nothing underneath.

Duncan stared at her, drinking in each lush detail, from her splendid breasts and small waist, to her long, shapely legs. Her hair was the cloud cloak of a sorceress.

His mouth went dry at the thought of her ripe nakedness so close at hand for these past hours. While she'd sat so poised and proper across the dinner table she had been waiting for him, all creamy white and softness under her elegant gown. Hot desire clenched his body.

Eagerly Duncan reached for her. "Darlin', you certainly took your time getting around to this." He covered her mouth with his in a voracious kiss, his hands roaming her naked back.

Blythe pressed against him, reveling in the friction of his chest hair against her breasts.

Why had she waited so long? she wondered. She'd stubbornly denied herself his fascinating male body, its unique textures, warmth and form. Desire sang through her veins. Blythe wanted Duncan. She wanted his body and as much of his heart as she could win.

She slid her hands from his waist to cup the tight curve of his buttocks and pulled him closer.

His head came up sharply. "Let's take it gently, darlin'. I'm . . . it's—" He paused abruptly and closed his eyes as Blythe's hands strayed. "You're not making this easy," he rasped.

Blythe dipped her head and kissed one of his nipples, pleased at its instant beading. "I don't want it easy," she whispered.

With the pointed tip of her tongue, she began to trace a path down his chest. Duncan grasped her arms, toppling them both onto the bed. Immediately he loomed atop her, pinioning her with his hands and legs.

"I aim to please," he assured, covering her face and throat with ardent kisses.

"Practice makes perfect." Blythe slanted her head to allow him access to her neck.

"In for a penny, in...for a...pound." Duncan lowered his head over her right breast. He parted his lips and lowered his head still more, until the pink tip was inside, but untouched. He breathed lightly.

Blythe shivered. "Duncan..."

Duncan ignored her unspoken plea. "If you don't want it easy, how do you want it?" He moved to her left nipple and warmed it. At her body's immediate response, profound satisfaction rippled through him.

"Hard," she gasped. "Real...hard."

Wet heat enveloped Blythe's nipple as he took it into his mouth, and when he laved it with his tongue she clasped his head to her. A tingling river of electricity flowed through her to connect with the molten ache between her thighs. As Duncan lightly used the edge of his teeth, she whimpered at the backlash of pleasure. Her neck arched as she pressed her head back into the pillow. When he favoured her other breast she was certain she couldn't survive another moment without feeling him inside her.

Duncan released her wrists and ran his palm across the ivory plane of her belly. Smooth. Inviting. He brushed his lips against it, lapped it with his tongue and felt her muscles quiver. He'd never been so affected by a woman's response to him. Never had it been so right. Never had he hoped, wanted, *needed* it to be so very right. Until Blythe.

He moved his body up hers to bind her to him with another kiss, teasing her tongue. He raised his head, enjoying the sweet sound of their labored breathing. "Real hard as in . . . rock hard?" He brushed himself against her.

Vivid images played through Blythe's mind, fueling her already incinerating desire. Desperately she raced her hand down his ribs, to his waist and angled it down between their bodies. He caught her before she could reach him.

"Not yet," he warned huskily. "That would be too *easy*."

Their gazes locked. Duncan kissed her palm. He licked her smallest finger, lavishing moist attention on the sensitive area at the base. Blythe shivered with delight, finding it difficult to draw in enough air. As she watched, her finger disappeared between his lips. He sucked lightly. A small sound wrenched its way up her throat.

"Love me," she breathed as she felt the promising heat of his manhood move against her thigh.

"Yes." His eyes were the eyes of passion—dark and burning. He sealed her lips with his.

His cunning fingers sifted through the blond curls at the apex of her thighs. She moaned into his mouth as he stroked the slick bud between her legs. His delicate, persistent touch brought Blythe climbing into frenzy, arching, rigid with shudders of pleasure, as she breathlessly voiced his name.

Finally she sank to the bed. For long moments she lay drifting in the honeyed cocoon of perfect contentment.

"Touch me." Duncan guided her hand with greedy urgency.

Blythe caressed him, marveling at the contrast between satin and steel.

"Yes...like that..." He squeezed his eyes shut and made a guttural sound. "*Just* like that...!" Abruptly he clamped his fingers over hers and eased them away from him. He parted her thighs.

Blythe felt the blunt tip of his manhood probe the threshold of that most vulnerable part of her body. He eased into her carefully. She was tight. It had been so long since she'd been with a man, and never with a man like Duncan.

Once he was fully within her, he paused, tense and still, his breath coming in sharp bursts against her throat. Blythe felt her stretched muscles adjust to the new fullness. She opened her eyes and looked up at him. Dark hair clung to his sweat-damp forehead. He stared down into her face, then took her lips in a searing kiss. Duncan began to move his hips, slowly at first, then with increasing power as the ancient rhythm built. Blythe clasped him with her thighs.

"Do you know how long I've waited for you?" he demanded thickly. He answered the question himself. "Forever. I've wanted you forever."

Blythe traveled through a galaxy of suns, buffeted by waves of celestial delight, which expanded and increased in intensity. In front of her shone a brilliant star. It eluded her, dancing just out of reach.

She raised her legs higher and heard Duncan's wrenching groan.

And then the star was within her astonished grasp. Sparks sizzled down her spine to ignite a shattering burst of sensation.

Duncan threw back his head with a hoarse cry as his body went taut, gripped by the force of climax.

WHEN BLYTHE AWOKE, only the flames of a few die-hard lamps illuminated the room. A glance at the bedside clock told her the sun would soon rise.

Duncan lay next to her, his arm crooked protectively around her as his shoulder cradled her cheek. She smiled, content as she'd never thought to be.

Who would have imagined an act as basic as sex could be so earthshakingly satisfying? So profound? So...holy? That was the only word she could think of to describe the deep awe she'd experienced at being that close, that connected with another being. With Duncan.

She turned her head slightly to look at his sleeping face. Thick black lashes formed crescents under equally black swept-wing eyebrows. His cheeks and jaw were darkly shadowed with new beard. Trying not to disturb him, she reached out to fulfill her need to touch him; fingertips to tousled jet hair.

Instantly his eyes shot open to stare at her. Then, more slowly, he blinked himself into wakefulness and smiled. "Hi, there." He hooked his arm around the back of her neck and drew her closer for a thorough kiss. When they finally drew apart, he murmured, "I was afraid it was all a dream."

Suddenly Blythe needed reassurance she wasn't the only one affected by what they'd done. "Dreams go away."

Without warning, Duncan rolled over, pinning her to the bed beneath him and bracketing her hands on either side of her head. The smile was gone. He held her gaze. "Hear me, Blythe. Dreams might go away, but reality doesn't. Last night was *real*. Damned real. It was better between us than a dream could ever be. And I'm not just talking about great sex. It was more than that." He searched her face intently, then relaxed. "I think you understand what I mean." Uncurling his fingers from her wrists, he framed her face with his hands and brushed tender kisses over her mouth, cheeks, eyes and forehead. "I *hope* you understand what I mean."

"I do," she said softly. "Oh, Duncan, I do. But I needed to know I wasn't the only one who felt it."

"You weren't." Duncan remembered how stunned he'd been, the *closeness* that had felt almost spiritual. "Not by a long shot." Until last night with Blythe, sex had never been like that for him. Until last night, he'd never wanted it to be.

Blythe's heart soared. She couldn't look into the future to see what was in store for them, but she could behold what happened now. Their relationship was changing. This morning it held . . . promise.

Duncan rolled to his side, facing her. "Ah, darlin'," he sighed, drawing her closer. "We're good for each other. Who could have known my aunts' stockbroker would capture my heart?"

"And what would you have done if you had known?"

Duncan grinned. "Why, I would have actually been eager to go to Winter Park. I would have stormed into your office sooner!"

Blythe dropped a kiss on his naked shoulder. "Why wouldn't you have wanted to go to Winter Park, anyway? That's where your aunts live."

"Uh, right. Don't get me wrong. I love my aunts, and I would do anything for them. But when I spend much time around them, things happen. There seems to be a perpetual line of miscommunication between my aunts and the world."

Blythe tickled his ribs and to her delight, found an immediate response. "Sounds like superstition to me."

He stilled her hands in his larger ones. Then, releasing one, he drew his nimble forefinger down the top of her breast almost, but not quite, to the tip. With a whisper touch, he circled the rim of pink. "So, you like to play tickle."

"Don't you . . . don't you want to see the sunrise?" She closed her eyes, giving herself up to his touch.

Duncan chuckled deep in his throat. "No, darlin'. I want to show you another way we can start the morning."

MONDAY MORNING, as Blythe sat in her office remembering her weekend in Atlanta, she smiled to herself. On Sunday, she and Duncan had toured Atlanta, but they probably would have had an equally memorable excursion if they'd never left Duncan's bed.

Well, now she'd seen Atlanta. It was a fascinating city, alive and diverse. As a hub of commerce and transportation, the city offered much, but its most important asset, as far as Blythe was concerned, was Duncan McKeon.

When he'd taken her to the airport, she'd missed him as soon as she stepped through the gate. All the way home she'd thought about their hours together, reliving each moment of delighted discovery.

Blythe blinked. She'd never get any work done daydreaming. Consulting her organizer, she found the first item on her list was the completion of the Chasen and Sons proposal.

She made a note of the *Standard and Poor* and *Value Line* volumes she needed, and took it out to Wendy, who promised to pull them in a few minutes.

"My, aren't we busy?"

The familiar voice made Blythe's skin crawl. She turned to face the speaker. It wasn't safe to leave your back exposed to Leonard Brock, thought Blythe with distaste. "Some of us have work to do."

His thin, reptilian mouth curved. "Ah. Putting up such a brave front. Who would know you'd lost so much of your business? I suppose it's especially important, now, to keep the confidence of your remaining clients." He watched her with small, dark, avid eyes.

"Is there a point to this little tête-à-tête, Leonard?" she asked flatly.

His look of hurt surprise was patently false. "I'm just trying to be neighborly."

Blythe gave him a short nod. "Goodbye, neighbor."

With a self-satisfied grin, Leonard Brock sauntered down the hall to his office.

Wendy looked up at Blythe. "He's always had a reputation as a back-stabber. Even where I worked before you hired me. Word gets around, I guess."

Blythe nodded. "Why am I not surprised?"

"Oh. Here. This man called while you were in the ladies' room."

Blythe accepted the message slip from her sales assistant and walked into her office. She read the name of the caller: Ethan Dodd.

"Damn." She really didn't want to go through another conversation with the heartbroken man. It was too painful.

A thought crossed her mind, trapping the breath in her throat. She could easily end up like Ethan. She could be the one left behind.

She wasn't going to think about that now. She would do Fiona's abandoned lover the courtesy of returning his call. Resolutely Blythe began dialing.

Relief flooded through her when she was greeted by an answering machine. Blythe left the message she'd called, then quickly hung up. "You're pathetic, Summers," she muttered, disgusted with her cowardly haste.

She dreaded talking to Ethan. For a moment she entertained the thought of refusing to talk to the Alaskan again. Maybe then he'd give up, find some nice, well-adjusted woman, get married and have a bus load of babies. He'd never know his first child even existed.

No, she couldn't cut Ethan off so cruelly. If Ethan gave up on her sister, then Fiona, Jr. might never know her—or his—father. Blythe sighed heavily. If Ethan called her back, she would speak to him.

Wendy tapped on Blythe's door and walked in. "I've got that information you requested."

"Thanks." Blythe cleared a space on her credenza and Wendy set down the armload of books.

"Is this all for that proposal you've been working on?"

Blythe smiled crookedly. "This is just some of the material."

Wendy's almond eyes widened. "Wow. This must be some big deal."

At eleven that night, as she put the completed proposal on Wendy's desk to be typed, Blythe recalled her sales assistant's words. Some big deal. It would be *the* big deal of the entire office, if Blythe could capture it. It would also launch her solidly in her new direction.

She locked up the office and headed home, envisioning how things would be when she was firmly established as a retirement fund specialist.

"Have you had dinner?" Fiona asked as Blythe walked in the door.

Blythe smiled wearily. "I warmed up some soup at the office." She was beyond hunger. All she wanted now was a comfortable bed. "And you? Did you have something to eat?"

Fiona nodded. "I made a salad and broiled some chicken."

"Nice and nutritious." Blythe glanced at her stack of mail. *Tomorrow.* She turned to go to her bedroom.

"Would you like some tea?" Fiona's question sounded hopeful.

She's here alone, all day. She's pregnant and afraid. Blythe repressed a tired sigh, and managed a smile. "Sure. Sounds good."

Immediately Fiona lifted the kettle from the stove, and poured steaming water into a teapot.

"Boy, you're prepared," Blythe remarked, setting her purse and briefcase on the kitchen counter and stepping out of her high heels.

"I've been keeping it ready for when you got home." Fiona grinned at her sister, then peeked into the teapot. She picked up a wooden chopstick from the utensil crock and poked the tea bags.

Blythe felt a little less exhausted. She grinned back at Fiona. "Thanks. I appreciate that."

They brought their tea into the great room, and settled on the couch.

Blythe sipped the hot liquid contentedly. "Mmm. This was a good idea."

"This has always been one of my favorite things—sharing a cup of tea with my sister." Fiona lifted her cup to her lips. Her emerald eyes smiled at Blythe over the china edge.

"We haven't done it much lately, have we?"

During the past months, increasingly frequent flashes of tension between the sisters and the demands of Blythe's work had made such interludes rare. Blythe mourned the erosion of their closeness, but she was at a loss as to how to halt it.

"So tell me, when are you planning to see the magnificent Mr. McKeon again?"

Blythe struggled to keep the sappy smile from her face. "This coming weekend."

Fiona raised her russet eyebrows. "My, my, it must be love."

It was a perfect opening to tell her sister Ethan had called, but Blythe hesitated. But this moment was so peaceful, so pleasant, she hated to risk ruining it.

"Must be."

Accepting she was in love with Duncan was sometimes still difficult. She felt foolish. She'd gotten careless and learned to care. Now, just thinking of him brought a rush of joy so intense she wanted to hug herself and laugh. Even more, she wanted to hug Duncan.

"Having a little trouble getting used to the idea?" Fiona asked in a casual voice. Her cup rattled softly against its saucer.

Blythe did not miss the tremor. She nodded slowly. "Yes. I alternate between feeling euphoric and feeling foolish. When I started seeing Duncan, I was certain our...friendship...was going to be temporary. Nothing that would have me thinking about the future. But somewhere, somehow, something changed.''

Fiona smiled. The edges of her mouth trembled slightly. ''Have you ever had just a nice little temporary affair?''

Blythe's gaze dropped to her lap. She fiddled with the handle of her cup. ''Actually...no.''

Fiona poured more tea for them both, then took up her cup and saucer, and settled back against the cushioned couch. ''I think women who can successfully plan and execute such tidy relationships must have awfully thick skins. I envy them.''

Blythe nodded. She did envy such women, but she wondered if they were so unaffected.

''If you were like them, you'd have missed what you had with Ethan. What you could have again.''

Fiona took a swallow of her tea, eyes downcast. ''No. It's over. He's written me off by now, and that's best.''

Leaning forward, Blythe put her cup down. She locked her gaze with her sister's, silently commanding the younger woman's attention. ''He hasn't written you off. He called today, Fiona.''

A tiny sound caught in Fiona's throat. ''He called?''

Encouraged, Blythe said, ''Yes. He must love you very much to continue to put himself through this torment. Please call him. Talk this out. Give it a chance.''

Fire flared in Fiona's eyes. ''Butt out, Blythe. You gave me your word you wouldn't tell Ethan where I was. This is none of your business.''

"The hell it isn't. You love him. He loves you. He's the father of your child, for God's sake! Don't you think he at least deserves to know *that?*"

Fiona slammed her cup down on the coffee table, marring the wood. "I said butt out!"

"How can I? Day after day I see you withering inside. This is a time that should be full of wonder for you, full of rapture. Instead, it's one of sorrow and pain. It hurts me to see you like this, baby. You're my sister."

"That's right," Fiona snapped. "I'm your sister. I'm not your possession, and I'm *not your baby!*" She stood and ran from the room.

"YOU CERTAINLY SEEM to have covered every contingency." Martin Chasen looked up from the proposal Blythe had completed three days ago. He smiled. "This is quite comprehensive."

It was the first smile Blythe had received since she'd arrived at Chasen's office to keep the appointment they'd set two weeks earlier.

"That's the way I like to do business," she said.

"I have to take this before the board. We meet in twelve days, on the twenty-eighth. I'd like you to be there to go over it with them and answer any questions."

Blythe thought she might have to anchor herself in her seat to keep from leaping up and dancing. "That will be fine."

They set the time, shook hands and Blythe left.

Now that he had her proposal, Martin Chasen could pick up the telephone and call her competitors, to get bids and propositions from them. He had something to use as a comparison. It wouldn't be the first time that had happened to her. Just thinking about it made Blythe's stomach knot. She fastened her seat belt, and turned the key in the ignition.

Chasen had seemed impressed with her work-up. His invitation to make the presentation to the board was a good sign. Blythe decided to hold that thought. All the way back to the office, she dissected every detail of her appointment with the comptroller.

When she arrived, she took one look at Ginny and Wendy and knew something was wrong. Dread chilled her.

"Tell me it's not what I think it is," Blythe implored them.

Wendy fiddled with her pencil cup.

Ginny chewed her lip and looked up at Blythe with worried brown eyes. "Another account was pulled."

CHAPTER TWELVE

"WE'RE SO LUCKY to have you, dear. We'd never manage without you to help us with these financial things." Martha set the brimming glass of iced tea on the desk, then bent to kiss her nephew's cheek.

Duncan smiled fleetingly and scraped his fingers through his hair. For the past hour and a half he'd been trying to untangle the mess his aunts had made of their checkbook. It was Saturday, or he'd be tempted to call the bank and talk to someone in their bookkeeping department. "Aunt Martha, you've got to keep track of the checks you write." He massaged his forehead.

"We have," Amelia informed him brightly. "We've been very careful to do just as you told us."

Martha nodded. "Yes, we did, Duncan, dear. We recorded the amount of each check we wrote." Martha looked proud of herself.

"Unless we forgot," Amelia added. "Then we couldn't, you see."

Duncan's headache throbbed harder. "You forgot?" Why was he still amazed? He'd been straightening out Martha and Amelia's checkbooks for more than twenty years. "It makes it easier for me if you at least note in the register that you *wrote* a check."

"Oh, but Martha made a note of every check," Amelia assured Duncan.

Martha looked surprised. "Me? Amelia, I thought we decided you would record them."

"Neither of you wrote anything."

Amelia's eyes widened. "Of course we did, dear. We wrote checks. How else would we pay our bills?"

Duncan sighed heavily. "You don't pay your bills. I do. At least the regular ones." And still they managed to annihilate their accounts.

"Not with your own money, Duncan!" Martha was clearly dismayed.

He took her hand, and smiled at her. "No," he agreed, "not with my money."

The women looked relieved.

"Good," Amelia said. "Father left us enough to be comfortable. We don't want you to use your hard-earned wages on us."

Duncan's grandfather had left his daughters more than comfortable—he'd left them rich. The old man had believed his only son could make his own way, and had divided his estate accordingly.

"Aren't you and Blythe going antique hunting in Mount Dora?" Amelia asked.

Duncan glanced at his watch. He'd thought this hour would never get here. With relief, he closed the checkbook and pushed away from the desk. He stood. "Yes, we are."

Martha smiled. "She's such a lovely girl. I wonder if her children will have that striking blond hair."

"Wouldn't that be lovely!" Amelia piped in. "And twins. You know, twins run in our family."

They both looked at Duncan.

He politely ignored the point of the conversation. "Goodbye, ladies. Don't wait up." He gave them each a kiss on the cheek.

"Our bridge group is here tonight, dear," Martha reminded him.

Bridge group, garden society, one volunteer committee or another, thought Duncan as he backed the old Cadillac out of the garage and headed toward Blythe's place. He was happy his aunts were so involved in the community, but it meant little privacy at their house.

No privacy at Blythe's house, either. According to Blythe, Fiona never left the place. Worse, he had the distinct impression his relationship with Blythe upset the younger woman, though she didn't seem to object to him personally. Duncan wondered if it had something to do with Fiona's pregnancy. No one had mentioned it, but he wasn't blind. And so far, Duncan hadn't heard one word about a husband.

Fiona answered the door.

"Hi." Her cheerfulness sounded forced, but he took heart that she'd made the effort.

He gave her his most winning smile. "Hi."

"Come on in and have a seat. I'll get Blythe."

While he waited, Duncan looked around Blythe's great room again. This was more what he'd had in mind when he'd talked to that creative genius who'd done his place. Maybe Blythe would be willing to help him redo his condo.

As he examined the craftsmanship of the mantel, soft lips pressed against his nape. He turned to find Blythe, dressed in camel slacks and a honey brown cotton sweater, her hair caught in a soft knot high at the back of her head.

He pulled her into his arms and gave her a proper greeting.

Fiona entered the room, and Duncan looked up to see her eyes widen and her cheeks turn pink.

"Uh, excuse me," she said, as she retreated into the hall.

He turned back to the kiss Fiona had interrupted.

Blythe eased out of his embrace. She took his hand and led him toward the front door. "Bye, Fiona," she called.

"Bye," came Fiona's voice from the next room.

When they were in the car, Duncan turned to Blythe. "What was that all about?" he asked. "Since when am I not allowed to kiss you in your own house?"

"Fiona—"

"Is an adult. I doubt she was traumatized to see us in a clinch."

"—is going through a bad time," Blythe continued patiently.

"She's pregnant, isn't she?" he asked bluntly.

Blythe bristled. "Yes, as a matter of fact. She is. Seeing us together, seeing how happy we are . . . well, she won't say anything, but I know it upsets her."

Duncan's mouth hardened. "Why?"

Blythe searched his face for a long moment. "She didn't marry the father of her child. She—she didn't feel it would work out. She came back here."

"To you."

"To me," she acceded.

"Correct me if I'm wrong. Fiona found out she was pregnant, left her lover and moved in with you. Now your lover isn't supposed to touch you because it upsets Fiona."

Put like that, Blythe had to agree it didn't sound reasonable. But then, life seldom was reasonable. She felt torn between her need to shield Fiona and her need to be with Duncan.

She reached out and gently touched his face. His scowl softened.

"Please don't put me in the middle," she said, tracing the curve of his cheekbones with her fingertips. "I love you, Duncan. I love my sister, too."

When he remained silent, Blythe pointed out, "We're careful of your aunts' feelings."

"It's their house."

Blythe smiled. "Tell me you wouldn't care how they felt if it were your house."

His silver gaze flicked aside, then returned to meet hers. "All right. Point taken."

That left them back at square one, Blythe concluded morosely. She looked at Duncan, hoping he had an answer.

Duncan looked back at her, obviously hoping for inspiration. The silence in the car grew deep.

Suddenly he pulled her into his arms, and without thinking, Blythe responded. As her lips moved against his in a frenzy of reacquaintance she indulged her fingers, sifting them through the thick blackness of Duncan's hair. He slid one warm hand under her sweater, pushing her bra aside, to touch her breast. Breath caught in her throat.

"I want you so badly, Blythe," Duncan muttered against her lips. "You're in my thoughts constantly. I can't concentrate anymore." He fingered her nipple.

She moaned in pleasure.

The roar of a lawn mower started up several yards from the car.

Blythe suddenly recalled it was Saturday afternoon, and she and Duncan were making out in her driveway. Hastily she straightened her clothing. When she looked up, Duncan eased back, his elbow resting against the door.

"Let's go," she said tersely.

"In a minute," he said.

The neighbor rode by on his lawn mower, smiled at them, waving.

Blythe smiled at the man, and waved back. "*Now* would be nice," she muttered, maintaining the pleasant curve of her lips for the benefit of the neighbor.

Duncan took a deep breath and let it out slowly. "Not yet."

"Why?" She turned to face him.

He lifted an eyebrow.

"Oh."

"If the only way we can be alone together here in Florida is to be tourists, we ought to take full advantage of the status. There are a lot of nice hotels in Orlando," Duncan pointed out. "If we take a room in one of them we'd have a good restaurant, a swimming pool . . . a bed."

Visions played through Blythe's mind: Duncan's hand, long-fingered and gentle, caressing her breast; intense emotion stark on Duncan's face as he parted her thighs for the first time; Duncan poised over her, sweat-damp and gleaming in the flame light. Blythe found it difficult to breathe.

She needed time alone with Duncan. She wanted to share the secrets and smiles lovers shared. She ached to join with him in that miraculous union of body and spirit.

But a hotel room? It seemed so illicit.

As if he sensed what was going through her mind, Duncan offered an alternative. "We could go to Atlanta." He pressed a soft kiss on her temple. "We have plenty of privacy in Atlanta."

Atlanta was a lovely city, and Blythe enjoyed her visits, but she lived in Winter Park.

"That isn't the answer, Duncan," she told him in a low voice, striving to curb her impatience. "We can't always go to Atlanta whenever we want to be together."

He kissed the sensitive area behind her ear. Blythe closed her eyes and leaned toward him. She felt his lips curve up.

"Why not?" he murmured. "Atlanta is a good place for a stockbroker. More wealth. More businesses."

Like a worm in an apple, suspicion ate through Blythe's titillated daze. She sat up. "Are you suggesting I move to Atlanta?"

Duncan straightened in his seat. "What we've got together is something special, something so extraordinary I can only believe it's rare." He took her hand and laced his fingers through hers. "We have a real, honest-to-God relationship, and I want it to continue. Given a chance, I think it could become a permanent part of our lives. But we need more time together, Blythe."

She gazed at their joined hands as she absorbed what he'd told her. Rare. Relationship. Permanent. Blythe found the prospect of believing in tomorrow both wonderful and frightening. She took refuge in caution.

"Your moving to Atlanta would be a practical answer to our problem. For a broker, there's more opportunity in Atlanta than in Winter Park—"

"Central Florida. I work throughout Central Florida. Not just Winter Park, or Orlando, or Casselberry, or Kissimmee." Even as the words tumbled out of her mouth, Blythe knew Central Florida was not as developed as Atlanta and might never be. Atlanta was a regional hub.

"All right. Central Florida. Atlanta still has greater opportunity for you. That's where you should be if you want to set up company retirement funds. I could help you move, help you get started."

"Duncan, I want us to have more time together, too. But what you're suggesting is impossible. It would be like me expecting you move to Florida. After all, there are a lot of hotels here, and with the continuing growth the potential for all your divisions is unlimited. You'd be getting in on the ground floor."

He shook his head and held to his line of reasoning. "You wouldn't have to give up anything. Most of your clients transact their business with you over the telephone, don't they? Get a WATTS line."

"And what about my clients who insist on doing business face-to-face? Duncan, when a broker moves, she—or he—can expect to lose about fifty percent of her or his business. You're talking about cutting my income in half." Blythe frowned. "Not to mention the people who depend on me. Most of my clients are retired, many of them elderly. I've been handling their investments for years. They trust me.

"Ginny and I have plans. She's getting her license. We're going to be partners. And then there's my sister. Fiona is having a hard time. I'm not going to let her down when she needs me."

Duncan ran his finger lightly along the curve of her jaw. "Think about it, okay?" he coaxed. "Atlanta has a lot to offer."

"Right," she said, impatient with this turn in their conversation. "And you think about moving to Winter Park."

He smiled. "My moving to Winter Park would entail a lot more than your moving to Atlanta."

"Oh, really? How so?"

"I own a large company. If I move it I'll lose personnel. Moving expenses for those who can come will be an enormous drain on the company's coffers, not to mention finding new quarters, the moving expenses for all of Macrocosm's equipment—"

"Macrocosm is a software company. Other than your copiers and word processors, and the machines you use in R and D, what equipment would you have to move? You don't have a warehouse of hardware. You lease your office space. It's not like you'd have to sell a building."

"Moving Macrocosm would have an adverse effect on a lot of my employees—especially the ones that couldn't relocate."

Impatiently Duncan turned the key in the ignition. "Just give Atlanta some consideration, okay?"

"Sure. When you do the same with Central Florida."

Blythe sat back as Duncan pulled out of the driveway. She'd lost her enthusiasm for their trip to Mount Dora. The only antique she wanted to find today was Aladdin's lamp. It looked as if the time Duncan and she needed could only be secured through magic.

WHEN DUNCAN RETURNED to his aunts' house that night, laughter from the living room reminded him his aunts were having a bridge party.

At that moment, Martha, accompanied by a man Duncan guessed to be in his late sixties, came into the kitchen.

"Oh, Duncan, dear," Martha exclaimed, brightening. "I didn't know you were home."

She introduced him to Philip Brock. Then she patted Duncan on the arm, poured some peanuts into a cut-crystal bowl and carried it back with her to the card players.

Martha's guest stayed in the kitchen. He took a diet ginger ale from the refrigerator, offering to pour one for Duncan, who declined.

"Don't let me keep you if you need to get back to the game," Duncan said.

The other man shook his head, and chuckled. "No, I'm the dummy."

"Oh."

Brock observed Duncan over the rim of his glass as he sipped his drink. "I understand you're seeing Blythe Summers."

Duncan wasn't pleased to hear his aunts had been chatting about his personal life to their bridge partners. Still, he had nothing to hide. "Yes, I am."

The older man set down his glass. "That surprises me."

Duncan frowned. "Why?" What damn business of his was it anyway?

"Well, her rather infamous past..."

"What do you mean?" Duncan asked tightly.

The bridge player pulled a pipe and tobacco pouch out of his sweater pocket, and began packing. "I guess you wouldn't have heard about it if you live in Atlanta, but it was in the news all over Florida. About three years ago she and her husband were hauled up on fraud. It made the newspapers." He touched a match to his pipe and drew, then exhaled smoke. "The husband was heavily fined and lost his license." The man blew a smoke ring that wafted for a second, then gradually lost its shape and dissipated. "*She* managed to get off scot-free. Don't know how. Maybe she had a better lawyer."

FOR MOST OF THE NIGHT Blythe fretted over her conversation with Duncan. During the afternoon, neither of them had brought up the subject of their future again, and now Blythe was regretting it. Duncan had spoken of permanence, and she believed he wanted it. But was there such a thing? There had been no permanent relationships between man and woman in her life, not even with her husband. Were she and Duncan just setting themselves up for a fall?

And then there was his assumption she'd have no trouble pulling up stakes and relocating in Atlanta. She had to admit he was right on one point: There would be more opportunity for what she wanted to do in Atlanta. But she lived here, in Winter Park. Her carefully nurtured business was here. Master's degree in economics in hand, she had *chosen* Winter Park as the place to start her new beginning, free of the entanglements of her mother's marriages.

By dawn Blythe had decided she and Duncan would have to accept the fact things would be inconvenient. She'd fly to Georgia when it was feasible. He'd come to Florida when it wasn't.

Blythe waited impatiently for a reasonable hour. She'd call him. The two of them would work things out calmly, rationally, over breakfast.

At seven o'clock the next morning her telephone rang. When she answered, Duncan greeted her briefly.

"Something's come up," he told her. "I'm leaving for Atlanta in five minutes. I'll call you."

"Oh. Okay," she said, surprised. "I hope everything works out all right."

And then he was gone.

It must have been a serious emergency at Macrocosm to have warranted such an abrupt departure, Blythe thought, worried. Clearly Duncan was troubled. The last time she'd heard him use that tone of voice he'd been standing in her office, accusing her of churning his aunts' account.

After she hung up, Blythe wandered restlessly around the house, doing a spot of dusting here, a little straightening there.

Did he regret yesterday's conversation? Did he think their relationship was too inconvenient? A dead-end street? She stopped to stare out the window at the bird feeder suspended from a bough of an oak. A red-winged blackbird poked its dark beak through a feeder hole, supping on millet and sunflower seeds, oblivious to human problems.

The door from the garage cum pottery studio opened and Fiona walked in. She wore tennis shoes, clay-smeared jeans and a chambray shirt. Her hair was pulled back in a ponytail, and her cheeks bloomed with color.

"I've come up with some interesting shapes," she said, clearly pleased with her accomplishments. "I'm ready for a break. Want some tea?"

Blythe nodded, and sat down on a stool at the breakfast bar.

Fiona looked more closely at her sister. "What's the matter?"

"Nothing. Everything." Blythe picked at her dust-ladened rag. "I mean, when you get right down to it, what does it all mean?" She gave her sister a crooked smile, a failed attempt at lightness.

"Knock it off, Blythe." Fiona dropped two tea bags into the fat, brown teapot. "What's wrong?" She fixed Blythe with a piercing look.

"Nothing."

Fiona waited. The only sound was the bubbling rumble of the water heating.

She didn't want to upset Fiona. If Blythe related the conversation with Duncan yesterday, Fiona might feel she was holding Blythe back from an opportunity. "I'd rather not talk about it." There was also the chance Fiona would fear she'd be left alone during her pregnancy.

On the other hand, she might not. And Blythe wanted to talk it over with someone. She drew a breath to speak.

"I see," Fiona said tightly. "I'm just the little sister. It's all right for me to tell you my deepest, darkest secrets, but you'd never consider confiding in me. Of course not. You've always got to be in control. If you cried on my shoulder like I've cried on yours, you wouldn't have that control."

Blythe gaped in astonishment.

"You don't trust anyone, do you, big sister?" Fiona continued, her hands fisted in fury. "Trust and control. You've always applied them to me. You've never

trusted me and you've always tried to control me."
Fiona laughed, a painful, bitter sound.

"I do so trust you!" Blythe protested. "You're dear
to me. I barely have control of my life, what makes
you think I want to control yours?"

Fiona leaned forward, ignoring the shrill whistle of
the kettle. "When *haven't* you tried to control my
life?" she demanded. "Fiona, go there," she mimicked, "Fiona, do this." Her voice rose with each
word. "Love him, Fiona. Don't be foolish, Fiona.
Face facts, Fiona!"

"Maybe it's time you did face facts," Blythe
snapped, stung. "You're pregnant and you haven't
done one thing to prepare for your child. You have a
man who loves you—*a man you love*—and you refuse to speak to him."

Fiona's face went white. "Oh, yes, let's tell Fiona
how to run her life. Well, dear sister, it seems to me
you haven't done such a bang-up job of running your
own."

The screaming kettle continued to spew searing
steam into the kitchen.

Blythe slowly rose from the stool, trembling with an
inner pain that mingled with the bubbling ooze of her
anger. "At least I had the guts to make a commitment." She had not allowed her heart to interfere with
the logic of her decision to accept Andrew's proposal
of marriage. Look where that had gotten her.

Tears sprang to Fiona's eyes. She dashed them away.
"That's right. You've always been the strong one. The
one who's never run from anything. But then it's hard
to move away when you're trying to keep something
pinned beneath your thumb."

Stunned silence crashed down between them, split by the furious shriek of the kettle.

Fiona glared at her sister. "Where's Duncan? I'll bet he's hightailed it back to Georgia. Probably wised up and saw you'd try to run his life." She paused, gathered her breath. When she spoke, it was in a calmer voice. "It's what I did."

"What?"

"I went to Alaska to get away from you, Blythe. You've always mothered me. I was being smothered. I had to get away and Alaska was as far as I could go."

Blythe stared at Fiona. It felt as if something inside her shattered, the shards sucked into an aching vacuum where her heart had been. She tried to swallow but the lump was too large. "I've only tried to protect you," she whispered, moisture burning in her eyes. She drew a sharp breath and tilted her head back. She straightened and warm tears channeled down her cheeks, rolling against the corners of her mouth to leave their salt. "I'm older than you. I felt responsible for you. I learned the hard way not to become attached to our mother's husbands. None of them cared about us, not even our own fathers. Two little girls— we were nothing but a nuisance to them. It hurt when they'd leave without so much as a backward glance. I wanted to spare you that, so I tried to compensate. Impossible, I know now. But I've always carried the guilt for not being able to completely protect you from the hurt. It was never my intention to smother you."

Fiona stood still for a moment, staring at her clenched hands. Again she met Blythe's gaze, then turned and walked quietly out of the kitchen.

Blythe went to the stove, and turned off the heat. The kettle's cry slowly faded.

MONDAY MORNING Blythe found it hard to get out of bed. After their argument, she and Fiona had spoken to each other only when necessary. Duncan hadn't called. The thought of facing the board members of Chasen and Sons, tomorrow, was daunting and she wanted to roll over and pull the covers over her head.

Instead, she forced herself to rise, shower and dress. By the time she was ready to leave, she still had not seen Fiona. Blythe peered down the hall. Fiona's bedroom door was closed.

Maybe it was better that way, reasoned Blythe, and headed the Volvo toward Stewart Duke.

No sooner had she entered her office than her phone buzzed. Blythe took a deep breath, straightened her shoulders, and lifted the receiver. "Blythe, here."

"Ms. Summers? This is Mrs. Blackwell, Mr. Chasen's secretary. I'm calling to cancel your appointment, tomorrow." The words were coldly impersonal.

"Has the board meeting been canceled?" asked Blythe.

"I can't say."

Blythe frowned. "Please connect me with Mr. Chasen."

"Mr. Chasen is in a meeting. Goodbye." The telephone clicked, the connection severed. A flat dial tone filled Blythe's ear.

She carefully returned her receiver to the telephone cradle.

The nightmare had returned.

CHAPTER THIRTEEN

DUNCAN TILTED HIS HEAD back and scraped the razor up the underside of his white-foamed chin, leaving a trail of smooth skin. With a practiced flick of his wrist, he flipped the shaving cream off the blade, as he considered the state of his life.

Orders for the new system were pouring into Macrocosm, and with them, large, cashable checks. Business was great. Duncan knew he should be ecstatic, yet it seemed to him nothing was going right. He sighed heavily. The only thing wrong was him.

He paused to study the reflection in the bathroom mirror. *Traitor.*

Blythe could no more swindle her clients than pigs could fly. He knew that. But Philip Brock's revelation had caught him off balance.

He almost wished she was guilty. It might explain why she turned inward, withdrawing at unexpected moments. Shame. Remorse. *Something* caused her to distance herself from him. Though they never lasted long, Duncan found the spells frustrating and curiously painful.

He raised his razor and resumed shaving. On the first draw he cut himself. The nick bled crimson, staining the foam pink. Duncan cursed under his breath and finished slicing his dark stubble away. After rinsing his face, he stanched the tiny wound with a piece of tissue.

As he went about dressing for work, Duncan tried to fathom Blythe's moments of withdrawal. What did she need from him? He tried to recall her every gesture, expression, and word, searching for an answer as he had countless times before.

His fingers froze in the process of knotting his tie. Trust.

It had never been a consideration with other women he'd dated—there'd been no need for it. Both parties had entered into the game with full knowledge of the rules: short and sweet. Trust was an element to which he'd previously given little thought. Maybe Blythe had sensed in him what he had not even been aware of until Brock dropped his bomb. When put to the test, his faith in Blythe had wavered. That disgusted Duncan.

But ultimately, his belief in Blythe's integrity held firm. She could never bilk her clients, of that he was certain. Only his responsibility to his aunts had forced him to verify their Atlanta broker was guilty of churning their account. He'd hated every minute of the task, feeling as if he'd spied on Blythe.

The guilt and shame were his. Blythe was innocent.

Since flying back to Atlanta two days ago he'd examined his life and what he discovered left him shaken.

He loved Blythe Summers. He couldn't bear to lose her.

Her troubled past didn't matter. If that was all that caused her to withdraw from him, he would reassure her. They could make it work.

They had to.

BLYTHE PULLED HER CAR into the garage and turned off the engine. She sat for a moment, too tired and too depressed to make the effort to enter the house for another evening spent being avoided by Fiona.

It had been another rotten day. The market had gone down and while she'd been able to take advantage of lower prices for some of her clients, she also had to contend with others who were nervous. And Duncan hadn't called.

Finally, releasing a weary sigh, she got out of the car and went into the house. She set her purse and briefcase on the kitchen counter, then opened the refrigerator. Clearly Fiona had once again neglected to do the grocery shopping. An empty carton of milk, some corroded leftovers, a withered carrot and various condiments were the only contents.

Blythe eyed the leftovers. Was mold considered animal or vegetable? She dumped the dubious portions, along with the carrot, down the garbage disposal, tossed the milk carton into the recycling bin, then set about making herself a cup of hot herbal tea.

The prepackaged chicken dinner she'd nuked in the office microwave would suffice for her dinner tonight, but what had Fiona eaten? Expectant mothers needed real food. Blythe decided she'd go shopping at the twenty-four-hour supermarket as soon as she finished her tea.

The telephone rang, and she glanced at her watch. It was past ten.

"Hello?" she said.

"Blythe."

She'd recognize that smooth baritone anywhere. It speeded up her heartbeat and filled her with an excited, wondrous glow. "Hi. I missed you Sunday. Did everything turn out all right?"

There was a second's hesitation, as if Duncan was confused by her question. "Pardon?"

"Your business. You know, what you had to go back to Atlanta for? Is everything all right now?"

"I'm still working on it," he assured her, "but I'm hopeful. Sorry for leaving so abruptly."

"Oh, that's okay. Duty called."

"Listen, sweetheart, I know it's late, but I really wanted to hear your voice."

Delight bubbled through Blythe, lifting away her fatigue. "I feel better already."

Immediately Duncan sounded concerned. "Is there something wrong? Are you ill? What is it?"

Blythe leaned back against the edge of the counter. "I'm not ill. But lately nothing seems to be going right. I've had a few accounts close, and an important meeting canceled."

"Why?"

It was a natural question, but Blythe couldn't bring herself to give a straightforward answer. What would Duncan think of her if he knew about the fraud charges in her past? She couldn't bear to see the contempt in his eyes that she had seen in so many others. She just couldn't. No, she would wait to tell him. Later. With any luck, much later.

"Oh, you know how people are," she said with studied vagueness. "Sometimes they get very strange about their money."

"I'll bet they do."

"Reason doesn't always figure into their decisions." Instantly Blythe cursed her galloping tongue.

If she babbled on she would sound suspiciously nervous—*and she was innocent!*

"Right. I can identify with that. Money makes people a little crazy."

She smiled. "Like causing them to swoop down on their aunts' stockbroker in a righteous fury?"

"No, that was probably the *smartest* thing I've ever done, though I didn't know it at the time. At the time I felt like an idiot."

Blythe kicked off her pumps. "And how do you feel now?" she asked softly.

"Desperate. I haven't seen you or touched you in three days, and I'm going nuts."

His words throbbed with the same yearning that gripped her. She missed Duncan. She missed the sight of him, the scent of him, the feel of him. She wanted to laugh with him. She wanted to—

"I want to make love with you, sweetheart," he said huskily.

"Yes." She sighed. Oh, yes.

She heard him draw in a long breath. He released it in a rush. "I have a meeting in Orlando on Friday, and I don't have to leave for Atlanta until Saturday night."

"Wonderful!"

"I've reserved a room for us at the Palmbrook Hotel."

Blythe was taken aback. Hotel?

"Wait a minute," she said. "We need to talk about this."

"Okay."

"Why a hotel?" She stalled, trying to dredge up a good reason to justify her distaste for using a hotel room.

"Privacy. Something that seems to be in short supply when I visit you. Of course we don't have that problem here in Atlanta."

She chewed her lip as she searched for an acceptable reason.

"What have you got against hotels, Blythe? It would solve a number of our problems."

"It's just ... I don't ..."

"Yes?"

"Meeting like that in a hotel seems so ... so *illicit*." She blurted the word. "Hotels are where prostitutes conduct their business."

Duncan laughed. "No one is going to mistake you for a hooker, darlin'. Hmm. Unless you want them to. That could be interesting. You can be Bambi Vavoom and I'll pretend I'm the shy virgin truck driver."

Blythe stiffened. "How very sensitive, Mr. McKeon," she said coldly.

"I'm sorry. You're right. This is a serious matter. Okay. Hotels are out. You come up with an idea."

She couldn't.

After a long silence, he said, "I see. So, what is it? The hotel? Or an evening with my aunts or with Fiona sulking? There's always Atlanta."

Blythe sighed heavily. "The hotel."

"Palmbrook. The Rose Suite. Friday," he told her. "It's the only way we'll get any privacy. I'll pick you up after work."

The dull hum of the dial tone filled the room. Blythe stared at the receiver in her hand, then placed it in its cradle. She picked up her mug, then realized the tea was cold and set it back down.

The man was aggravating. Honorable, sexy, arrogant and aggravating. Especially when he was right.

LATE FRIDAY AFTERNOON Duncan walked out of the offices of Central Florida Software, Inc. The meeting had gone as well as could be expected. The president of CFS was furious; he'd called Duncan a fool.

Duncan stepped into the elevator with his attorneys and absently pressed the button for the lobby.

After his realization that he needed Blythe in his life, he'd called Central Florida Software and offered them the chance to make him a new proposal. This time they'd come to the table with a sweet deal. A very sweet deal. Duncan's informant at CFS had sent word they were so confident of success they'd begun the process for a new stock issue. Capital would be needed for the purchase.

They'd offered to buy Macrocosm for a good price, with a contract retaining him as CEO for four years. They'd told him they wanted to move the company to Orlando, making the transfer as attractive and as easy as possible.

Duncan had turned the offer down. His informant had confirmed his suspicion that buyers were already lined up waiting for CFS to divide and sell Macrocosm as soon as the acquisition was complete. That would mean loss of jobs for many of Duncan's people. CFS planned to exercise their right to use the name Macrocosm—the name associated with Duncan McKeon—by assigning it to their experimental language group. This group was renowned for their numerous failures.

No matter how sweet the offer from CFS, Macrocosm was not for sale under these circumstances.

The doors opened onto the atrium of the downtown office building where CFS had their headquarters. The contingent from Atlanta walked out the towering Oz-like doors.

In the car, on the way to pick up Blythe, Duncan considered what her reaction would be. He knew without asking she would not be happy with his decision not to sell Macrocosm. She'd take it as a refusal to move to Winter Park.

He sighed, looking out the window. He hadn't mentioned the possibility of selling Macrocosm for just that reason: he didn't want Blythe to be upset if the negotiations failed. He decided to keep it that way.

THE ELEGANT SUITE was furnished with every thought to the guest's comfort and convenience. Fresh cut flowers, thick fluffy towels, immaculate appointments.

Blythe hated all of it.

While Duncan popped the cork from the champagne bottle, she wandered the room, restless, careful not to touch anything.

Duncan was right, of course. A hotel room provided them with the privacy they lacked in Winter Park. The important thing was they were here together. During the short time they'd have, Blythe would try to suppress her edginess.

When he called her name, she turned. He held out a glass of bubbly wine to her.

They sipped in silence for a moment. Blythe drank in more of the vital presence of Duncan than champagne. He was infinitely more intoxicating.

He set his empty glass on a side table, moving closer to her. She regarded him, tingling with anticipation.

Duncan gathered her into his arms and nuzzled her ear. "God, how I've missed you."

Her eyelids drifted down as she luxuriated in the male-scented heat of his body, the reassuring shelter of his embrace. She encircled his waist with her arms as he trailed light, slow kisses down her cheek. Blythe turned her head to intercept his lips.

With dizzying thoroughness, Duncan's mouth moved over hers. He framed her face with his hands. She parted her lips, offering him access. He teased her with flickered strokes of his tongue, followed by withdrawal, stroke and withdrawal. Moaning with frustration, Blythe slid her hands up under his cotton sweater and around to the smooth skin of his back. She reveled in the feel of his warm flesh against her palms. The small of his back presented a fascinating curve. How well she recalled it, accentuated by the low-riding jeans he'd worn that first morning in Atlanta.

Blythe trailed her fingertips across his flat belly. His muscles contracted reflexively.

"Witch," he growled, tightening his arms around her.

"I'm going to cast a spell on you."

"You...already have." The muscles in his abdomen tensed again as her fingertips briefly edged inside the bulging front of his jeans.

"With a magic wand like this," she breathed into his ear, "you must be a powerful sorcerer."

His smile in no way diminished the hot glitter of his eyes. Slowly he advanced toward her. Staying just out of his reach, Blythe retreated, step by step, mesmerized by the bold promise she read in his face. When she backed up against the bed, she stopped, her gaze still locked with his.

"I'll be happy to demonstrate my magic," he drawled. He took hold of the ribbing at the bottom of his sweater. "I'm working on a new love charm." The black knit landed on the seat of a Louis XV chair. He dispensed with his shoes and socks.

Duncan propped his hands on his hips. The glow of the table lamp cast his face into angles of light and dark, and gave shaded definition to the muscles of his arms, chest and abdomen.

Blythe knew beyond doubt she loved him, and the only magic involved was what they created together.

Sensing the change in her mood, Duncan drew her down on the bed, and came down next to her, half lying on his side. He gazed at her for a moment. "I find you in my thoughts more each day," he murmured.

When he traced the line of her jaw with his knuckles all her senses centered on that delicate touch. It would have soothed a butterfly. Blythe covered his hand with hers, holding it in place as she closed her eyes and focused on the warmth of his touch. She turned his hand to press a lingering kiss into his palm. Then she dipped her head and kissed him again, this time touching him with the tip of her tongue.

He stood and drew her up with him. They helped each other shed their clothing. He swept her to the bed.

Duncan burned for Blythe. Her slightest gesture became, for him, inflammatory provocation. She possessed the secret of fire and now sent it searing through his veins.

He touched her breast, felt her nipple harden against his palm. He suckled, and skillfully worked the turgid tip between his teeth until she brought her legs up to hug his hips.

Blythe whispered encouragement to him. He captured her mouth, sending sparks through her.

Duncan ignited. When he fought for the control to enter her slowly, she thrust her hips up, urging him deeper.

He groaned heavily. "So hot. So ready for me."

He stroked into her, hard and full, and in her frenzy she raked him with her nails. They were slippery with their mingled sweat, and the steamy room echoed with their hoarse panting and wordless mating noises.

She had to know him, had to feel him, taste him, claim him. She wanted to absorb him into her being, down to the smallest atom. She wanted all of him.

Duncan couldn't get enough of her. Nothing had ever been this good. Warm, and tight, and creamy, her body welcomed him, enfolded him, shared with him. His thrusts lifted her up the bed.

Blythe arched, crying out.

Duncan believed Blythe was most beautiful like this, her face rapt, her breasts swollen and rosy. He felt her convulse around him, wrenching him over the brink. He froze, locked in the exquisite agony of unrivaled pleasure.

Through the sparkling haze, Blythe saw Duncan's face spasm. She felt his gleaming body tighten and shudder.

Seconds melted into minutes as their breathing gradually slowed. Blythe floated in sweet contentment, luxuriating in Duncan's nearness, his masculine warmth. He moved to lie on his side, behind her, drawing her up against him, one strong arm curled around her waist.

"Mmm." She snuggled closer.

Duncan nuzzled her hair, planting a soft kiss at the curve of her jaw. "I want this for us," he murmured. "I want this closeness to become a regular part of our lives."

She wondered what it would be like for them to share more than the odd weekend. Cautiously she turned the idea over in her mind, examining it. It appealed to her so strongly she thrust it away. Wisdom dictated they be satisfied with occasional moments such as these. The idea of a more complete relationship was fantasy. She sighed. Everyone was entitled to a fantasy.

As if he had read her mind, Duncan said, "We could see each other all the time if you lived in Atlanta." He kissed the back of her ear.

Blythe stiffened, dreading the argument that was sure to follow. "Yes, but I live in Winter Park."

"In Atlanta there's more potential for the kind of business you want to develop."

"I don't doubt that for a minute, Duncan, but I have obligations here. Under the circumstances, it's impossible for me to even consider moving." *Here it comes,* she thought unhappily.

"Just think about it," he said.

Blythe frowned, waiting for him to continue. But he seemed inclined to drop the subject and after a few seconds, she relaxed.

A knock on the door broke the brief silence.

"Who could that be?" Blythe asked uneasily.

Duncan lifted his arm from around her and glanced at his watch. "Room service, I think."

She struggled up, clutching the sheet. "Room service? Oh, no!" Hastily she scooted out of the bed and, wrapped in the sheet, fled to the bathroom. She locked the door behind her.

Inside, Blythe listened at the door, hot-faced. She told herself again that taking a hotel room seemed to be the only way Duncan and she could obtain a portion of privacy, but the rationale didn't relieve her disquiet.

When she was certain the server had left, she emerged.

Duncan, now wearing a midnight blue velour robe, stood with his back to her, facing the set table. He turned to face her, his gaze caressing the length of her body.

"You're beautiful," he said softly. He smiled and held out his hand. "I thought you might be hungry."

Blythe adjusted her sheet, pulling it more tightly around her, and crossed the room to the table. He pulled out her chair for her. There, at her place, was a delicate white orchid. This was not a gesture from the hotel, she knew. The flower was too exquisite.

She cupped it in her hands, studying the perfection of its petals. The bloom was the embodiment of romance. Lovely, captivating and short-lived. Madeline had always received flowers from her men, though they had usually taken the form of roses. Madeline had pressed them. The dried flowers had lasted longer than her marriages.

Duncan watched with sick helplessness as she withdrew from him. *Don't leave me, Blythe. Not again!* Desperate to close the abysmal distance, he took her into his arms and covered her lips with his, employing all his skill, pouring into that single kiss the depth of his feelings for her.

Finally he lifted his head and searched her face. He found confusion there, question.

"Duncan?"

"I love you, Blythe," he whispered urgently. "I love you." He held her closer and rested his jaw against her temple, recording in his mind forever the softness of her.

Now was the time to reassure her. She had his trust. If she knew that, perhaps those damnable moments of distance would cease.

Blythe could sense the underlying tension in Duncan, but she couldn't explain it. His mind-reeling kiss distracted her from her concern.

He drew away, enough for her to look up at him. She couldn't read his expression. When he spoke, his words fell on her like drops of acid.

"I know about the fraud."

CHAPTER FOURTEEN

ICY CHILL flooded through her body, driving out the warmth, numbing her. How had he heard? What did he know? It sickened her to think he'd discussed it with someone in her absence. Betrayed faith and youthful ignorance had been responsible for soiling her reputation, a priceless treasure. She had worked hard to restore her good name in the following years. It seemed she had not been successful.

She pulled away from him, needing the distance to cope with her despair.

He seemed unwilling to let her go, his arms resisting at first, then slowly releasing her. "It doesn't matter to me," he said.

"Doesn't it?" She rubbed her hands up and down her arms, chilled to the depths of her soul. Both friends and strangers had spurned her in those dark days. "What went through your mind when you learned I'd been accused of fraud?"

She found her answer on his face.

Pain washed through her. "You thought I was guilty, didn't you?"

Dark color washed the high planes of his cheeks. "I—"

Abruptly Blythe began gathering her clothes, jerking them on.

Out. She had to get out, away from here. Blood pounded in her head. She wanted to find a private place, a place to scream, to tear her hair, and beat her head against the wall for her stupidity. A place where no one could witness her hurt.

In three strides, Duncan crossed the room. She turned her back on him, continuing to dress.

"It caught me off guard," he said. "Damn it, stop and give me a chance to explain."

From the corner of her eye she could see his fists clench, open and clench again. He laid his hands on her shoulders. She tried to shrug them off but his grip was firm as he turned her to face him.

Blythe stared at the base of his throat. She remembered its taste, its warmth. Resolutely she forced that thought aside, and refused to meet his eyes.

"Look at me." There was a peculiar edge to Duncan's voice.

Her gaze remained fixed.

"Look at me, Blythe," he demanded raggedly. "We can't talk if you won't even look at me."

With a hard-worn expression of indifference, she complied.

"I didn't start the conversation," he said. "I didn't pry into your past. Hell, I don't care about your past—I'm more concerned about our future."

"Oh, right."

Duncan shook her slightly. "The guy dropped the story on me like a ton of bricks. It was clear he believes you were guilty."

"A lot of people believe I was guilty." She backed out of his hold, away from him. Her stomach clenched as she remembered his abrupt departure from Winter Park.

He made no move toward her. Frustration was scrawled in the tense lines of his face. "That's not the way it was," he insisted stubbornly. "I . . . might have hesitated. But I know you could never cheat your clients."

"You went back to Georgia. Was that your statement of faith?"

Slowly, as if he was afraid she'd take flight, Duncan walked toward her. Gently he framed her face with his hands. He met her accusing stare. "No," he said softly.

Blythe tried to plumb the gray depths of his even gaze, searching for truth. She drew a long, unsteady breath. "Then why did you leave like that?"

He dropped his hands to his sides. "At first I thought guilt might explain the way you keep a part of yourself from me." His sharp laugh echoed with pain. "God, I *hoped* it was guilt. Then I realized you're incapable of dishonesty. You're too scrupulous. You care about your clients. Which left me back at square one. Why do you withdraw when we're together?"

Startled, she glanced up at him. Withdraw? Immediately she sat down on the love seat.

"You're not sure of me, are you?" Torment rang in his raw voice. "You have moments of such doubt *you run from me.*" His eyes silently pleaded for an answer. "I've given you everything I've got to give, Blythe, but it doesn't seem to be enough. I don't know what else to do."

She searched his face, looking for answers, but all she found were questions. When had she turned into herself, away from Duncan?

Quiet smothered the suite like a wool blanket on a humid summer's day. Outside in the hall, children shrieked and giggled, the sound of their merriment fading as they passed.

Blythe combed her memory for evidence of her withdrawal, absently lifting the orchid to her nose. A faint, sweet fragrance lingered, evidence the flower was freshly cut.

The roses her mother had received held no scent. The only dimension of their beauty had been visual. Like Madeline's marriages. Like romance. All had withered.

Hands gripped her upper arms, shook her once. "Damn you, stop that!" The anguish behind Duncan's words pierced her thoughts like an ice pick. She focused her eyes. He was down on one knee in front of her, his face level with hers. When had he crossed the room?

I've given you everything I've got to give. It doesn't seem to be enough. Realization dawned slowly. Duncan said he'd been trying hard to please her. What did men believe women liked? Intimate dinners for two. Flowers. The answer clicked into place. *Romance.* The harder Duncan tried to please her, the more romantic his gestures, the more alarmed she became.

She smoothed an errant lock of black hair from his forehead. "Duncan, I never meant to hurt you. All this time... I didn't know I was hiding."

He studied her face. "Why? Why are you hiding from me? I love you. Can't you believe that?"

She opened her mouth to tell him, and stopped, surprised. The things he did to please her—she liked them. They made her feel special, and she found, more than anything, she wanted to be special to Duncan.

"I believe you," she told him. Blythe framed his beloved face with her hands.

Duncan kissed her, tentatively at first, then with growing hunger. Quickly he helped her off with her clothes, and dropped his robe to the carpet.

They made love with a new tenderness that haunted Blythe afterward, as Duncan held her in his sleep. There was still the matter of her own doubt. She was a coward, pure and simple, and she knew it. Blythe also knew if she couldn't overcome her fear, the loss would be immeasurable.

SATURDAY AFTERNOON, they left the room to explore the hotel grounds, but Duncan devoted himself to filling his senses with Blythe.

Even in a simple dress, with her hair pulled back into that bun, he found her irresistible. She radiated an energy equal to her physical beauty. He'd seen her in action. He knew she was sharp. She'd excel at whatever she undertook, including sitting at the head of a boardroom table. His eyes drifted down to her mouth and he was immediately flooded with erotic memories. Blythe was a woman of many talents.

Boardroom and bedroom.

Before he could examine that startling thought, Blythe asked, "Would you like to walk around the lake?"

"Certainly." He swept out his arm in a courtly gesture.

They made their way to the lakeside promenade. Small individual gardens dotted the landscape, offering benches where passersby could sit to soak up the sun and the serenity. A black swan caught his attention as it glided through the water, sending widening ripples in its stately wake.

"This is lovely," he murmured.

Blythe sighed contentedly. "Yes, it is lovely." She regarded him from the corners of her eyes. "*Florida* is lovely." He slowly turned his head to look at her, and she batted her eyelashes at him.

"Atlanta is, too," he replied.

Yes, it was, she thought, wishing some magic would change Duncan's mind and make him fall in love with Winter Park, make him choose it as she had.

They walked in silence for a while, yet Duncan did not feel their quiet was strained. It was...he searched for the word... it was *comfortable*.

That surprised him. Comfortable was not a description he would have applied to his past romantic relationships. Tense, sexual, brief—these were the words he would have chosen had he ever sought to analyze his previous alliances. He welcomed the ease he felt with Blythe. There was too little calm in his life. Most of his hours were filled with the concerns of Macrocosm.

But was that still necessary? He thought about it a minute, turning this new concept over in his mind as he walked side by side with Blythe around the picturesque little lake.

For the past ten years he had devoted his time and all his resources to nurturing his enterprise. Now... now Macrocosm was no longer an infant. It had reached maturity. And so he had another new concept to examine.

"Oh, look." Blythe directed his attention to a duck followed by five down-covered ducklings. The six of them marched from the grass, across the walk and into the lake, where they formed a small flotilla. "Aren't they precious?"

Duncan smiled. They were cute; a little awkward, still learning how to move. He tried to remember the last time he'd noticed anything so young. Or anything not directly related to business. Was he missing so much? Was life slipping through his fingers?

Suddenly he wanted to stop and draw Blythe into his arms, to hold her. Just hold her. He wanted to feel the silk of her hair against his cheek and smell the clean sweetness of her. He needed the reassurance of her return embrace.

But something held him back, an unexpected uncertainty he found distressing. He settled for twining his fingers through hers, absorbing the warmth of her skin.

She smiled at him, and gave his hand a reassuring little squeeze. The ache inside him faded.

Blythe broke the silence. "It looks like the paddleboats are all rented." She looked up at him, smiling, her eyes reflecting her pleasure in the day.

He looked at the empty little marina. "We'll come back sometime," he murmured, and drew her fingers to his lips.

A squealing bundle of honey curls and blue eyes burst from a garden and trundled into them. The toddler, unsure on his legs, sat down abruptly, and gazed, surprised, up into their faces. Suddenly an enormous grin opened up, pebbled with tiny baby teeth. He bubbled laughter, waving his pudgy arms, inviting their smiles, confident of his power to enchant. A thread of drool dribbled from his pink mouth, but he crinkled his eyes and chirruped, unconcerned with social graces.

"Christopher," called a young mother pushing an infant in a stroller. She caught up with her errant offspring. "Christopher, you've got to watch out," she scolded, picking her son up and settling him on her hip. Christopher appeared not at all repentant.

"I am sorry," his mother apologized. "Sometimes it's hard to keep up with him. This stroller slows me down." She grinned and planted an adoring kiss on her child's forehead. "I think he knows just when to make a break for it."

"He's beautiful," Blythe said, offering Christopher her finger. He grasped it in his small fist. He frowned slightly at the peach-tinted nail and promptly stuck it in his mouth.

"Oh, no!" The younger woman quickly extricated Blythe's wet finger. "He bites," she explained. "He's going through that stage, you know? Sorry if we disturbed you."

Christopher waved goodbye with both arms as he was carried away.

Chuckling, Duncan glanced at Blythe—and froze.

Raw yearning etched her face as she stared after the baby. Naked longing shimmered in her eyes. She swallowed hard. The corners of her mouth trembled.

And then it was gone. That maternal need was no longer visible.

But he knew it was still there, buried within her. And it hurt to think she wouldn't share with him something so important to her.

They resumed their stroll, but Duncan's mind refused to relinquish what he'd seen so clearly in Blythe's face.

Why hadn't she told him she wanted children? Was he just expected to *know?* Maybe she didn't think such things were important to him. Maybe she didn't trust him enough to tell him.

Revelation slowly flooded in. Maybe she didn't think there was any purpose in telling him. Children needed security. They deserved a foundation based on bedrock.

Marriage.

That was another subject Blythe and he had never discussed. In honesty, marriage had never occurred to him. He'd always been married to Macrocosm.

As they walked, Duncan examined how the patterns of his life were changing.

"Well, I guess we'd better go back. You have a plane to catch," Blythe said.

They checked out of the hotel, and drove to the airport.

After taking his suit bag from the trunk, Duncan turned to face Blythe. He touched his fingertips to her temple, pretending to smooth back her immaculate hair. "I'll call you when I get home." He kissed her deeply, tenderly, and found a measure of reassurance in the fullness of her response.

"I'll miss you," she breathed.

Truth wrenched at him. "I'll miss you, too."

THE THOUGHT OF PACKING up and slipping away—*far away*— was beginning to hold appeal for Blythe. In the week since Martin Chasen had canceled their meeting, two more investors had called to close their accounts; fortunately, small ones. She had written and called her ex-clients, trying to learn their reasons for pulling their accounts. Not one of them had answered her letters. None would talk to her on the telephone. And Martin Chasen remained "unavailable."

Ginny's obtaining her license should have been a ray of sunlight through the gloom, but Blythe wasn't sure there would be any business to bring her friend into if things continued as they were.

Then there was Fiona. She'd shut Blythe out, refusing to speak to her except when absolutely necessary, and then only in monosyllables.

Ginny appeared in her doorway. "Orange. I need orange!" Ginny brought the back of her hand to her forehead in a theatrical gesture. "I'll not go over another file until I have an orange soda."

Blythe straightened. "You had a soda only this morning," she told her new partner with mock sternness. "It's only 9:00 p.m. and you already want another one. Pass a few lousy little tests and you turn into a sloth."

"Ha!"

Grinning, Blythe opened her hand to reveal six quarters. "My treat."

They walked into the employee lounge and got their drinks.

"How is Fiona, these days? Has she seen her baby on the sonogram, yet?" Ginny regarded Blythe evenly.

"I don't know. I'd like to think she has sense enough to be going in for checkups, but I hardly see her anymore. She always manages to be in the part of the house where I'm not." Frustration nagged Blythe, and a wistful ache. Fiona rarely spoke to her these days. Things hadn't been the same since that evening they'd argued. The only bright spot had come on the telephone bill: two lengthy calls to a number Blythe recognized as Ethan Dodd's. Fiona had mentioned neither.

"She's how far along now? Six months?"

Blythe nodded, and took a large, sweet swallow. "Just."

Ginny slowly shook her head. "That girl needs a good kick in the butt if she's not seeing a doctor."

"I won't argue that," Blythe said, heading toward the door.

They walked back to Ginny's office. "It's tough, going through that alone," Ginny observed.

Blythe looked at her friend. "She's not alone. I'm there for her—if she'd let me be."

Ginny smiled and patted Blythe's back. "I know you've done your best. But this is a time when a woman needs her man."

Her choice, Blythe thought.

"Speaking of men, that Duncan of yours is really something." Ginny rolled her eyes as she whistled, and shook her hand loosely from the wrist. "Hot stuff."

Blythe found herself smiling. "Yeah, he is, isn't he?" She knew just how hot he could be.

"What are you going to do about him?"

The smile vanished. "I don't know."

Ginny fixed Blythe with an admonitory stare. "Lotta dumb women in your family."

It was a statement Blythe couldn't, in honesty, deny, and she was still thinking about it hours later as she stood looking out her bedroom window. Oak and bay trees altered by night to form eerie black silhouettes.

They had worked out a system, Duncan and she, that scheduled one weekend in Winter Park, the next in Atlanta, the following weekend in Winter Park and so on. But for how long would they be able to keep up a long-distance relationship?

Duncan. The thought of him warmed her as nothing else could. What was she afraid of? But deep in her heart she knew. Risk. The pain of being left behind again.

Emotion filled Blythe, closing her throat, stinging her eyes. She could expect Duncan to be patient for only so long. And her time was nearly up, she could sense it. Who could blame him? He had proven himself trustworthy again and again.

Truth trickled across her consciousness, and she grasped at it, recognizing it. She wasn't afraid Duncan would be like her mother's husbands. That wasn't the heavy anxiety chafing her soul.

She was afraid she'd be like her mother. That she, Blythe Kay Summers, would be unworthy of trust—and that when Duncan discovered it, he would reject her.

Blythe walked to the armoire, opened the door and examined her reflection in the full-length mirror.

She was a different person than her mother. Eyes, hair, stature—distinctly different.

They were different inside, too. Madeline was not afraid to take risks.

Fiona. Blythe had never realized how alike she and her sister were. Both of them were looking for the sure thing.

Blythe chided herself for having been blind. Her investment experience had taught her what she needed to know: the greater the risk, the greater the possible return. No risk, no return.

Unlike Fiona, Blythe wasn't willing to stand by and lose an exceptional man because she couldn't bring herself to take a risk. And if what she and Duncan had didn't last forever—well, nothing in this life was certain.

Slowly Blythe closed the armoire door. She'd lived too long with the past. Tomorrow she would see to her future.

DUNCAN NODDED a short greeting to the portly matron passing in the hall as he unlocked his condo door. He hefted Blythe's suit bag. "Good evening, Mrs. Farnham."

The older woman eyed the suit bag and sniffed. "Good evening, Mr. McKeon," she answered stiffly, and lumbered past, heading toward the elevator.

"She makes me feel like a scarlet woman," Blythe muttered as Duncan ushered her into his home.

He grinned at her and closed the door. "That's fine by me. You can be Scarlett, and I'll be Rhett." He dumped her luggage and took her into his arms, holding her close. "Let's play Atlanta burning." He nuzzled her ear. "Mmm, darlin', I can feel the flames now."

Before she could answer, he covered her mouth with his in a rough, hungry kiss.

There was only now, only this moment mattered, thought Blythe hazily. The future was yet to unfold. She would show Duncan, and make him believe.

She cupped the back of his head, lacing her fingers through his hair, and deepening the kiss, opened to him. His tongue aggressively moved in, touching, stroking, reclaiming its territory.

After a moment, Duncan drew back slightly and studied her face, his expression unreadable. "This was my week to go to Florida. Why did you decide to come to Atlanta instead? Tell me now, while I'm still coherent."

She kissed him, hoping to postpone the conversation, to delay it until after he'd had time to see for himself. Under her coaxing, his sensual mouth, usually so responsive, remained still.

"It's better to learn for yourself. Later. Later, Duncan." The last was almost a plea as she tunneled her arms under his tweed jacket to clasp around his waist.

He stayed her arms with his. "I don't like surprises. I prefer you tell me now."

She reluctantly met his gaze.

He sensed her nervousness, and it triggered his. In the course of silent seconds, Duncan felt as if he lived three lifetimes. Whatever she had to say was important enough for her to fly to Atlanta. Was she there for the kiss off? To try to let him down gently?

Blythe drew a deep breath and let it out again. It had seemed such a good idea, yesterday, but suddenly it was embarrassing. What if he didn't care anymore? Her throat tightened, remembering the things they'd just shared. What if he no longer saw it as sharing, but rather as a service?

She met his gaze. "I—I've done some thinking. A lot of thinking." Blythe felt her courage deserting her. "I love you, Duncan, and I don't want to lose you," she blurted. "It's not guilt that made me withdraw, it was the past . . . hurt. I'll work to overcome it." His continued stillness terrified her. "I mean, I think I've settled things in my mind now. Anything . . . just . . . You're precious to me," she ended haltingly.

When had he become so dear she was willing to remove her armor? It was too late to seek safety now. Her words could not be taken back.

Wood-smoke eyes stared at her. Then, a slow, beatific smile transformed Duncan's face. He laughed and hugged her. "My God, woman, you had me scared."

"*You* scared? What were you afraid of?" It seemed incredible this strong, vital man could fear anything she could do. Relief rushed through her, leaving her weak and trembling.

He pulled the pins from her hair, and nuzzled the gilded-silver tumble. "I thought you'd come to say goodbye," he said quietly.

Something inside her melted at his words, and resurrected stronger than before.

He gently twisted his hand in her hair and lowered his face close to hers. "I love you," he told her, his words a low rumble. "Have no doubt of that. And now I know you're mine." He bent his face closer. "Mine."

Duncan took her mouth with a fierce possessiveness that left no question of his feelings in Blythe's mind.

Blythe felt the turgid mass of him through the front of his corduroy jeans as he pressed against her. His immediate, strong reaction to her satisfied and excited her in a way distinctly feminine; a realization of power. She lowered one hand, and with one lacquered fingernail traced the outline of him through the corduroy. She breathed into his ear, "I'll never be hungry again."

With a groan, deep in his chest, Duncan fell upon the buttons of her raw silk jumpsuit, swearing under his breath, fingers flying. She caught the hem of his sweater and ripped it up over his head, then attacked the fastenings of his jeans. Socks and panty hose went flying, shoes scattered.

He pulled her down on the foyer carpet, and poised over her. The sound of their harsh, shallow breathing echoed and charged the air with primal electricity.

Duncan applied lips and tongue, and worshipful hands, until every nerve, every fiber in her body sang shrill with need.

"I was afraid the excitement would lessen, the longer we were lovers," he murmured. "But it hasn't. It keeps getting better." He slid slowly into her. "And better."

Through heavy-lidded eyes, Blythe watched Duncan's face. It was tight, contained. She knew he reached for control for her sake, and she wanted none of it. She couldn't wait to feel his friction. Boldly she thrust up to meet him. "And better."

His heavy, deep strokes propelled her where she wanted to go, and Duncan followed.

"*UNNG.*"

Blythe was reluctant to disturb the blissful peace in which she floated. She compromised by snuggling closer, back into Duncan.

He groaned again. "Have mercy. Isn't ten times enough for you?"

She laughed and turned to face him. "Ten times? I could have sworn it was only—"

"Ten," he said firmly, and lightly tugged a lock of her hair. "At least."

"My suit bag is still downstairs," she pointed out.

He stroked her hip. "Good place for it. You don't need it anyway. You're perfect as you are, all warm, and soft, and rosy. You belong in my bed, it agrees with you."

"Your *bed* isn't what agrees with me."

He smiled smugly.

"What if I get up to make coffee?"

"That's allowed."

Blythe climbed out of bed and reached for the closest robe—Duncan's.

"You look good in my robe," he said with a friendly leer, "but you look better naked."

"You sweet talker, you." She picked up a pillow and dropped it on his head, then darted out of the bedroom as he surged up to grab her.

Duncan caught a glimpse of thigh as Blythe flashed out the door. That expanse of woman-soft skin was quite sensitive, he remembered fondly.

He got out of bed and padded into the bathroom where he showered and shaved. Quickly he pulled on a pair of jeans and went down to the kitchen.

The wonderful fragrance of food teased his nostrils. He found Blythe checking something in the oven and leaned over to kiss the back of her neck. "Smells great. You didn't have to do this, you know. I was going to take you out to eat." He nuzzled her nape. "But this is much nicer."

She turned and wrapped her arms around his waist. "I'm going to run upstairs and get dressed. Pour yourself some coffee. If the timer goes off, take the blintzes out of the oven."

"Blintzes? Where did you get the stuff for blintzes?" He knew his refrigerator's contents were meager.

"I brought everything." She grinned and pointed to the red thermal bag sitting on the counter. "I got up, last night, and put everything in the fridge."

"I love blintzes."

"I know. Martha told me."

He sniffed deeply. "Cinnamon."

Blythe smiled. "And toasted almonds."

Duncan pulled her into his arms and kissed her quickly and firmly on her mouth. "Go get dressed. I'll just sit here, drinking coffee and counting the minutes until the timer goes off."

He watched her stride briskly from the kitchen, and heard her climb the stairs, then he went to the coffee-maker and poured a cup.

She had gone to considerable trouble to make his favorite breakfast. It had been years since he'd had blintzes. They were a treat Eula had made for him on special occasions. He associated the dish with birthdays and good report cards.

Duncan sipped his coffee. *Mmm.* The coffee was unusually rich. Blythe had even seen to that detail. There was something warmly intimate about a woman fixing a man's favorite breakfast after a night of passionate lovemaking.

And they had done just that—made love. After Blythe's halting declaration last evening, Duncan had soared. He'd tried to share with her what he was feeling. And what he'd received in return left him profoundly moved.

Duncan was startled when the timer went off. He set his full cup of cool coffee on the table and opened the oven door. A mouth-watering aroma rolled up to engulf him in a cloud of heat.

"Just made it, I see," Blythe announced as she entered the room, now clad in corduroy jeans and a turtleneck pullover.

A few minutes later, she set two plates of blintzes and freshly chopped Delicious apples on the table. When both of them were seated, Duncan eagerly took a bite. He rolled his eyes in blissful enjoyment.

Blythe grinned. "You like?"

Duncan swallowed. "I like." He grinned back at her. "Definitely."

When they had eaten every bit of breakfast, they cleared the table. Duncan rinsed the dishes and Blythe arranged them in the dishwasher.

He found he enjoyed sharing this moment of domesticity with Blythe. His mornings were usually so solitary. He never ate breakfast, except for the occasional scrambled egg or bowl of cold cereal. Passing wet dishes to a beautiful woman was infinitely more enjoyable.

A man could get used to this.

After they finished with the kitchen, they divided the newspaper and found comfortable spots in which to sprawl.

Duncan pointed to a stock in the New York Stock Exchange listing. "What do you know about this?"

Blythe came over to him and looked where he pointed. "Not much, I'm afraid. It's not one of the stocks I regularly cover. They have a lot of debt. Who would you be buying it for? Your aunts? I think you could do better."

"Why do you ask if it's my aunts?"

She lifted his finger, uncovering the minute abbreviation "pf." "Because it's a preferred stock."

"I didn't see that."

"Better dividends than common, but usually not as much potential for growth. Depends on the market."

"Nope. Preferred stock isn't me. I'm just plain old common stock."

Blythe smiled. "More like *un*common stock. There's nothing common about you."

He grinned. "You only say that because it's true."

As they went back to their reading, quiet settled back in place, disturbed only by the occasional rustle of a turning page. Yes. A man could certainly get used to this.

"Duncan, who told you about my...about my fraud charges?"

He looked up. "One of my aunts' bridge-playing friends."

"Do you remember her name?"

"Philip..." What *was* that guy's last name? It had rhymed with crock, appropriately enough. Lock? Bock? "Bock. No...Brock. Philip Brock."

A startled expression passed over Blythe's face. "Brock. Are you sure?"

He thought about it. "Yeah. I'm sure. But I can ask my aunts if you want. They could tell me."

"He plays bridge with them?"

"Yeah."

Frowning, she turned back to her paper.

"What about him, Blythe?" Duncan asked, unwilling to let the subject drop. He was missing a part here, and it bothered him.

"There's a broker in my office who gloats every time I lose an account. He's never forgiven me for getting the office he wanted. His name is Leonard Brock. I wonder if they're related."

Duncan realized he was crushing the paper in his hands, and loosened his grip. If he had been used... Abruptly he relinquished that thought. It was over. Blythe would tell him the details of her past if or when she chose. He knew she was innocent. That was enough. Still, he filed the name of Leonard Brock in his memory.

''We should be doing something,'' he objected halfheartedly after they had read in companionable silence for about an hour. ''What about a museum?''

''I'm going to the Orlando Museum of Art with Martha and Amelia, next week, to see the samurai arms and armor exhibit.''

''Okay, then, what about Central City Park? I want you to get to know Atlanta better.''

''We've been there. Besides, I'd rather get to know Duncan McKeon better.'' She attempted a leer, but that delectable mouth was incapable of looking anything but tempting. Her eyes, however, conveyed her message clearly.

Duncan felt his body harden in response. ''I'd really like you to get to know Atlanta better,'' he persisted faintly.

Blythe left her chair and walked across the living room to where he sat in front of the picture window. The smile of Eve touched her lips as she held out her hand to him. ''I'm more interested in one particular resident of Atlanta.''

AFTER PORING OVER her client book all afternoon, Blythe went to the employee lounge for a soda.

Steven Howard sat alone, hunched over a soft drink can at one of the small tables, chain-smoking.

She went to the vending machine and selected a diet cola. ''What's up?'' she asked. ''How can a man with a brand-new Mercedes look so miserable?''

''I won't be able to keep it,'' Steve lamented.

''Why not? I thought you said there was a new issue on the horizon.'' Blythe and everyone in the office acknowledged Steve as the new stock issues expert.

"I got word today it's a no-go." He took off his glasses and began cleaning them with a handkerchief. "I don't understand it. Central Florida Software made a beauty of an offer. A good price, a contract for the present owner to stay on as chief executive officer for four years at a princely salary, plus bonuses. The strategy was to move the acquisition to Orlando."

Blythe took a sip of her cola. "Sounds like inside information to me, Steve."

He shifted in his chair and rubbed the lenses harder. "Yeah, well. I didn't take any action on it—other than to count my chickens before they hatched—and I didn't tell anyone about it until the deal was dead. No one expected the guy to turn down such a cream puff offer!"

She sympathized with Steve. Clearly he'd expected to sell a lot of the stock that would have been issued to raise capital for CFS. "It does sound like a great proposition. Who is the dummy?"

Steve slid his glasses back on. "The CEO of Macrocosm. Duncan McKeon."

CHAPTER FIFTEEN

THE HARSH ILLUMINATION from the overhead lights failed to flush out the gloom lurking in the far reaches of the garage. Duncan locked his car and headed toward the elevator that would take him to his condominium. His footsteps echoed in the concrete cavern.

God, he was tired. He really did need to start delegating more work. The days when he made every decision were definitely gone. It was time to start giving his staff more authority.

A taxi pulled in and stopped. The back passenger door opened. Blythe got out.

Duncan's delight at seeing her pierced his fatigue. "Blythe! Darlin', this is a great—" The expression on her face froze him. "What's wrong?"

The taxi driver refused to wait, so Blythe paid him, too angry to worry about the return trip to the airport. As he drove away, the sound of his engine reverberated against the walls of the garage like the roar of a war machine. After the echoes from the taxi faded, tomblike silence descended.

She walked forward until only a few feet separated them. "Is it true?" Her voice rang hollow against the concrete walls and pillars.

Wariness and dread filled him. "Is what true?"

Silence pulsed with the anguish that churned through Blythe's heart. During the time it had taken to get from Winter Park to this garage her hurt had crystallized, fragmenting into fury. Now it grated along her nerves, squeezing the air from her lungs.

She wanted him to say he hadn't turned down a wonderful offer so he wouldn't have to move to her town. She wanted his reassurance they had a future together. But she wasn't certain she'd believe him anymore, even if he spoke the words she wanted to hear more than anything. His action had been too articulate.

Desperately she tried to sort through her thoughts, knowing how much depended on her question, and ultimately, his answer.

She moistened her dry lips with the tip of her tongue. "I need to know..." She swallowed. "What do I mean to you?"

Duncan stared at her for a moment. "What's this all about, Blythe?" he asked quietly. His words murmured through the garage like a subterranean river.

"Why didn't you tell me CFS offered to buy Macrocosm? That they made a remarkably generous offer?"

"It was business."

"Business."

"That's right," he said firmly.

"We've discussed business before. In fact, we've discussed your business and mine several times. Suddenly it's a taboo subject?" She took a step toward him. "Come on, Duncan," she challenged. "You can do better than that."

The skin over his prominent cheekbones tightened. "It was *just business.*"

"You made a decision that affected *us* and you didn't bother even to mention it to me. Why?"

"Because of this." His arm swept out to encompass the whole scene. "I knew you'd make a big deal out of it, and you didn't disappoint me, Blythe."

"I can't help but think there's more to it than that. I thought we *trusted* each other. Or was that one-sided?"

He scowled.

"What happened to all this honesty you believe in, Duncan? Does that only apply to other people. You're not bound by the same rules? My God," she exclaimed softly. "That last Friday in Winter Park when you picked me up. You were coming from the meeting with CFS, weren't you? You knew then…and you said nothing to me."

"It was a business decision. I knew you'd take it personally, so I decided not to say anything." He slashed the air with his open hand. "That's *all*. You're making too much of this."

Alarmed, Duncan watched her wide eyes fill. He could take her anger. That he could cope with. Tears were new between them. Her hurt, so visible now, tore at him. He moved toward her.

She backed away, shaking her head. "You had the opportunity to move to Winter Park. No more hopping a plane every weekend." Angrily she dashed away her tears. "All I want to know is why you turned the deal down—the *true* reason. Was it because you don't want to move to my territory? Because you really don't want our relationship to get any more serious than it is now? Or should I *trust* the reason you've given, even though you hid everything from me?"

He plowed his fingers through his hair. "I have a habit of telling the truth."

"Or withholding it."

He fastened his gaze on hers. "It was a done deal. One I suspected you'd take exception to. Damn it, I couldn't see any need to rake over the matter. There was no other decision I could have made. CFS wanted to take Macrocosm in a direction I opposed. My signing that contract would have given them the right to do so. If you want details, I'll give you details. It was never my intention to hurt you."

In her eyes he could see the shadow of internal struggle. He took advantage of it and took a step closer toward her, then another, until he enfolded her in his arms. "I should have told you," he murmured into her hair.

"Yes," she mumbled. "You should have."

"But that's not the real problem, is it, darlin'?"

Blythe raised her head and searched his face. Then she sighed heavily, accepting the truth of what he said. "No, it isn't."

"Why don't we go upstairs and talk it over?"

She sighed again, softly. "All right."

They rode the elevator in silence. As she stood next to Duncan while he unlocked his door, Blythe tried to fight off the foggy depression that settled over her. This discussion had been a long time coming. It was no longer avoidable. She'd thought she'd be prepared. She wasn't.

Duncan went directly to the kitchen and, to Blythe's surprise, took a milk carton from the refrigerator. He set about making hot chocolate via the microwave.

"What? No brandy?" she asked, a halfhearted attempt at humor.

He smiled slightly. "No. What we have to talk about requires clear minds."

She nodded, and wandered into the living room, staring out at the view. When Duncan handed her a cup of cocoa she was drawn from her memories of sweet, stirring times. Of the laughter they'd shared.

He stood behind her, close, companionable, as they sipped their steaming drinks.

"It's all about compromise, isn't it, Blythe?" he asked at last.

She nodded, moving away to lean against the back of the easy chair, needing that little distance. "Neither of us seems to be able to make it."

Duncan didn't answer. He smiled sadly.

A lump swelled in her throat. "I love you, Duncan."

He looked away and swallowed hard. He looked back at her. "How could you possibly believe I don't want more for us?"

"I was afraid."

They fell silent. The mantel clock kept time with eternity, ticking off each sonorous minute. In the distance, the thin whine of a siren warned of an emergency.

"What we have to decide is whether or not we have a future together," Duncan said evenly. "We can't go on as we are, Blythe. Planes and hotels aren't enough anymore."

Her brow crumpled and she pressed her lips together. "I know."

"I don't want to live separate from my wife."

Her eyes widened. She had hoped for this moment, but now it brought her only pain. "Oh, Duncan, please don't," she whispered. "Not now, not at this moment."

"I want so much for us, Blythe. I want children."

"That's not fair, Duncan," she cried.

His jaw muscles worked for a second. "I can't afford to be fair. Our future is at stake," he persisted softly. "Without compromise we'll lose everything we have together. Everything."

Locked in misery, Blythe couldn't deny the truth of his words. They had reached a turning point. A choice had to be made. A compromise.

Duncan set his cup down. "I want to marry you, Blythe. But I can see you obviously need time to consider. Go back to Florida. Let me know when you've made your decision."

Her vision blurred with tears. Unable to speak, Blythe wearily nodded.

BLYTHE TOSSED A MORSEL of bread into the water. An old turtle with moss growing on his back regarded her for a moment, then leisurely paddled to the floating bread and took a bite.

She leaned her forearms on the rail of her dock, and looked out over the lake behind her house. Here she could pretend all was well with her world. Here she was insulated with silence, isolated from emotion. Removed. Untouched.

But she couldn't stay in her cocoon. There were problems to be faced, a choice to be made. Regret wouldn't solve anything.

Blythe knew she had to face her situation. Her relationship with Duncan was hanging, and enough of her accounts had closed to indicate her career was in serious danger. For almost a week, now, she'd shied away from the painful prospect of coping with it all. She'd told herself she didn't care anymore. But that wasn't true, and Ginny was too new a broker to be saddled with the entire responsibility of their business. What was left of it.

Inevitably her thoughts settled on Duncan, and she imagined what life with him would be like. For a brief moment she was pierced with joy. Then reality returned to tear at her.

Compromise. She had never liked the word, and she liked it less now. For her, things were either one way or the other. Straightforward. All or nothing. To Blythe, compromise had always represented failure to achieve one's goal. Settling for less.

There had been too many failures in her life. Blythe wasn't sure she could handle another one.

At the sound of footsteps on wooden planks, Blythe turned. Fiona approached, a small ice chest cradled in her arms.

"Care for a little company?" she asked.

This was the first time Fiona had approached her since their argument. Usually their conversation was limited to a few monosyllabic words.

Afraid to hope for much, Blythe shrugged. "Sure."

"I made us lunch. Thought you might be hungry." There was a nervous edge to the brightly spoken words. Fiona looked at Blythe as if expecting an answer before proceeding.

"Thanks. I am." She was not, but Fiona was clearly trying to be friendly and Blythe didn't want to discourage her.

Fiona set the cooler down and opened it, removing two sandwiches in plastic wrap. With a tentative smile, she handed one to Blythe.

"There are apples, too," she said. "And brownies." She offered her sister a soft drink.

They ate in silence for a few minutes. Then Fiona cleared her throat.

"Blythe, I've been trying to say this for weeks." She looked down at the sandwich half she held.

Blythe waited, not knowing what to expect. Nothing was as she'd expected it to be anymore.

"I'm sorry," Fiona said.

The wood of the railing was rough under Blythe's palm. Anger, hurt and hope twisted inside her, knotting in her throat. Truth had a way of feeling like a blade against a bone. "Fiona—"

"No. I've put this off too long." Fiona walked over to her sister. "You deserve better than I've given you. I've been a bitch. I don't like myself much, for it."

Blythe stared down into the peat-colored water. Sunlight sparkled on the dorsal fins of small fish darting through the lily stalks. "That's past, now."

Fiona shook her head. "I was wrong."

Blythe looked up to meet her sister's gaze. "We were both wrong."

"Yeah." Fiona's throat closed, clipping the word short. After a moment, Fiona dug into the cooler and came up with two brownies. "I have something to tell you."

"You've been in touch with Ethan," Blythe said quietly, and took a bite of her brownie. She hadn't realized she was so hungry.

Fiona threw her a startled glance. "Yes. How—?"

Blythe smiled. "It showed up on the telephone bill."

"We're going to get married."

"That's great!" Blythe hugged her sister, delighted by the younger woman's happy grin. "When?"

"As soon as we can. A week."

"What did Mom have to say about it?"

Fiona laughed. "I haven't told her yet. I wanted you to be the first to know."

Blythe swallowed. "Thank you." Her eyes stung. Their relationship would never be the same. *They* would never be the same. Now, each had accepted responsibility for her own life, her own happiness.

EARLY THE NEXT MORNING, Blythe strode into Ginny's office and shut the door. The new broker looked up in surprise.

Blythe drew a deep breath, and let it out, steeling herself. "I've had time to think, Ginny. Hooking up with me as your partner isn't a good idea."

Ginny scowled. "Are you trying to dump me?"

"No! Don't even think that. It's just not safe for you. I don't know how, or why, but obviously my reputation has been trashed again. Yours is still fresh and clean. I think—"

"No, you aren't thinking," snapped Ginny. "I don't need a martyr, I need a partner. And you're it, lady. You're smart, you're experienced, and you're honest. You can just forget kicking me out into the cold."

"I'll give you accounts, I wouldn't let you starve—"

"Forget it, Blythe. A deal's a deal. You're my partner. I don't want anyone else, and I don't want to be on my own. I could never do better than to have you as my mentor."

"Any new accounts withdrawn this morning?" She set her jaw, expecting the worse.

"No."

"So far. Remember, I've been through this before."

Ginny nodded slowly. "Maybe you should remember I was there, too."

"Yeah . . . well. Think about what I said, okay?"

"Okay." Ginny rolled her eyes toward the ceiling. She tapped her foot twice. "Okay," she said, "I've thought about it. I haven't changed my mind."

Blythe released a heavy sigh of mingled frustration and relief. Her friend hadn't abandoned her. Against the odds she had chosen to stay. There had been no compromise.

There could be no compromise between Duncan and her, either. He had made the first move. He'd tried to reach an agreement with CFS and only certain ruin had stopped him. The ruin of a dream.

Her choice determined their future.

Ginny picked up a client folder from the pile on her desk. "What happened in the Meads' account? Was this a contested entry time?"

Together they went over questions and problems that constituted the everyday maintenance of accounts, all the while keeping an eye on the market and making the necessary calls to clients. Blythe found they worked as smoothly as the team she'd hoped they'd be.

Around noon, Leonard Brock showed up. Instead of his usual self-satisfied smile, he wore a serious expression. Blythe studied him through narrowed eyes.

"Ginny," he said, "please excuse us. I need to talk to Blythe."

Blythe and Ginny exchanged puzzled glances. This was a Leonard they'd never seen before.

He waited until Blythe walked out into the corridor. "Let's talk in your office," he suggested, surprising her. He'd never before admitted the coveted large office was hers. He'd always referred to it as his, and occupied by her only temporarily.

Once inside, he quietly closed the door. He stared at the floor for a minute, as if assembling his words, then dragged his hand through his perfectly groomed hair. Blythe had never before seen him distressed. Leonard was always so smooth, so aloof, even in his cruelty. She waited for him to speak.

He looked up and met her gaze. "I know why you're losing your accounts."

Blythe eased herself against the corner of the front of her desk, hoping she looked more collected than she felt. To her puzzlement, Leonard didn't look pleased.

"Tell me," she said.

It had been so long, she had tried so hard to uncover the reason for the defections, and now her nemesis, a man who took pleasure in baiting her, came to her with the answer. Blythe didn't doubt Leonard was telling the truth. Even he was not that malicious.

"Late yesterday, I had calls from Ada Kernfelder and Donald Hanlon."

The knot in Blythe's chest twisted, but she remained silent.

"They told me," he continued, "they play bridge with my father, who'd recommended me."

Bridge. Why was that familiar, the association of bridge and Leonard?

He walked over to the plate-glass wall, looking out at the bull pen, yet Blythe didn't think he watched the furious activity of the new brokers. As he again raked his fingers through his brown hair Blythe's anxiety increased.

"Blythe, you lost your clients because Martha Bevane and Amelia McKeon told them you'd churned their account."

The world spun around Blythe. Blindly she clutched at the edge of the desk, missed and felt herself falling. Strong hands gripped her shoulders, supporting her. Gradually her balance returned. She looked up into Leonard's eyes and found concern.

"I'm—I'm okay now," she managed to say. "Thanks."

He released her, but regarded her closely.

She swallowed hard. "Please. Go on."

"It was a mistake. An innocent mistake, I'm sure. I've seen those two in here. They're flaky, but harmless, and anyone can see they're fond of you."

"Then how...?"

"Dad said everyone was talking about investments, one evening, and the McKeon sisters related how their broker had churned their account. Then Ada Kernfelder asked, 'Who is your broker?' and the sisters said, 'Blythe Summers.'"

That's all it would take. A spark to a dry prairie. A career ruined.

Blythe looked away, her throat closing in grief. Finally she was able to ask, "Who plays bridge with Martha and Amelia, do you know?"

Leonard withdrew from his slacks pocket a folded piece of paper, which he handed to her. She opened it and read the names.

Donald Hanlon
Helen Mabry
Oren Johnson
Ada Kernfelder

Marianne Chasen
Philip Brock

Marianne Chasen. That figured. Doubtless a relative of Martin Chasen. His wife, maybe.

Blythe's eyes continued down the list until it reached the end. Philip Brock. Now she remembered. The man who'd told Duncan she'd been involved with Andrew's fraud.

She looked at Leonard. He had nothing to gain by coming to her. She imagined herself in his position. It would take courage to face another broker with the news that clients—ex-clients—believed her dishonest.

"Why are you telling me this, Leonard?" she asked quietly, swamped with the fatigue of defeat.

Color flared in his face. "I suppose you think I'm gloating," he said bitterly. "Well, I'm not. My father recommended these clients to me. He's always resented your having the largest office. He wanted me to have it. But I'm a good broker. I don't need to get business this way."

"Leonard, I believe you. I know it was hard for you to tell me people think I'm corrupt. I'm not sure I'd have had the courage, in your place."

Courage. The word struck a chord in her. Never in her life had she needed courage so badly. Did she have enough not to lose what she'd built with Duncan?

Leonard frowned slightly. "If our situations were reversed you'd have come directly to me. You always do the right thing. It's one of the reasons I admire you," he admitted grudgingly.

Blythe absorbed the shock of that statement with an uncertain smile. Leonard Brock admired her?

You always do the right thing.

"What do you plan to do now?" he asked.

"I suppose the first thing I need to do is call Martha and Amelia, and have them talk to their friends."

Leonard smiled tightly. "I guess I won't set up any new accounts for their bridge partners, then."

Blythe offered her hand and he took it. "Thank you, Leonard."

It seemed she hadn't figured the man out after all, she thought. She found she was glad.

After he left, Blythe picked up her paperweight and walked to her chair. She sat, thinking.

Things happen.

Duncan had been right. Things did seem to happen around Martha and Amelia. She recalled the way he'd arrived at her office, ready to roast the broker who had churned his aunts' account, only to find the card they'd given him was from the wrong broker.

There seems to be a perpetual line of miscommunication between my aunts and the world.

Their bridge club had unwittingly plugged into the perpetual line. She, too, had borne the brunt of their miscommunication. Twice. In his life, how many times had Duncan borne it? Too many times, she suspected.

She realized now, Duncan would never be comfortable living in Winter Park. He needed the buffering distance of Atlanta.

Blythe knew he loved his aunts. She'd seen how protective he was toward them. Martha had told her he'd visited them regularly since they'd moved to Winter Park. He was, however, entitled to his desire for self-preservation.

Ginny stuck her head through the doorway. "Well? What happened? Leonard mysteriously drags you off, and I find you sitting here, staring into space."

Blythe blinked, then recognizing her new partner, smiled. "Ginny. Just the person I wanted to talk to. Please come in and close the door."

After quietly shutting the office door Ginny took a seat. "It must be serious."

"I need perfect honesty from you," Blythe said.

Ginny examined her neatly trimmed fingernails. "I have a feeling honesty isn't going to feel so perfect."

Blythe stood and walked around to the front of her desk. She sat down in the chair next to Ginny, and caught her friend's gaze. "I want to marry Duncan."

Brown eyes flared wide. "That's wonderful!" Ginny exclaimed. "Finally you've come to your senses. When is the wedding?"

"It's not that simple."

Ginny sighed heavily. "I knew it."

"I would have to move to Atlanta."

"Uh-huh," was the new broker's noncommittal reply.

"That doesn't mean I want to dissolve our partnership. Not at all."

"Uh-huh."

"I could develop new accounts in Atlanta. There are more companies of the size I need if I'm going after retirement accounts, pension funds. You want to deal with individuals. You can do that here. About half the clients won't want to transfer their accounts to Atlanta—they like having their broker close by. Eventually, if things work out, and if you want, you can be in charge of all the individual accounts, and I'll handle the retirement funds and anything nonindividual.

"There are a couple of Stewart Duke offices in Atlanta. I'll be coming in with a client base, so I'm sure one of them will take me. We'll get Tom to set the partnership up for us so we can work in separate offices. I'll work with you before I move, and I'll be available to you by telephone, after. But only if you're satisfied with it, Ginny. You and I have a deal. We're still partners." Blythe waited for an answer.

Ginny sat quietly for long seconds, then said, "Go for it. You'd be crazy not to. I have only two conditions. Well, three." She held up three fingers. "One, I get to be the matron of honor."

Blythe grinned. "You read my mind."

"Two, you work with me before you move. I've worked with the clients for years. It's the fine points of this broker stuff that still have me a little nervous."

"Of course."

"And three, you leave immediately for Atlanta and seal the deal with Duncan!"

"Okay."

"Now, I mean *now!* And call me."

Blythe hugged Ginny tightly. "Sure thing, partner."

BLYTHE CRADLED the telephone receiver between her ear and shoulder, corralling her suit bag with her legs. "I'm at the airport, Wendy. I have a few minutes before I board. Are there any important messages—anything that won't wait until tomorrow?"

"I thought you'd already be in Atlanta by now," Wendy said. "Ginny said you said you were going to the library there. Yeah. Right."

Blythe grinned. "I'll tell you all about it when I get back. If things don't go right, I'll need to cry on your shoulder."

"I'll buy a big box of tissues. There's only one message Ginny or I can't handle. Are you ready for this?"

Blythe straightened slightly. "Okay."

"Martin Chasen wants to talk to you."

Pulse normal. Heartbeat regular. Wonder Woman was alive and well. "That so?"

"Yep. You want me to call him back for you and tell him to kiss your—"

"Not yet, Wendy. We'll try peaceful negotiations, first. Give me his number." She jotted down the number Wendy gave her.

"Have a good trip, Blythe. Have fun at the... library." Wendy chortled.

As soon as she hung up, Blythe dialed Chasen. This time Chasen's secretary was almost cordial.

"Martin Chasen, here. Thank you for calling, Blythe. I'd like to get together with you to discuss your proposal. I apologize for the delay. My daughter in Buffalo had her baby prematurely and there were some complications. My wife and I felt we needed to be there with her."

"Boy or girl?"

"A beautiful girl." Pride filled Chasen's voice.

"Is this your first grandchild?"

Chasen laughed. "No. The fifth. But each one is special."

"Do you have pictures?"

"What grandfather doesn't? I took five rolls of 'em."

"I look forward to seeing them."

They set an appointment and said goodbye. Blythe just made it to the gate, the last passenger to board.

At the airport in Atlanta she took a taxi to the main library, armed with rolls of change for the copy machine.

It was four o'clock by the time Blythe decided she had enough information on potential business in Atlanta. Her cab delivered to the building where Macrocosm was headquartered. Blythe hadn't called to say she was coming, so she knew she was taking the risk Duncan wouldn't be there.

She left her suit bag with the building's concierge and proceeded up the elevator.

The first thing she noticed in the reception area was the colorful arrangement of flowers.

"Mr. McKeon's in a meeting," the elegantly suited receptionist said. "Is he expecting you?"

Blythe smiled. "No. If you'll be kind enough to leave him the message Blythe Summers is here, I'd like to wait for him."

The receptionist made the note, then indicated the waiting area. "Please make yourself comfortable."

It was a very long hour.

When the receptionist began tidying her desk, Blythe realized it was closing time.

She returned to the lobby to claim her bag. There was no way to tell how long Duncan would be tied up in his meeting or if it was even in this building. Her coming to see Duncan, unannounced, had been a long shot that hadn't paid off.

"Is there anything else I can help you with, ma'am?" the clean-cut young man asked as he handed her luggage to her.

She could either catch a flight back to Orlando or spend the night in Atlanta and try to reach Duncan tonight.

"Yes, thank you. Can you recommend a hotel?" What she had to say to Duncan needed to be said in person.

"That won't be necessary."

At the sound of that familiar voice, Blythe turned to find Duncan standing at her shoulder. He took the suit bag from her and nodded to the concierge. "Thank you."

Silence thickened between them like ice on a pond in winter until they stepped inside Duncan's condo.

"A hotel?" he demanded. "You were going to leave me with a message you'd been to my office to see me, and go to a *hotel?*"

"I didn't know where you were or how long you'd be tied up. What was I supposed to do? Camp out in the lobby?"

"You could have come here."

"To do what? Stand around the hall until Mrs. Farnham called the police?"

"Just use your k— Oh, that's right." He looked sheepish. "We never got around to making you a key."

"No. We didn't."

He passed his hand across his face. For the first time Blythe noticed the dark smudges under his eyes.

She brushed her fingertips along the high ridge of his cheekbone. He captured her hand with his, pressing it against her face. His silver gray eyes searched her face.

There was no question in her mind. This was right. Their futures were inexorably intertwined, and she would do her best to keep them that way.

Blythe summoned her courage. "Duncan, do you think there's much potential here for new pension funds?"

He blinked. "Pension funds?"

Well, that lead-in had failed. She'd have to try the direct approach. "Do you still want to marry me?"

Duncan smiled as he took her into his arms. "Oh, yes," he murmured as he lowered his face to hers. "I need the love of an honest woman."

EPILOGUE

"HOLD ON A MINUTE, Ginny." Blythe covered the receiver with her hand and turned a fond eye on her three-year-old daughter. "Amanda, Mommy is on the telephone right now. Go find Daddy. I'll be there in a minute."

A mutinous pink bottom lip came out.

"Amanda." There was warning in the word. "Go find Daddy."

The child eyed her mother, gauging, then turned around and walked slowly—too slowly—from the office.

Blythe sighed. "Sorry, Ginny. Amanda is in a power-play phase. She tries to dominate."

Ginny laughed. "Now I wonder who she got that from?"

"Not me. I was a perfect child."

"What about Matthew?" Ginny asked, referring to Amanda's twin brother. "Is he going through the same stage?"

"Yes. I have two beautiful, intelligent, hardheaded children. Ah, but when they're good, they're like little angels."

"You should try raising three boys, sometime."

"No, thanks. I'm not feeling especially suicidal. I don't know how you do it."

Blythe thought of how far she and Ginny had come in four years. They had their own firm with an impressive roster of clients. Ginny supervised the Winter Park office of McKeon and Rodriguez, Inc., while Blythe headed the office in Atlanta. They handled personal accounts and pension funds for select investors and companies throughout North America.

"Have you heard from Fiona lately?" Ginny chuckled. "When are they going to start on their third baby?"

"I wouldn't be surprised if they haven't already. I spoke to her two weeks ago. She's trying to persuade Ethan to take an engineering position he was offered in Tampa. She wants to go back to Florida."

Duncan walked into her office holding Matthew. Like his sister, the child had auburn hair and green eyes.

"We have to get your mother and Spence to the airport or they'll miss their plane. And—" he glanced at his watch "—Martha and Amelia are due in."

Blythe nodded to Duncan. "You hear, Ginny?"

"Good grief. It sounds as if you're running Grand Central Station."

"Spence needed to do some research here for his latest story, so Mom took some vacation time. They celebrated their fourth wedding anniversary with us." Four years with one man. That was a record. "Mom and Spence spoil the kids something awful. I think they must hit every toy store in New York before they come to visit. And Martha and Amelia are just as bad."

Duncan pointed to his watch. "Give Ginny my love. Tell her to say hi to Victor for me."

"I heard," said Ginny. "Bye!"

Quickly Blythe grabbed her purse and gathered up Amanda, pressing a tender kiss to the little girl's cheek.

She smiled up at Duncan.

He leaned round Matthew to kiss her. "We are lucky, aren't we, darlin'?"

"Oh, Duncan, yes."

The reward had definitely been worth the risk.

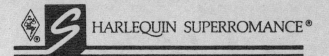

HARLEQUIN SUPERROMANCE®

COMING NEXT MONTH

AVAILABLE NOW:

*O*nce upon a time...

There was the best romance series in all the land—Temptation.

You loved the heroes of REBELS & ROGUES. Now discover the magic and fantasy of romance. Pygmalion, Cinderella and Beauty and the Beast have an enduring appeal—and are the inspiration for Temptation's exciting new yearlong miniseries, LOVERS & LEGENDS. Bestselling authors including Gina Wilkins, Glenda Sanders, JoAnn Ross and Tiffany White reweave these classic tales—with lots of sizzle! One book a month, LOVERS & LEGENDS continues in March 1993 with:

#433 THE MISSING HEIR
Leandra Logan
(Rumpelstiltskin)

Live the fantasy....

LL3

HARLEQUIN®

Temptation

**Harlequin is proud to present our
best authors, their best books and
the best for your reading pleasure!**

Throughout 1993, Harlequin will bring you
exciting books by some of the top names in
contemporary romance!

In February,
look for
Twist of Fate by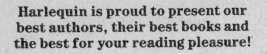

Hannah Jessett had been content with her
quiet life. Suddenly she was the center of a
corporate battle with wealthy
entrepreneur Gideon Cage. Now Hannah
must choose between the fame and money
an inheritance has brought or a love that
may not be as it appears.

Don't miss TWIST OF FATE ...
wherever Harlequin books are sold.

BOB1

Where do you find hot Texas nights, smooth Texas charm and dangerously sexy cowboys?

DEEP IN THE HEART

Wedding Bells—Texas Style!

Even a Boston blue blood needs a Texas education. Ranch owner J. T. McKinney is handsome, strong, opinionated and totally charming. And he is determined to marry beautiful Bostonian Cynthia Page. However, the couple soon discovers a Texas cattleman's idea of marriage differs greatly from a New England career woman's!

CRYSTAL CREEK reverberates with the exciting rhythm of Texas. Each story features the rugged individuals who live and love in the Lone Star State. And each one ends with the same invitation...

Y'ALL COME BACK...REAL SOON!

Don't miss *DEEP IN THE HEART* by Barbara Kaye. Available in March wherever Harlequin books are sold.

HARLEQUIN SUPERROMANCE®

HARLEQUIN SUPERROMANCE NOVELS WANTS TO INTRODUCE YOU TO A DARING NEW CONCEPT IN ROMANCE...

WOMEN WHO DARE!
Bright, bold, beautiful...
Brave and caring, strong and passionate...
They're unique women who know their
own minds and will dare anything...
for love!

One title per month in 1993, written by popular Superromance authors, will highlight our special heroines as they face unusual, challenging and sometimes dangerous situations.

Dare to dream next month with:
#541 CRADLE OF DREAMS by Janice Kaiser
Available in March wherever Harlequin Superromance novels are sold.
